Evil Lives After

by

Toni V. Sweeney

Dedication

For Those Who Remember the Old Stubbs Place,
And to the Memory of
my Aunt Shirley
(1935-2023),
Who Once Lived There

The evil that men do lives after them;
the good is oft interred with their bones."

~William Shakespeare
Julius Caesar, Act 3, Scene 2

Chapter 1

Though I was unaware of its significance at the time, on that particular day which I would later refer to as my "Gothic summer," I was at the office, reporting in after finishing a roofing project.

Being a simple roof replacement, it hadn't been a difficult job. Originally, it was to be merely repairing a few shingles blown off during a recent hurricane that had decided to come inland, transform itself into a tornado, and brush the outskirts of town. Being so close to the sea coast as our town was, we got a lot of summer storms, blowing lots of business to every construction company in town—Estonko has several—and this year had been no different.

Once the homeowner saw our estimate, he decided to simply have the entire roof restored. *It's several years old, so why wait?* was his reasoning. One of the crews, myself included, did the work.

Since I was foreman, it was my duty after we finished, to turn in the reports to Dad, along with an itemization so he could bill the customer.

That was why I was at the office that afternoon.

I'd given some of the guys rides to the site, and now had brought them back to where their own wheels were parked. The first thing I noticed as I braked the pickup at one of the stops was the car already parked in the customer area. Noticed and paused to momentarily drool

1

over.

A British sportscar convertible...sterling gray in color, meaning it was just a touch away from being totally black, with a noticeable metallic gunmetal glint.

Beautiful.

Could anything have been more out of place in front of a construction company's office?

Not that Roth Construction was housed in a rickety tin tub of a trailer looking as if a stiff wind would send it tumbling. My grandmother had made certain of that. She'd informed Grandpa early on that his place of business wasn't going to look like it was slung-together, a fly-by-night ready to be torn down and moved under cover of darkness. Result: Grandpa and his brothers renovated the building themselves, making it into something to brag about.

When my dad and *his* brothers, my uncles Cliff and Rick, took over, they did more updating, urged on by Mom, who had stepped into Grandma's shoes.

It was good advertising, she told them. In fact, we'd had several customers compliment us on its looks, so she, and Grandma, were right.

The women in our family are always right. Ask them. They'll tell you so.

I remember thinking, *Man, I'd love to have a car like that,* then remembered I'd *had* a car like that. Once. BD...*before the divorce.*

Now, it languished in my former apartment's parking garage, probably never driven and simply accruing rental fees, because Jilly, my ex, preferred her own car, a foreign four-door sedan. If she hadn't sold it to one of my former friends who'd often slavered over it.

Probably Tim Pittman, that douche. He'd also

salivated over Jilly. Oh God, I hope he isn't banging her. Well, guess it wasn't any of my business now if he was. Jilly was no longer mine and neither was the car.

That angry thought brought me out of my envious haze and back to the present. It also took me out of the truck. We had three models. Dad drove one, and my brother Ben used one for the heaviest of the loads to be carried. I owned the smallest, the half-ton, light-duty, used mainly to haul employees back and forth from construction sites. Yes, I know. Technically, having people riding in the back of a truck is in violation of the law, but we had special permission from the sheriff, providing we didn't take them six miles outside his jurisdiction, meaning onto the Interstate.

The others had already clambered out of the truck bed, clocked out, and driven away while I was in that momentary sports car daze.

I hurried inside, curious to see the dude earning my envy.

A buzzer sounded as I pushed open the door, courtesy of a small plate under the welcome mat, a three-by-six-foot piece of ribbed rubber designed to catch Georgia dirt and mud.

Iced air wafted over me.

The inside of Roth Construction consisted of a show room, with several rows of samples of roofing, flooring, carpeting, window constructions, and catalogues of all the rest. It resembled a smaller version of any big name home improvement store. To one side of the entrance was the reception area with the usual chairs and end tables holding magazines relating to house design and renovation, and beyond that a counter with computer, usually manned by Jennie, our receptionist/cashier.

Today only Dad was in sight because it was Jen's afternoon off.

Standing before the counter was a girl. Young woman, really, but I, from my mature aspect on the cusp of thirty, designated her a *girl* because she looked at least six years younger than I.

So...the object of my auto envy is a dudette?

And a very pretty red-haired one, at that.

She was dressed in fairly subdued summer wear, meaning she wasn't wearing cutoffs that an older generation would've called 'suicide shorts' but instead had on skinny boy jeans and a tank top. As she slung the tote off her shoulder and extracted a handful of folded papers from it, the tank's low neck revealed some fairly lush cleavage but she didn't seem to be making the maneuver with the intention of titillating or teasing. It just happened as she moved.

She looked all business and very serious.

Dad noticed the bulging boobies but flicked his gaze quickly away before it could be called staring. Hey, he might be in his mid-fifties and married for thirty-two years, but he's always appreciated womankind in general.

He loves only one woman in particular, however.

Realizing I was standing with the door open—I could almost hear Mom saying, *Were you born in a barn, Dyl?*—I let it swing shut behind me and walked over to the drink cooler on the other side of the room.

It was camouflaged by a surround of potted plants, the ones with the big, oval-shaped leaves. Some people call them 'indoor magnolias' but I've yet to learn the actual name. There were some other bushy tree-types as well. The cooler was like those generally found at checkout stands in convenience stores, an upright, glass-door model, shelves neatly stocked with bottled water and soft drink cans. There was no charge to take one, and customers and employees alike were encouraged to partake.

I opened the door and partook. A diet, caffeine-free soda. Hey, a guy's got to watch his manly figure or no one else will.

Come to think of it, maybe I should drink more of them. It had been a while since anyone watched me for any reason.

I popped the top on the can, expertly prevented it from overflowing, and took a sip. Leaning against the cooler. I pretended to survey the showroom while returning my gaze again and again to Dad's customer.

"Nice, huh?"

My brother Ben stood beside me. Shouldering me out of the way, he opened the cooler door, and selected a regular can of pop. Ben didn't worry about calories or caffeine.

"Better than nice. Definitely hot." He flipped the tab, took a swig, and gestured with the can. "A feast for the eyes…as you've been doing."

"How long have you been standing there?" I asked, not looking at him.

"Quite some time, but you wouldn't know. You were too busy ogling."

"*Ogling?*" I glanced at him, studying the sunburned face so like mine, except it wasn't on eye level. Ben always hated the fact that I'm two inches taller. "Aren't we using big words today?"

"Hey, you're not the only one who has a college education, even if I choose to use my hands rather than my brain nowadays." He raised the soda as if indicating something obvious, "I've seen what using the gray matter gets you," and returned to his original subject before I could react, "Man-oh-man...wouldn't you like to have that wriggling under you for fifteen minutes, bro?"

I gave a short, sharp sigh that was almost a snort. I could see where this was heading. Ben was one of the few who dared to bring up the forbidden subject of my novel-writing calamity, and its marriage-dissolving aftermath. Kinship has its privileges.

"Ben..." I put a warning tone into my voice.

No use. He was off and running on his second-favorite subject, his big brother's sex life, or lack thereof.

"...or maybe twenty minutes...or an hour." He took another sip of soda and raised his eyebrows, wiggling them suggestively. "Scratch that. You've been so deprived recently, it'd probably be only five minutes."

At pelvis level, his body jerked abruptly, the hand not holding the pop can fisting with a piston-like back-forth movement.

"One, two...oops...all done."

"Ben..." This time, I raised my voice, though still keeping it quiet enough that Dad didn't notice.

At the counter, the girl shifted her weight and the way her buttocks rippled beneath the tight denim made something shift within me, too.

Damn, is she wearing any underwear? Maybe a thong? I envisioned a teensy strip of cloth rising from the division of those rounded globes.

"Oh, come on, Dyl. I'm fully aware you've intentionally deprived yourself of feminine companionship since you came back to your former stamping grounds." It was amazing how poetically descriptive Benjamin got whenever he wanted to rag me. "While I admit none of our local beauties can match your lovely, lamented ex, I doubt if you've gotten any in the past two years, unless it's the one-sided kind."

Leave it to my little brother to get directly to the point, hitting the nail of my malady on its celibate head as neatly as he did a real nail driven into a two-by-four. I'd dated once or twice since I came back, but it went no further than that. Jilly's memory always managed to get in the way. If I'd gotten any action, it was of the egocentric kind, as he said…late at night, with visions of Jilly riding me until I filled a hand towel, to be immediately buried at the bottom of my laundry hamper while I told myself Mom would never notice.

Who was I kidding? Mom did all the laundry.

My God, I'd regressed into my adolescent self. Shit.

"Shut up, Ben." That sounded so feeble. What I really wanted to do was swing around and plant my fist on his smart-ass jaw.

I didn't. Brawling in the showroom? That would be bad for business.

"Look…I'm only thinking of your physical welfare, bro. Mental, too." He drew in a long sigh. "If you're not interested…"

He turned away, taking a last swallow and crumpling the can in his fist before dropping it into the recycling bin half-hidden by yet another set of foliage.

The weird thing is, he was sincere.

Since his marriage, Ben was so mired in wedded bliss, he'd become an acolyte for Cupid. He and Liz had been married for three years now but were still in the honeymoon stage, often so public about displaying their affection that even Dad was occasionally moved to tell them to 'get a room, for Crissakes.'

The World According to Ben was that people were only happy when they had a helpmate, and the idea especially extended to an older brother who'd already taken that route and made an unholy hash of it.

"Your loss." He gave one final try.

I didn't take the bait. Instead, I shook my head.

At the counter, the girl raised a hand, twiddling her fingers.

"Tomorrow at seven, then. No use wasting time."

"I'll have someone there at seven sharp," Dad promised.

She re-shouldered the tote and walked away. I noticed she was wearing flat-heeled gladiator sandals that didn't add an inch to her height. Made both Ben and me look like giants as she sidled past.

Well, it wasn't exactly a *sidle*, more of a *glide*. She moved like well-oiled gears working together…

…*moving back and forth while I plunged upward…plumbing that slick, smooth mechanism…*

I shifted slightly as a sharp pinch stung into my crotch. Jeans felt too tight. Maybe I'd better lay off those sodas. Or was it more than that? Thinking of this lovely creature as some kind of machine and me the mechanic making sure she was kept running smoothly?

Dylan, you have been deprived too long. My mind echoed Ben.

As she passed us, I thought her eyes flicked our way…*my* way…slightly. I was certain she was aware we'd been talking about her.

I studied her silently. She was really pretty, bordering on beautiful. Like most redheads, she had that milky, near-translucent skin, but where most looked bleached out and spattered with freckles, there was barely any discoloration blemishing her complexion. Those visible were more like decorations. Instead of that weak-eyed look coming from having red lashes, her eyes were rimmed by a fringe so thick and dark it looked artificial. I wondered if it was. The eyes that had glanced at me weren't, however. They were a fantastic olive-green.

She stepped on the pressure plate. The buzzer squawked again, and she went out, the door closing.

"Dylan," my father called from the counter.

"Right here, Pop." I walked over, setting down the soda can and digging into my hip pocket. "Job finished for the Andersons. Here's all the paperwork."

I laid it on the counter, glancing back at the door. If I hurried, maybe I could get outside before she drove away.

He picked it up, riffled through the pages, and without looking up, asked, "Did you get an eyeful?"

"Sir?" I attempted not to understand.

"The girl." His eyes twinkled. "Don't think I didn't see both my boys trying to be cool and stare at the same time. Put your eyes back into your heads."

"Now, Dad, you know…" I began.

"I'm sure Dad knows. Very well." Ben joined us at the counter. "Got that little ol' repair job for Miz Bailey done, Daddy. You going to charge her this time?"

Adelia Bailey was a widow, a lady whose husband had been our grandfather's best friend. Dad kept doing repairs for her and telling her she didn't owe because her husband had overpaid somewhere back in the long-forgotten past. So far, she believed him.

"What do you think?" Without waiting for an answer, Dad picked up a clipboard with papers attached, the top sheet filled with neat black ballpoint. "Got a new job for you, Dyl."

"Yes, sir." I reached for the clipboard, but he pulled it out of reach.

"The old Mercier place." He studied the top sheet.

He looked as if he was expected an overt reaction. The Mercier place had been abandoned for years, maybe centuries. I couldn't remember a time when it had been inhabited. Now someone wanted it repaired?

Uncertain what to say, I finally came up with, "Did somebody buy it?"

"Hardly." He looked up from the clipboard. "Looks like one of the Mercier chicks—if you'll pardon that description—has come home to roost." He nodded toward the door. "That young lady has just hired Roth Construction to do a complete renovation. I want you to go over tomorrow morning…"

I remembered what she'd said. *Seven o'clock…no use wasting time*. I was sure that didn't mean seven pm. Damn it, there went my sleeping in this Saturday.

"…to do a walk-through, see what needs fixing right now, and a future projection. Oh…don't forget to ask her whether she wants the Saturday option or not."

I perked up a little at that. Dad had this rule about Saturday work; he let the customer decide. Some demanded construction run six days of the week. Others didn't want people hammering and sawing when they were sleeping late, or the kids were home from school and underfoot, so they opted for Saturdays-free and work five days only. If there were no projects available, and that had never happened in the thirty years I'd known my

Dad, meaning my entire life—then everyone had the weekend off. When a job was finished, Saturdays were theoretically free, but most of our employees asked to be reassigned to whatever was available, to earn extra money.

"Is this budget standard, or the sky's the limit?" I asked.

We had various levels of construction. Thinking of the sportscar, I figured it'd be the latter.

"At the moment, it's open to interpretation." Dad studied the clipboard again. "Seems she works for Dream Home Unlimited."

Dream Home Unlimited was a company dedicated to the repair, renovation, and updating of houses. DHU, as it was usually abbreviated, was so well-known their magazine feature stories had made the futures of several construction companies. They also had their own cable series, kind of like those home construction reality shows, aired through the auspices of the Georgia Film Commission.

"They've given the go-ahead to make the place into a—and I quote—'contemporary dream farmhouse,' end quote. The results will be in their magazine with plenty of credit to us."

He held out the clipboard.

"I'll get right on it." I took it and started to the door.

Ben was by my side as I went out.

"You're getting a second chance here, bro," he stage-whispered into my ear.

Usually I ignored his razzing. Today, for some reason, it galled. I wanted to smack him. More than *smack*. I wanted to give him one of those swings with my fist like I used to when we were kids and he was such a pest, the kind earning me a spanking from Dad and a lecture from Mom.

A guy can only take so much, even from a brother. *Especially* from a brother.

Instead, I tightened my grip on the clipboard, and swung around, giving him what he used to call my 'killer glare.'

"Hey…" He backed away a couple of feet, hands raised. I guess he thought I was going to swat him with the clipboard.

Maybe I still had a little bit of that "bad older brother" charisma left.

"…just saying…" He let it go at that. Shrugging, he walked back to the desk, trying not to look as if he were retreating.

I went outside, staring at the empty spot where the sportscar had been. It was gone, too long ago for me to catch up, not even a puff of red Georgia dust floating in the air, taking with it any hope of me chatting her up.

Oh, well, to paraphrase a certain fictitious Southern belle, tomorrow would be another day, and on that day the aforementioned young lady, whose name I had yet to learn, would meet me at the old Mercier place.

I had no idea what I was walking into.

Chapter 2

According to those novel-writing manuals, this is the point at which I should put in some information—expository and otherwise—as to why I'm where I am today.

So, here goes…

To be dramatic, and also to show off my literary knowledge, let me start with a quote from Oscar Wilde:

…each man kills the thing he loves… The coward does it with a kiss, the brave man with a sword…

…and the writer does it with a computer keyboard.

That's the way I committed my 'crime.'

With my usual hunt-and-peck system, brandishing forefingers like daggers, I destroyed everything I had, everything I loved.

Dylan Roth, verbal slayer.

My forefathers came from somewhere in Middle Europe, and my contemporary surname is a corruption of one that in its original Serbian or Transylvanian or whatever, was unpronounceable to American tongues, so…we ended up as 'Roths.' Marrying me, by the way, was Jillian's only act of rebellion against dear ol' dad. He was preparing her for an engagement to an up-and-coming young congressman he'd set his eye on, but my girl stuck to her guns and got her Georgia Cracker instead.

Did Daddy Dear ever rage in private while smiling

for the cameras in public!

The Old Man had two faces, and he was careful which one he presented that day, though in the wedding pictures, he did look as if he'd swallowed a walnut, shell and all.

He's had it in for me ever since and was simply waiting to pounce. Two years ago, he got his chance.

Before my very ignominious fall, I was an investigative reporter for a well-known DC newspaper. In those days, I was the fair-haired poster child for journalistic daring, a boy wonder fearless for one so young, but idealistic at the same time, determined to get the truth 'before the people.'

Also a complete fool, as what follows showed.

After having written three very powerful and explosive exposés and winning myself a couple of journalism awards, I let my forty-five minutes of fame go to my already swollen head.

I got cocky, I admit it, relishing the spotlight, sucking in the adoration like a thirsty horse does water. This Georgia boy fit right in. I was now part of the crowd of beautiful people ruling the District...dining with senators, congressmen, celebrities...I'd even met the President while I was getting those exclusives and garnishing those awards of merit for the way I ferreted out the truth.

"What's next? A Pulitzer-winning novel?"

How many times did I hear that? Unfortunately, I listened, and thought, *Why not?*

They say the novice author always writes about what's familiar. I was no exception, much to my regret.

Glory of Princes was the title. It was a political thriller, something I slaved over for months when I wasn't working, neglecting wife and friends in the process. Using the pull I then had, I found an agent who in turn found a publisher and…

…the rest…?

That's the very sad history.

The book was an immediate bestseller, thanks to my then-reputation. Six months on both United States and international bestseller lists. Its popularity lasted longer than mine, I'm sad to say.

I thought I was being so clever. I wrote about what I knew, all right, but I was an idiot. I should've realized my wife's father would retaliate after recognizing himself in that thinly-veiled portrait of the senator, a Washington politico who'd taken so many bribes and made so many enemies he couldn't remember who he'd double-crossed and who he hadn't.

In the novel, he's murdered. Unfortunately for me, in real life, he stayed very much alive.

The day after the novel's release, he confronted me, breathing fire and smoke…and threats. I suppose it's a good thing I refused to discuss it beforehand, always brushing aside his questions with the statement, 'It's bad luck to talk about a book before it's finished.'

It was even worse luck to talk about it afterward, if you can call our one face-down "talking." I'd describe it more as the single slam of a battering ram against a barred door.

If he'd had any idea…

He'd probably have made arrangements to steal my laptop. As it was, he didn't dare raise too much of a fuss, couldn't sue me for slander, for then he'd be admitting what I'd written was true. So he remained silent, smiling and laughing when someone indiscreetly called his attention to my character's similarity to himself. The old bastard fought dirty, hitting me in my weak spot.

He got back at me through my wife.

I guess I should be grateful he didn't ask some of his more felonious friends to escort me to a terminal swim in the Potomac.

As for Jillian, my darling Daddy's Girl…

She'd been thrilled to think I was branching out, was writing a 'little old novel,' as she so quaintly put it. She was less than happy with the finished product, however, especially my portrayal of the senator's daughter, married to my hero, who happened to also be—surprise!—a reporter. I swear my description of her as a 'pseudo-nymphomaniac who was too cowardly to become a real one' was meant to be nothing but hyperbole. In bed, the love of my life was a tigress, even if it was only after she'd had a few drinks to dissolve her inhibitions, her reticence for carnal contact while sober a result of her all-girl boarding-school education, no doubt.

I had no complaints.

Jilly didn't see it that way, thanks to my vindictive father-in-law, who hovered like an evil genius, a parental devil whispering into her ear. Instead of listening to my feeble attempts at explanation, hoping she'd see reason and laugh it off, she lost her sense of humor. She listened to Daddy and filed for divorce, for mental cruelty and psychological brutality.

What mental cruelty? I asked when served with the papers. *Psychological brutality? Really?*

I fought it, of course. I loved her, I argued, and enumerated: I was faithful. I wasn't a violent man, didn't drink or smoke. To my mind, there was no reason for us to even separate, much less dissolve our marriage.

Nevertheless, the Senator got her the best divorce lawyer the District had to offer, demanding a trial when I stubbornly refused to sign the papers. *Let a judge decide*, he said. A few months later, in spite of my protests and humiliating pleas, I walked out of a courtroom bloody, bowed, and single. In the space of an hour I lost everything…wife, home, all the stocks, bonds, and properties…and my job. Despite their stand on freedom of the press, within moments of that judicial gavel smacking against wood, my editor notified me it might be better if I sought employment elsewhere.

Did I mention he and the Senator were old fraternity brothers?

Jilly, bless her little daddy-dominated soul, was very understanding about my loss of income, however. Because I wouldn't be able to pay her the alimony designed to keep her in the way she'd always lived, in lieu of payment, she most graciously allowed me to sign over to her all royalties from sale of the novel, as well as any movie, television, or other media rights and residuals.

I hope you can appreciate the irony as I say that. I can't.

I've always been grateful we decided to wait to become parents. Don't get me wrong, I want kids and I wouldn't mind the child-care payments, but the Senator would definitely interfere in my visitations. To have a child and never see it would be sheer torture. And I hate to think what he'd tell the kid about his absentee father.

Anyway, to continue:

While I was still reeling from this, the Senator struck the final blow. A few weeks later, I found myself back in court, this time facing a libel action, i.e., defamation of character because many people had remarked on the similarity between my fictional senator and the real-life one.

His reputation was upheld by prestigious witnesses. Mine was downgraded by the divorce and my current lack of employment. When the verdict was returned in his favor, he was also as merciful as my ex-wife. (Note sarcasm here.) He didn't press for restitution but simply requested a public apology, which I delivered to the press on the courthouse steps.

It was an effort not to choke on every word I spoke, but I managed. At least he didn't force me to do it on my knees.

The celebrity-based magazines all had a field day, with feature articles…all told from the Senator or Jilly's point of view. No one asked me for my opinion at all. I rated a couple of paragraphs in one of the most prestigious magazines, in an article about the Senator in which I'm mentioned as "the scandalously misguided former son-in-law with a talent for exaggeration." Other questions were brushed away by the old bastard with, "For my daughter's sake, I think it's better if we don't bring up that unfortunate incident."

Yes, within a couple of weeks, I'd gone from son-in-law to an 'unfortunate incident.'

My friends turned out to be fair-weather, also. Future employment in DC was nonexistent, so there I was…no job, no wife, no life…

Boy wonder falls so low he has to reach up to touch bottom.

Faced with the sudden cold shoulder Washington turned on me, there was nothing for me to do, except…

…crawl away and lick my wounds.

That's why, at the age of twenty-nine and a half, I found myself once again living with my parents.

How the mighty have fallen…all the way back to Estonko, Georgia.

It's said you can't go home again, but I did. With my tail well-tucked between my legs. Surprisingly, it didn't hurt as much as I expected.

…and that brings us up to speed, to a certain summer of this year, and back to my story…

****

The next morning at six am, I was showered, dressed, and trotting up the stairs from my basement lair into the kitchen.

When I originally left home, my old room had been converted into a sewing room so Mom could take her machine out of the den where Dad was always complaining he couldn't hear the TV while it was running. Around the same time, he'd paneled the basement and added a kitchenette and bath, intending to rent it, but when I reappeared, it became my private domain by default. They didn't charge me rent, but I insisted on paying my part of the utilities and groceries.

It was only fair since I ate a lot.

I heard Dad as I reached the top step.

"…if they've decided to let bygones be bygones, I say…"

"What do you say, Dad?" I asked, stepping into the kitchen.

He looked up. "Good morning, son." To my question, he replied, "I say, eat your breakfast and get going. Paperwork's right there." He gestured at a clipboard lying on a counter near the door.

He finished his coffee, set the cup in the dishwasher as Mom had trained him to do, and headed to the door opening into the back yard where we parked our trucks. It was still early enough in the morning to be cool, so the door was open, the screen latched.

Okay, so he wasn't going to answer my question. Maybe it wasn't anything important, or maybe it was none of my business.

Mom diverted me momentarily by placing before me a plate filled with scrambled eggs, bacon, and grits swimming in butter. A wedge of wheat toast covered in melted cheese balanced on the plate's edge.

Cholesterol City, here I come!

As I stabbed a spoon into the grits, I thought again how, if I'd eaten like this while I was reporting, I'd have *bounced* down DC's streets. A cup of coffee had been my morning fare back then. Currently, the manual labor performed on a construction crew, combined with the hot Georgia sun, kept me at an even one ninety-five with no fat to spare.

Maybe it was time I started thinking about finding my own place and going back to bachelor-style meals, namely chips, dips, peanuts, and beer, with an overflowing hamper and dust-laden furniture.

Nah.

I shoveled in grits and eggs and washed it down with the coffee she poured into the mug I'd used since high school. *Coffee,* the writing on it read, *the Elixir of Life.* It had been in the back of one of the kitchen cabinets. Once I was safely ensconced at home again, it appeared at the table next to my plate and stayed there.

Yes, I was definitely regressing.

"There's not any problem about this project, is

there?" I tried to sound casual as I swigged coffee with chicory.

Damn, I'd missed that special taste. Jilly and I had a top of the line coffeemaker, and its most expensive mixture had been the morning beverage of choice. The one time I suggested buying a little electric percolator and a can of coffee, you'd have thought I'd asked her to start doing the neighborhood's laundry.

"Problem? Not that I know of."

The way Mom turned away, avoiding my eyes and returning the coffeepot to the counter made me wonder.

"Why do you ask?"

"Oh, I heard the tail-end of what Dad said, and thought…"

"Don't worry about that," she interrupted, picking up a sponge and getting very busy wiping down an already spotless countertop. "That's nothing to do with you."

I hadn't considered that it did. I'd simply thought it was something to do with the project. I couldn't think of anything I'd done that might've elicited a remark ending in 'let bygones be bygones.'

Not lately, anyway.

She looked around. "Eat your breakfast. So you can get to doing what needs to be done."

"Yes'm." I answered her as I had when I was a kid, and applied myself to eating, but her reply left a lingering dissatisfaction.

I didn't pursue it further because there was the sound of a vehicle stopping outside.

In a moment, the back door opened and Ben lumbered in.

"Hi, Mom, hi, bro."

God, I don't know where he learned it, but I wished he'd forget he ever heard that word. It got old the first time he used it.

Mouth full, I nodded a greeting and reached for a bacon strip.

"Hey…bacon!" He plucked the piece out of my hand and shoved it into his mouth, chomping happily.

"Have some bacon," I snapped.

"Thanks, don't mind if I do." He calmly slid the other two pieces off my plate. They went the way of the first.

"Mom," I appealed to her. "Is it okay if I slap him upside the head?"

"No." Calmly, she went to the fridge, taking out the package of bacon. "It might rattle his brains."

"What brains?" I couldn't believe he'd taken the food right out of my hand.

I should've. He'd done that more times than I could count when we were little. He stole so much food from me back then it's a wonder I didn't starve to death and he didn't become a walking tub. Lucky for Ben, he has a high metabolism.

Lucky also that then, as now, Mom was there to replace what Ben had eaten. Bacon was already sizzling in the pan.

"That hurt, Dyl," Ben looked pained. "You know I've an IQ of—"

"—more than you need," I interrupted. I gestured toward the stove. "That's mine, by the way. Hands off."

"I'm cooking enough for two," Mom said, without looking away from the pan. Like she always did.

"Can I have some cheese toast, too?" Ben asked.

"Of course, dear."

Of course, dear, I mimicked wordlessly, grimacing at my brother.

He smiled, smugly, the baby of the family, always indulged. I wished his metabolism would suddenly screech to a halt and he'd inflate like a balloon.

That made me laugh.

"What?" Ben asked.

I shook my head, knowing not to tell him would irritate him. God, how petty and childish a grown man can sometimes be.

"What are you doing here, anyway? Did Liz throw you out?"

Best way in the world to distract him was to talk about his wife. Even after three years, the bloom still wasn't off that particular rose. If there was one way to drag him away from food or beer or any of the more manly pursuits, such as shooting pool, watching a ballgame, or talking about some modification he'd made to his truck, Elizabeth Ann Turner Roth could do it simply by being present.

"She told me she wanted to sleep late and I should get lost." He looked appropriately hurt. "Can you believe that? She told *me*...her adoring hubby...to beat it."

"Apparently, you've beat it too much," I muttered in an undertone. "Maybe she's tired of you waking her up whenever you get an early-morning hard-on."

I broke off a toast crust and began to drag it through the remnant of my grits. There were a few forkfuls left, butter congealing fast.

"Watch it, Dyl..." His voice dropped, glancing at Mom.

Ben had this odd delicacy. He'd never talk about anything remotely involving sex around Mom. He might gibe at me mercilessly in private, and hug Lizzie and kiss her, even nuzzle her ear in Mom's presence, but *say* anything?

Never.

He hit me on the shoulder, nodding toward Mom, and shaking his head.

I pretended not to understand. "If I were a woman, I doubt I'd want some overweight lunk pounding on me when I was trying to get some well-deserved Saturday morning shuteye."

"Actually, she said she wasn't feeling well," he admitted. "Got a touch of a stomach bug or something."

"Or something," I echoed, and looked up, grinning widely. "Hey! Maybe all that hard work's gotten some results." I let my voice drop to a whisper. "If it's a boy, will you name it after me?"

I'll admit the idea that Liz and Ben might give me a little niece or nephew made a jolt inside me, a happy one.

"Damn it, Dylan."

It gave me a different kind of jolt to hear the same irritation in Ben's voice my own had held the day before, as well as the measure of embarrassment. How a man sounding so crude could be embarrassed when that crudity was turned back on him was beyond me. I still couldn't figure out why Ben was so verbally licentious. He'd been no worse than anyone else before he married, and afterward, he was fully domesticated.

Maybe he thought that gave him a license to jeer.

One day soon, I need to have a serious talk with Brother Ben and convince him to shut up before he gets into trouble.

I started to say so, but at that moment, Mom turned, holding a plate of bacon with a single slice gripped in the teeth of a pair of tongs.

She dropped three more pieces onto my plate.

"Thanks, Mom." I arranged them onto the rapidly-cooling cheese of my toast, folding the bread over them. "Got to go. Work awaits."

As I went to the door, Ben shot me a glare before turning back to the bacon and toast Mom was putting on his own plate.

Grabbing clipboard and papers, I went out, carrying the scent of bacon with me into the open air.

Chapter 3

Okay, another momentary digression. About my home town, Estonko, a brief history, to give you the 411 and put everyone in the know:

My hometown lies on the northern entrance of Rowen County, in extreme south Georgia, the best part of the state as far as I'm concerned.

I'll make this brief. Chartered in 1871, current population of around 2,500, there's always been a mystery about where the name came from. Otherwise, it's a sleepy little Georgia town where we still follow traditions, such as stopping traffic for funerals and by observing Mother's Day by wearing a red rose if Mom's still around and a white one if she's gone to her reward.

Ya'll come...why doncha?

And the Roths did...in 1919. We've been in residence quite a while.

My great-grandfather had been a carpenter in the Old Country. Does anyone call it that anymore? Seems America is now old enough to be called the Old Country and Europe the *Older* Country. Anyway, my grandfather followed in great-granddad's footsteps. By the time my own father came along, the family business had become a construction company.

As a teenager, I did more than my share of driving nails and putting up houses, as did my younger brother. Now I was once again working for my dad.

From blue collar to white and back in one generation. A true American success story.

Dad and Mom were as glad as everyone else to have me home...*where I belonged*, they said. That seemed to be the general consensus.

Who needs them Northerners, anyway?

The majority of the town was on my side through the recent unpleasantness of my life and rarely referred to the divorce or the novel. It's amazing how close-mouthed everyone was about an event that would usually be gossip fodder in a small town. Whether out of kindness or whatever, even if they spoke of it behind closed doors, in public these folks knew how to keep a buttoned lip.

The local bookstore even relegated their copies of *Glory of Princes* to their archives, a storeroom, available only if specially requested. That was their way of keeping Jilly from getting her few ounces of flesh from my royalties.

Everyone truly seemed glad to have me back.

Okay, enough background. If you want to know more, check out their website. Yes, they have one. Otherwise, read on...

****

I drove directly through town, passing Chauncey's Grocery and other buildings, turning at the courthouse and around a couple of corners before driving onto the county road. The property was on the other side of town, but I figured it wouldn't take long to get there. With one hand on the wheel while I fed myself with the other, I thought about my destination.

The Old Mercier Place.

That was how it was always referred to whenever

anyone mentioned it, which wasn't very often nowadays. Of course, most people mispronounced it, calling it "Mercer," instead of using that "i" that made the correct pronunciation "Mer-shay." I think Dad, Ben, and I were the only ones calling it by its proper name, and I admit I occasionally let my tongue get lazy and say it like everyone else.

As I said, the place had been empty for as long as I could remember, and I had no idea why. It was just *there*…unoccupied, as much part of the scenery as the yellow pines surrounding it. Like most abandoned houses, legends grew up about the place, tales of ghostly lights shining from the windows and the sound of shouts and gunshots no one investigated. Kind of like those old houses featured in the made-for-TV movies featured on the television at two o'clock in the morning.

We kids never questioned those stories but simply accepted them as part of the trappings of a house no one wanted any longer. There weren't so many stories now, not like when Dad was a teenager or I was small. Once, when he thought Ben and I weren't listening, at one of those get-togethers where adults sat around drinking beer, talking, and telling dirty jokes after the kids are put to bed early, I'd sneaked back downstairs and eavesdropped. I'd heard him reminisce to my uncles about having a beer party and getting routed by the sheriff.

I'd never had that pleasure, not at the Mercier place, at least. I'd never even seen the house up close. Under pain of a punishment he wouldn't even mention, Dad had forbidden either Ben or me going there. Fear of my father's anger was stronger than my desire for beer or any other substance, so when my peers did their annual

Halloween *dare-the-ghosties* thing, I held back, admitting, *Hell, yes, I'm afraid...of my dad...*and let them hoot at me as they drove away.

That didn't stop me from beer parties at other venues, however.

All I knew about *Chez* Mercier was that it had been deserted since the late nineteen twenties, and at this point, no one in my generation really knew why or cared. It was simply a ramshackle, familiar landmark like the sign at the entrance to town.

I swallowed the last bite of bacon-and-toast, sucked a morsel from a back molar, and concentrated on getting to my destination, with a single wish that I'd brought my coffee with me in a driving cup.

I missed the guestimate by five minutes. I'd been driving for about twenty when the turn-off came into sight. Since I was the only one on the road at this point, I stopped the truck, studying what I could see of the house.

From the road, it was barely visible, a weather-bleached hulk in the middle of two hundred acres of pine forest destined to be pulpwood. Every couple of years, someone hired a crew to come in and cut the trees and plant new ones to replace them. At least the owners were conservation-savvy, if absent.

At some point, someone had strung barbed wire fencing, now rusty and probably tetanus-laden, around the roadside edge of the property, leaving a gate-space for the tree cutters to drive through. At the far edge of the fence, there was a partly visible upright post driven into the edge of the ditch running parallel between it and the road. That was a usual sight around here. Most roads had deep ditches on either side.

The mailbox that should've been atop the post was long gone. Now it was merely a jagged and weather-rotted, termite-infested stump barely three feet high. The box had been replaced by a sign reading, in handwritten and nearly illegible red paint, "POSTED. DO NOT ENTER. TREPASSERS WILL BE PROSECUTED." The sign now hung by one nail, most of it hidden by the weeds into which it dipped. What I could see of it was shot full of holes, probably by kids trying out the rifles they'd gotten for Christmas and birthdays.

Guess they stood in the road as they fired. To avoid prosecution.

I imagined if I dug around in the ditch, I'd find plenty of shell casings hidden by the vegetation, mostly coffeeweed and beggar lice, so high they nearly hid the stump. In the fall, an occasional flash of goldenrod would complete the picture.

After backing up, I turned the wheel and guided the truck across the bit of ground connecting the property to the road. There was a rumble as tires struck earth, an echo going through the two-foot diameter cement storm drain in the ditch, dirt hard-packed around it, allowing heavy rains to flow from one side to the other and not flood the road. Some of the dirt had washed away during the last rain, and the pipe protruded slightly. The truck rolled across, bouncing roughly.

As I turned onto what was left of the road leading to the house, there were more bounces and jouncing. I could hear the swish and scrape as weeds caught by the undercarriage were crushed or jerked out of the ground by their roots. It was obvious someone had come through earlier because the tracks made by tires were visible, with weeds sticking up like a Mohawk haircut between the ruts.

I wondered how that little sportscar had liked passing over that. I made a note to ask Miss What's her name Mercier if she wanted to have the road graded a bit. Otherwise those weeds might do some real damage to the underside of that little car. If she was planning on selling the place after Dream Home Unlimited got through publicizing it, she wouldn't want potential buyers losing their mufflers and such when they came to view it.

On one side, pine trees lined the road; on the other, what had once been a meadow was now filled with more coffeeweed, some volunteer lupines and clover, and plenty of sorrel and other indigenous Georgia plants and grasses happily propagating for the past near-century. The land had lain fallow all that time. It was probably so fertile by now that a seed dropped into it would sprout within an hour.

The road rounded a grove of pecan trees stretching back behind the pines, and the house came into full view.

The car was parked in front of the steps, its paint job hidden under a glowing patina of red Georgia dust giving odd coppery highlights to the sterling gray finish. Somehow, it looked dejected, as if ashamed of its appearance.

I stopped the truck next to it, turned the key and set the parking brake, and prepared myself for my first close-up view of the Old Mercier Place...

Instead, all I saw was the impatient young woman standing on the porch.

****

Excerpt from Dylan Roth's journal, April 24, 1921:
Had to go to the hardware store today for nails. Saw a very pretty girl there. I made bold and introduced

myself. She was polite and told me her name. Anna Belle Rowen. I wish to see her again and told her so. I hope she doesn't think me an insolent foreigner.

Chapter 4

She was tapping one sandaled foot against the porch's planks while her forefinger beat a corresponding rhythm on the face of the sports watch on her left wrist. *Click, tap...click, tap...* both sounds made an odd syncopation in the early morning silence, drawing my attention away from the house immediately.

Opening the door and sliding out of the truck, I raised a hand in greeting.

"You're late," she said, before I could make a sound. The forefinger tapped the watch crystal again. "I said, seven o'clock." A pause. "It's five minutes *after* seven."

She spoke with the disapproving primness of a teacher confronting a student trying to sneak into class after the bell had rung.

Taking the clipboard from the passenger seat, I slammed the truck door and marched around it, stopping at the steps and the wild outcropping of hedge on either side to look up at her. Today, she was wearing one of those shirts with the shoulder cut-outs, and denim leggings with her gladiators. With that red hair pulled back into a low ponytail, she was a pretty sight, even for that early in the morning, annoyed as she was.

I forced down my own irritation. *The customer is always right, even when she's being rude about it.*

"It's Saturday," I said, as if that was an excuse.

"Surely Mr. Roth's paying you for today, as he does

33

any other day?" She looked a little uncertain.

"Of course he is," I shot back. "He never asks anyone to work for free."

She'd better not be hinting Dad was a slacker where his employees were concerned.

Her expression underwent another change, a *Well, then...?* grimace.

"In that case, you should've been here on time, Mr...?" She left the sentence hanging.

"...Roth," I supplied. "Dylan Roth," then added, as if it meant something, "the Second."

Recognition glimmered.

"Are you..." She started to ask but I beat her to it, hoping I'd squelch any further questions, especially about my novel.

"Yes, we believe in practicing nepotism at Roth Construction."

"Nepotism? A definite five-dollar word. You're an educated man?"

One eyebrow lifted as if she couldn't believe it.

"University of Georgia." I paused, then added, "*Cum laude.*"

I didn't usually brag about graduating with honors, but something about her attitude made me say it. Hell, I'd had a 3.9 Grade Point Average, so why shouldn't I?

"Yet you work in *construction.*" She smirked.

Score one for the opposition. Why did I feel as if I were heading into some kind of scrimmage with this pretty girl I didn't know? She hadn't moved from the porch and I still stood in the yard, looking up at her. I decided it was time to put us on the same level. I started up the steps.

"Careful," she cautioned. "They may not hold your

weight."

Is that a dig? I knew damn well I wasn't overweight, but to someone her size (five-two or less, possibly one hundred and one pounds if I squinted), I might look bigger than the average bear.

I stopped, boot hovering over the bottom step. I didn't bother asking how she'd managed to get to the porch. She was right. If those planks were the original ones, they were probably filled with dry rot, hollowed out with termite infestation, and warped by sun and weather. She weighed about ninety-four pounds less than I did. She could've probably sprinted up them safely, while I…would hit a weakened board and crash through like an elephant walking on a straw mat.

"Thanks for the warning." I meant it.

She chose to take it as sarcasm. "I don't want my company paying out liability insurance because you got careless and fell through."

"They wouldn't," I retorted. "It'd be considered workman's comp."

Gingerly, I placed my foot on the step, testing it.

It held.

I started up, resting one hand on the banister, stepping carefully all the way to the porch, five steps in all. If I fell, the banister wouldn't be much help. Only one was still standing, and it swayed when I gripped it. The other had fallen away, only a single upright post remaining. A couple of the step-boards were cracked and splintered on one side, one had a foot-sized hole where someone, some time, had fallen through, but otherwise they were in surprisingly good shape for being so old.

She didn't say another word until I reached her.

"Now then…" I cut in before she could speak.

"Let's start over." I took off my Roth Construction ball cap, ducked slightly, and put it back on. "Hello, Miss..."

"*Ms*," she corrected. "Scarlett Mercier."

My eyebrows shot up. "Because of your hair?"

That came out before I could stop it. It was certainly a beautiful copper-colored mass, the sun making it look even redder.

"Because my mother liked the name," she answered dryly. She sounded as if she were gritting her teeth slightly.

From her tone, I imagined she'd gotten that question a lot in her life, and probably a great deal of ribbing, too.

"They call me 'Letty,'" she added.

I'll call you Ms Mercier, I decided, and did so, "Ms Mercier..." as I nodded an acknowledgement. "I'm Dylan Roth and I apologize for being late. My only excuse is that I'm securely ensconced in the slower method of moving here in the South, and I've forgotten the rest of the world generally runs at a faster pace."

"Did you once think otherwise?" Her mouth twitched as if suppressing a smile.

As if she didn't know.

"I worked in Washington, DC, for a while," I admitted.

Right. For four years, the last two of which I wish I could expunge from my memory, or do over with a different result. Still, if that happened, I might not be standing here talking to red-haired Miz Scarlett.

"Washington?" She looked surprised. "What brought you back *here*?"

As if I'd turned my back on Paradise, electing to live in the hinterlands of Hell. I forced myself not to bristle. Where did she get that attitude? *Dream Home Unlimited* might be filmed all over the country, but it was based in Atlanta. Of course, Atlanta was getting metropolitan, but still...

"A jet plane," I answered.

Could it be she really didn't know about me?

Referring to the current headlines about misfortunes occurring to certain airplane passengers, I added, "And I didn't get bumped or ousted, either."

"Pity." She gave me a direct stare, then looked away, as if not impressed with what she'd seen, and back again, with a frown. "Did you say *Dylan* Roth?"

Uh-oh. *Now*, she remembers. If my infamy was about to again rear its ugly head, I didn't want anything about me jeopardizing Dad's being hired for this project.

"Whatever you've heard—"

The sound of a vehicle and the insistent honking of a horn kept me from finishing.

We both spun, looking toward the road as an SUV swerved around the curve of trees and skidded to a halt next to my truck, sending dirt flying.

The doors opened and two men tumbled out into the settling dust. They were dressed in jeans and tees, the shirts with the *Dream Home Unlimited* logo. Both looked to be husky, homegrown products.

Bodyguards?

"Hey, Letty." The one getting out of the passenger side raised a hand.

"You're late, Biff." She said it in the same tone she'd used with me.

"Sorry." He didn't look worried, as if accustomed to that admonition. "Bill got lost."

Bill and Biff? That sounded like a Grade C comedy team.

"Yeah." The other came around the front of the SUV. "Took a wrong turn at Albuquerque."

"Ha-ha, very funny. That's getting old." Her reply indicated he was often late and this was his usual response. "Don't let a certain rabbit hear you." Apparently, bodyguards weren't given any slack, either. This little lady was a hard taskmaster. "Get unpacked and let's get started."

The one called Biff slid back the side-panel door and leaned in. Bill hurried to help him drag out something in a black case.

They huddled together for a few moments, then came around my truck, trotting to the steps. I saw that Biff now had the black case attached by wide backpack straps over his shoulders with whatever it held in front, similar to those baby carriers I'd seen with the little guy fastened on his mom's chest, chubby legs dangling.

Whatever was in the case wasn't an infant, however. The top was unzipped and lines from those sound silencer-type earphones were firmly in place over Biff's ears. On his shoulder, he carried a metal rod with something looking like an elongated gray feather duster attached to the end.

I stiffened. Memories from my divorce hearing and the libel trial returned, of coming out onto the courthouse steps to be met by people holding similar items—microphone booms—while others recorded my humiliation with the cameras they aimed at me, just like the one Bill now held.

"Hey…what…?" I looked from them to Ms. Mercier, confusion and sudden suspicion dawning.

Was this some news story trick? She didn't want to have the house renovated? That was simply a ruse to get me alone and do a followup to what should've by now been old news? *Dylan Roth: Two Years After the Storm.*

Surely I wasn't that newsworthy. Not now.

"Listen, Ms. Mercier, or whatever your name is..." I prepared to tell her where she and her camera crew could go, even if it meant arousing the ire of whatever newspaper she was from and tarnishing Dad's reputation a bit in the bargain. I'd gotten enough hounding even after I came back home, though it eventually died down, and now...

Damn it, I deserved my privacy.

"Call me 'Letty,'" she answered blithely. "After all, we're going to be working together for quite some time."

"We are?" That stopped my tirade before it began. "I don't understand."

She didn't answer as Biff flipped open the top of the case. He fiddled with visible knobs, listened to something, then started toward me, holding out the dust mop.

"Say something," he ordered.

"Something." I chose to take him literally.

He listened again, did some more knob-twirling. "Say something else."

"Something else." I stared at him.

He nodded, and gave Ms. Mercier a thumbs-up.

"Oh, didn't I mention?" she continued as if there'd been no interruption. "*Dream Home Unlimited* is not only paying for the renovation, they're planning on using it as one of their televised projects."

She smiled as she said it. She knew damned well she hadn't mentioned it, not to me or to Dad. He'd have said something if she had.

It made sense. If they were shelling out X-number

of dollars on this project, they'd want to get as much back as possible, and making it into a week's worth of episodes would more than do that. But…

That meant these two would be following us around, filming every move we made and recording everything I said. Eventually millions of viewers would see it, and I'd be in front of the public again.

Oh God…

The Senator wouldn't like that. Me, before the cameras? It'd be rubbing a raw spot. Since Dad sent me to do the walk-through, that meant he was designating me as his liaison, go-between, whatever. I wondered if I could get him to let someone else take over. Ben, maybe. He'd love to be in my place. No one would associate Ben with the scandalous Dylan Roth.

"Ready to start whenever you are, Letty." Bill had been fiddling with his camera while she was talking. He looked at me, "Okay…uh…"

"Dylan," she introduced. "Construction owner's son. One of them." She glanced at me. "I imagine that hulk I saw you with is another Roth boy?"

"My brother Ben." I acknowledged her introduction, saying, "Hello," relieved she didn't go into detail and also that they didn't seem to recognize my name. Maybe neither was a reader or didn't remember something from two-year-old gossip columns.

"Dylan…" Bill nodded. "…right…now then, what I need you to do is get into your truck and take it up the drive. Count to ten, then drive back down again."

"Like I'm just getting here?" It was a stupid request and an even more stupid question. Of course I should do that. I'd seen enough of their shows to know how they all started out. They needed an opening for the episode, and they hadn't been here when I arrived.

"Like you're just arriving," he confirmed. "Then, park the truck, get out, and greet Letty. Like you did before."

"Not like I did before," I said, giving her a sideways glance. "I hope."

"Oh, I don't know…it'd make it more authentic, but don't worry, I'll play nice for the camera," she said. "You need to move the van," she reminded Bill.

"Right." He tossed keys to Biff and took boom and sound-set from him. "Park it over there." He nodded to a patch of thick brush broom directly in front of the house but bordering the field.

"Better not," I cautioned.

"Why not?"

"See those fallen branches and pieces of board sticking out of the grass?"

Biff looked where I pointed and nodded.

"High grass like that, with places to hide under the wood…might be snakes. It's late May, the right time of year." The minute I said that, Biff gave a very visible shiver. That meant he was a city boy. I gestured. "Just pull it on down the road a bit and leave it."

I remembered someone, at some time, mentioning that the road went past the house, continuing through the woods and on around the property, coming out on the other side a couple of miles away, where it reconnected to the county road. It was only used by the woodcutters on those occasions when they came in to thin the trees.

"Hey, that'd make a good side piece…beware of snakes," Bill said. "Maybe you can re-enact that later?"

I shrugged. "Guess so. Why not?"

It was going to seem *really* strange if any little thing

I said might have to be duplicated for the camera. I'd better watch what information I volunteered.

Biff nodded and climbed into the van. I did the same to the truck. He very politely let me leave first. Since I was going to be driving down the road again, I backed the truck around the trees and toward the gate, looking over my shoulder.

At the gate, I stopped, shifted into drive, and sat, counting.

"One…two…three…"

At "ten," I tapped the pedal and started the pickup down the road, driving slower this time, thinking how a cloud of dust wouldn't do the camera lens much good. I also told myself I had to remember to keep my head down and turn away from the camera as much as possible. I knew that was going to be difficult, what with zoom lenses and such, but it wouldn't matter, because as soon as I got home, I'd ask Dad to send Ben in my place when work started.

As before, the truck rounded the grove of pecan trees. Biff had parked the van several yards down the road and the space beside the sportscar was clear. He'd also reclaimed the sound unit.

Camera resting against his shoulder, Bill stood behind the car, looking up at Letty. She was still on the porch, speaking to an imaginary audience. Biff was beside him, boom hoisted up and over the camera, the protective grayish covering designed to filter out extraneous sounds already acquiring a distinct reddish tinge. As they heard the truck, both turned, aiming the lens and mike in my direction.

I pulled in beside Letty's car, braking as I had before, and cut the engine.

As I climbed out, waiting for the dust to settle, I heard her call out, "Hi, I'm Letty Mercier. You must be Dylan from Roth Construction."

As friendly as could be, as if we hadn't already met. As if we hadn't been carping at each other only minutes before.

"That's right." I came around the truck, clutching the clipboard, heading for the steps, forcing myself not to look at the camera. It was going to be difficult ignoring it and the boom when they were only feet away.

This is stupid. I remembered how actors had to shoot and re-shoot a scene any number of times. *God, I hope we don't have to do that.* Repetition was not in my vocabulary. I never was one for hiding my impatience or boredom, either. I could never be an actor.

"Careful," she cautioned. "Some of the steps are in awful shape."

She said it naturally, not as if she were reading from a script of our previous meeting.

"Right." Wishing I had a copy of that script, I went up the steps in a parody of the way I'd tested them before.

Once I was on the porch beside her, she got right to business, stating the plot succinctly. "Well, Dylan, as you know, I'm the current owner of this property..."

I hadn't, but it was logical, so I nodded as if it were common knowledge.

"...and *Dream Home Unlimited* has agreed to renovate and repair it with the idea of selling it, so..."

"...so let's get started on the dream."

She obviously didn't like that I'd stolen her punch line, the way each episode of *DHU* began. Nevertheless, she was professional enough to merely smile, and continue, "Since we're outside, I suppose the best place to begin is right here."

"We'll start with those steps you warned me about." I'd show her I could improvise with the best of them.

At the same time, I wondered why I hadn't seen her on any of the *DHU* shows. Dad and I watched occasionally, always looking for hints on construction and variations on décor. Could it be I'd simply missed the ones she hosted? Or maybe this was a kind of audition for her, as well as a renovation of her family home.

"…then work our way inside and upward." I glanced up, getting my first real look at the house itself.

Like most southern farmhouses of that era, the house was elevated, set on pillars fashioned of stacked red brick, lifting it three feet off the ground. A pillar stood at each end of the porch, two behind the steps, and at intervals down the sides and back.

I remembered how my grandpa's hunting dogs slept under his porch in the summer. Ben and I, with my cousins, would crawl under the house and play in the dirt during those same hot days.

The bricks appeared in good shape, no washing away of the mortar holding them together, and none missing. Flecks of paint still visible showed they once might've been painted white, as probably the house had been, also. The porch stretched across the entire front, but only the part where we were standing was still intact. On either side, the boards had fallen away, so it was as if we stood on a bridge attaching the steps to the house.

Directly above the roof overhang, an arched balcony projected from the second story, broken-paned windows on either side. The only reason I could see it was because most of the roof was missing and that on the sides was also gone, probably its falling was what had taken out parts of the porch. Above it was a smaller gable, no doubt an attic. Most of the shingles were gone from the roof, and there was a gaping hole on the right side. Here and there some of the gingerbread wood trim was still visible.

This place definitely had been an attractive home back in its day.

As I thought that, a cloud must've passed over the sun, because everything darkened...the windows became wide, staring eyes, the doorway a deep gaping mouth... I glanced at Letty. There were shadows under her eyes, making them so dark they seemed to be dripping down her face like overdone mascara...

What the...? I blinked.

Everything brightened. Letty stared at me, frowning.

"I see there are two stories." I flashed her a smile to cover my confusion. "That means more steps inside, naturally."

She nodded, apparently thinking of something to say. I didn't give her a chance. Shifting the clipboard, I pulled a pen from my pocket, clicked the point, and made notations on the first sheet.

"Five steps...two banisters..." I glanced down. "Definite repair to porch. Check."

...and we got started.

Chapter 5

The front door was gone, probably carted off by vandals, though why someone would want to steal a hundred-year-old door...

I nodded at the open doorway "One front door..." and scribbled. That would include the frame, lintel, transom, and side pieces. Those last two had probably been glassed. I made a note...*plain or beveled*?...and turned to look at the room itself.

We were in what was the foyer, not large, as those things went, but big enough. Sunlight sifted through the hole in the roof, lighting stairs and part of the floor where we stood.

Behind us, Bill panned the camera from left to right, taking in the scene.

"Not particularly inviting, is it?" Letty muttered.

On either side were doorless openings. To the back, and behind the staircase going up the right side of the wall, was another open passageway. Directly to my right was a surprise.

An actual door, still on its hinges.

"Let's see what's in here." I seized the doorknob, twisting slightly but being careful not to put much weight behind it in case the thing decided to come off in my hand.

It didn't move. I applied a little more pressure. With a loud grating, the knob turned. I looked down at my hand. Dark red grains lay on it.

Bill immediately took a step closer, camera focused on my palm.

"Rust," I said, unnecessarily. "I'm surprised it even works. Looks like an application of lubricant is in order." I studied the knob. It was ceramic, a discolored white, the surface crackled. Ground-in dust darkened the cracks. "Nice...you might want to see if that can be transferred to the new door."

She made an assenting sound. I wrote another note before I pulled the door open.

It had fallen slightly, and scraped against the floor. Inside was nothing but a sagging shelf and a bowed and half-splintered wooden rod extending from one side to the other.

"I think this must've been the coat closet." I pushed the door shut, and nodded at the opening on the right. "After you."

She gave me a look and went inside.

This was the parlor, I guessed, a room larger than the foyer, well lit because of the long floor-to-near-ceiling windows. A couple still had all their panes. The rest were nothing but pieces of shattered glass on the floor. We'd have to do a general sweep-up before working inside.

There was wooden wainscoting that I imagined would look great with the paint removed and a natural stain applied. At one side of the room was a large brick fireplace and hearth.

I studied the mantel, running my hand over the shelf. The frame itself was underside-beveled, with large scrolls supporting it. Vines, flowers, and leaves had been carved into the surrounds leading down to a gently rounded, solid base.

"This is beautiful," I said, and meant it. "You should see about having it restored. I can't tell what type wood it is, but it was made to last."

I knelt, looking up into the fireplace itself. Wind blew down the chimney. A bit of soot trickled out. I jerked back before it could hit me.

"Might need to have the chimney checked, clear out any bird nests, et cetera." I got to my feet, dusting my knees. "You *do* want to keep the fireplaces?" I asked, in afterthought.

"We'll have some kind of heating and air put in," she answered, "But…yes, the fireplaces stay. In working order."

I nodded. "If the rest are as ornate as this one, it'd be a shame to junk them."

I scribbled more info on the clipboard. Then I pulled out a retractable tape and took some measurements…length and width of the floor, the hearth, the windows. I would do that in each room.

We went into the next one.

Its fireplace shared the chimney with the parlor but was otherwise large and empty. At the end of a small passage was a swinging door, surprisingly still on its hinges and workable. Behind the door was a long room running the width of the back of the house.

"Guess that was the dining room and this is the kitchen, with a swinging door for hands-free entry and exit, convenient for someone carrying dishes." I gently moved the door back and forth. It squeaked a short protest. "I'm surprised it has both."

"What do you mean?" she asked.

"Most family houses of this period…we're talking

early-1920s, I guess…only had kitchens. That was where the food was cooked and eaten." My grandparents' home was set up that way. Mom and Dad still ate in the kitchen, though we had a dining room now, but it was used mainly for parties and holidays. "Your great-grandfather, wasn't it?"

She nodded.

"He must have been pretty welloff."

"I suppose he was." The sudden stiffness of her answer made me glance at her. "As I'm sure you're aware…" Her tone became strained, almost icy. "…he owned quite a bit of forestland that still supplies pulpwood."

I nodded, though I wasn't aware. At all. On-camera wasn't the time to say so, however.

She seemed to hesitate, then added, "He was also an investor in the Springtime Tobacco Company. They manufactured Good Puffs cigarettes."

"Good Puffs *then*, but not for the smokers later on," I quipped.

She didn't look amused. In fact, she looked downright angry, as if she'd been prodded into admitting something she'd prefer to forget.

I didn't try to figure that out. Instead, I turned my attention to the window looking into the back yard. From where I stood, I could see what appeared to be a well, with a narrow, upright building beyond it.

On the wall on either side of the window were cabinets, their doors intact. Below was a long sink with shelves underneath. The sink itself was much-chipped ceramic over cast iron, self-rimming, with a long, built-in, ribbed dish drainer, and…I stopped and stared…a hand pump.

"Oh, wow…" I didn't mean to let the awe in my voice be heard, but it came through anyway.

"What is it?" She sounded anxious, coming to stand beside me.

I gestured to the pump, seized the handle, and worked it. Nothing came out.

"Probably needs priming," I grunted.

The handle was rusted. It took a lot more effort than turning the doorknob had. I released it, glancing at my palm. It was streaked crimson, both from the pressure of my grip on the handle and the rust. I wiped my hand against the hip of my jeans.

"Are you going to want to keep this?"

"For ambience," she answered promptly. "We'll have faucets put in, of course."

"Of course." I echoed, barely able to keep the flippancy out of my voice.

She said it so casually. *Oh yes, we'll have air conditioning, and heating, and running water and…* I decided to burst that bubble right away.

"That may be a problem."

"What do you mean?"

"There's no water service this far outside town. Nothing to run pipes from."

Her expression showed no one had thought of that. "Then why is *that…*" She gestured at the pump. "…here?"

"There's a well out back." I gestured through the window, wondering what else they hadn't thought of. *Dream Home Unlimited* generally dealt with fairly modern houses, circa 1970 and onward.

She peered out. The well, a square, brick construction to the far right, was barely visible through the weeds.

"That's what the pump's connected to. The pipes have probably rusted through, gotten clogged with dirt. That's why there's no water. Anyway, I imagine they're lead and will need to be replaced with copper or plastic. Water'll have to be tested, too, to make certain it's still potable."

Her eyebrows went up as I said that. I was certain I was using the word properly and she knew it. It was merely a silent comment on my education and current employment status.

"Drinkable," I clarified, for the ignorant in the viewing audience.

She didn't answer. I could see her totting up the totals for that little bit of reconstruction.

"Don't worry." I smiled in a way I hoped would convey a positive attitude. "There's no industry around here that might've polluted the ground. We'll get a plumber to give us an estimate."

She smiled also, but I think it was more at that "we" I'd used than anything else.

"Now then..." I turned, saw something standing against the far wall. "What have we here?"

"What is it?" She looked around.

I approached the object. The last time I'd seen one of those was when my grandparents renovated their kitchen and donated theirs to the Estonko Family Museum where the Estonko Historical Preservation Society met. That one was much newer, however.

"This is the original kitchen work island." I waved a hand at the cabinet-like structure.

There was a small counter, a hutch-like front with cabinets, and a rolltop below them. I reached for the glass knob to the rolltop, pushing gently in case some of the slats didn't work.

"In here…"

The rolltop shifted upward. A frightened squeak sounded inside.

"Hey!"

Letty echoed a more feminine version of my shout of surprise. We had a brief glimpse of a gray, furry body about half the size of my fist before it leaped from the counter to the floor and scuttled across the room, disappearing into a hole gnawed in the wainscot baseboard.

We looked at each other and laughed, that shaky sound realizing there was no danger and how silly we must've looked. She put a hand to her chest, as if trying to slow her heartbeat. All it did was draw my attention to the perfect mounds her boobs made under the cut-outs.

Eyes right, Dylan!

"Looks like you've got one squatter, at least." I indicated the little black droppings inside the cabinet. "He's made himself right at home. I imagine once we start working he'll vacate fast."

"I hope so. I'd hate to have to put out traps."

She was softhearted to vermin? I got back on track.

"As I was saying…this is a work table. Canisters for coffee, sugar, et cetera, went in here…" I indicated the area inside the rolltop. "Canned goods up here." I tapped the door above that but didn't open it. No need having a repeat performance in case that little rodent's partner was lurking there. "And here…"

I seized the handle of a long door-like contraption on the left, pulling it downward.

"…flour was poured in here…to be sifted…"

Releasing the handle, I shut the bin and indicated the built-in sifter attached to the underside. "…into a bowl and made into biscuits here." I patted the countertop. "Below…"

I opened the large door underneath the counter. That sent a cloud of leaf bits and bark into the air.

"…we have Mr. Mouse's nest…" I waved a hand to clear the air and the fragrance of *eau de mouse* wafting into it. "…where pots and pans should go."

She snorted and sneezed. "Excuse me."

"Bless you," I muttered, and went on, tapping the drawers to the right of the door. "Utensils, tablecloths, and the like went in here."

I stepped back.

"This is in great shape, considering its age. You should really consider having it cleaned and fumigated…" I smiled and gestured to the mouse hole in the baseboard. "…and keep it…for the ambiance."

I couldn't resisting adding that.

"Good idea," she said, with grudging reluctance. "I think I will. Make a note of that." She tapped the clipboard. "'Keep the kitchen work station thingy.'"

"Yes, ma'am, Miz Scarlett."

Her smile wavered, then settled, and abruptly she laughed. It sounded genuine.

I got my measurements and we continued our tour, going through another doorway and avoiding the door propped against the wall. There was no doorknob, so I thought it might've been a swinger also.

We were now in a room nearly the length of that side of the house, with a fireplace bisected by a wall.

"That's odd."

"What?" Her voice went up slightly.

"The wall." I gestured. "See how it cuts through the fireplace…so part of it is in this room, and part in the room on the other side?"

I studied the wall. It was in door-sized sections, each piece made of solid wood, no veneer or hollow doors here. They were staggered slightly so they weren't aligned end-to-end but overlapping each other. That was an odd configuration. There was something else different, also. None of the panels touched the floor. They hung about a half-inch above it. Neither did they touch the fireplace but stopped directly before it.

I looked up. The doors hung in a metal track affixed to the ceiling, extending the width of the room. Where it met the wall, it curved and ran alongside it.

Walking over to the one nearest the wall, I saw there was something embedded in the center, a brass plate affixed to the wood, with a metal-rimmed circle set into it.

"I think…"

Thrusting my forefinger into the circle, I pushed against the panel. It struck an obstruction in the track and didn't move. I pushed again, and it slid reluctantly, as did the one behind it, revealing itself to be a folding door, what today we'd call a pocket door, though I'd never seen one this long or heavy. A rain of red dust filtered over me, making me cough, as they ran along the track, slid through the curve, and lined themselves neatly against the wall, revealing the other half of the room.

In the center of the second room lay a mass of broken glass and a twisted mangle of blackened metal with soggy decaying leaves and branches protruding from it. The top of the object held a piece of chain. Looking up, I saw a corresponding length dangling from the ceiling, and gave a soft, involuntary "Ahhh" as I realized what it was.

"Is something wrong?" she asked.

Bill came around me, aiming the camera at the thing on the floor. Biff hovered, making certain the boom was out of sight but close enough to catch my words. He made some kind of adjustment to a knob.

Until that moment, I'd actually forgotten they were there.

I knelt, reaching into the blackened mass and lifting out what looked like the strands of a broken necklace. Sunlight struck crystal beads, making them sparkle.

"Do you know what you have here?" I couldn't keep the surprise out of my voice.

"No. What?" She was plainly puzzled by my reaction.

"This is a ballroom." I got to my feet, holding out the strand.

She took it, running the beads through her fingers. She held them up, letting the sunshine again be captured in each one.

"The pocket doors can be shut to make a smaller room for little dinner parties, then opened for dancing. And this…" I indicated the beads and where they'd come from. "…is a beaut of a crystal chandelier." I gestured at the chain hanging from the ceiling. "It probably held a hundred candles and lit this entire space. I doubt if it can be recovered, but you might be able to use some of the crystals in a reproduction."

I made several notations on the clipboard and thought of something.

"That's another problem. No electricity."

"Don't tell me there are no power lines this far

outside town?" There was dismay in her voice.

I could see she was thinking this project was fast going down the tubes.

"There's power. Didn't you see the poles? Electricity *and* telephone lines, but the house will have to be rewired. Whatever's here has probably been chewed through by our little furry friend..." I nodded toward the kitchen. "As well as deteriorating with age." I looked around and sighed. "I'll bet this place looked great when there was a party here."

I could imagine a couple of fiddlers, maybe a piano tucked into a corner, a table holding a punchbowl filled with syllabub or fruit ade, men gathered around it, spiking the punch with whiskey, while the ladies huddled together, talking behind their fans. Would they do square dances or waltzes...or the Charleston? That would've been the era of the flapper, fringed dresses, and windblown bobs.

I had a sudden vision of the lady of the house dancing with her husband. She was wearing a drop-waisted dress and had bright copper hair, looking remarkably like her great-granddaughter.

I gave her a smile.

"Ready to tackle the upstairs?" I offered my arm.

Smiling in answer, she grasped it. "Let's."

"...and cut!" Bill interrupted. "Letty, we need to take a break."

"...and I need to take a leak," Biff complained.

"Told you not to drink those three sodas on the way here," Bill said.

Biff didn't answer, just leaned the boom against the wall and looked definitely uncomfortable. With my cup of breakfast coffee, I was surprised I didn't, also.

"Where can I…" He paused.

"There's an outhouse in the back." I jerked my head in the direction of the kitchen. "I saw it through the window. Don't know what shape it's in, but if you go there, better watch out for…"

"…snakes," he finished. "Yeah, I know." Carefully, he slid the straps off his shoulders and lowered the sound case to the floor.

"…or there are plenty of trees around."

"Thanks." He hustled through the door, then paused and looked back. "I won't get arrested for indecent exposure or anything, will I?"

"I doubt it. Haven't seen a sheriff's car patrolling, have you?"

He disappeared through the door. In a moment, we heard his footsteps crossing the porch.

"That reminds me." I turned to Letty. By now I'd begun thinking of her that way, though I told myself to keep speaking to her formally. "Aside from the dry-for-now wet sink in the kitchen, there's obviously no indoor plumbing. There's no sewage service this far out. You'll have to dig and have a septic tank put in."

"I'll talk to that plumber you're going to find," she replied.

Silence fell, the awkward kind, as in all cases where strangers find themselves together with nothing in common to talk about. I searched around for something to say to keep things moving until Biff got back.

"So…your great-grandfather was solvent enough to be an investor in that cigarette company?" I said.

She nodded.

"Guess that means he didn't farm, huh?"

"I believe he might've. Corn, soybeans…" She

waved a hand vaguely, looking as if she wanted to change the subject.

"I remember the cigarette factory was demolished in 2000." I smiled as I thought of something. "Too bad *Dream Home Unlimited* wasn't around back then."

The company had only been in business nine years, the TV show on the air for three.

"Why's that?" She frowned as if wondering what smart-assery I was about to come up with.

"There was heart pine lumber in the foundation, and good bricks. You could've purchased some of those and used them here. That would've been some good publicity…material from the factory used in one of its investors' homes. Why'd your great-grandfather leave, anyway?"

She hesitated. "You can ask that?"

Biff's arrival back preventing me from answering.

****

Excerpt from Dylan Roth's journal, May 1, 1921:

Today I asked Annie's father for her hand. We have known each other a short time but I am certain she is the one for me.

Chapter 6

The upstairs consisted of three bedrooms and two smaller rooms.

The master bedroom took up most of the entire upper right side of the house, with a smaller one next to it. Like the downstairs, it had wainscoting with shreds of wallpaper still visible. It also shared the chimney from the parlor and dining rooms. It was empty, except for a bed frame. So far, other than the work center in the kitchen, that was the only furniture.

That bed was a magnificent specimen. Wood, with a headboard as tall as I was, scrolled and carved with roses and vines. The footboard was shorter, only waist high and plain. All the artistry had gone into the panels at the head. It was a double bed but looked small compared to the king- and queen-size versions now available.

Jillian and I had owned a queen-size. I tried to imagine sleeping in a bed this confining, with a body so close to mine each of us only had about two and a half feet of personal space.

At that moment, Letty shifted her weight, and I glanced at her.

If it were someone like you, I thought, *I wouldn't mind the lack of space. Yes, indeed, in your case, Miss Letty, constriction would be downright welcome… What the hell am I thinking? I sound like Ben.*

I forced my unexpectedly lascivious thoughts back to business.

"No closets, but I imagine there were wardrobes in each room to hold clothes." I studied the bed, running a hand over the curving edge of the top boards. "I think this might be salvageable. If dry rot hasn't set in."

"Or damp from that hole in the roof," Letty said. She stood at the foot of the bed, hands resting on it. It must've been around four feet high. She looked as if she were peering over a fence. "I hope not. I'd love to keep this for myself."

I had a flash of her lying in it, that copper hair vivid against white sheets. I shook my head.

"You don't think so?" She sounded disappointed.

No way was I going to tell her what I was thinking. "Just wondering who we might get to see about restoring it."

Out of the corner of my eye, I saw a flash of something white and fluttery in the doorway. I whirled, looking at the door.

"What was that?"

"What?" She looked in the same direction.

I walked to the door, peering out, up and down the hall.

Nothing.

"I thought I saw…" I looked up at the gaping hole. "The roof's open. Probably a bird got in and was flapping around trying to find its way out again. Guess we'd better watch where we step. There may be droppings."

We went into the smaller room. The door was missing its knob and lock.

"Looks like someone tried to force it open." I

indicated deep grooves cut around the hole where the lock had been.

The door was in such bad shape it was a little difficult to tell, but I guessed it had been locked and the doorknob removed because that was the only way to get the door open. Whoever had done it must've been desperate, for the door was battered and chopped as if someone had taken an ax to it.

Maybe one of the kids had locked himself in and then couldn't get the door unlocked. I'd done that when I was four, locked myself in the bathroom. Luckily, Dad had an extra key.

This room was obviously the nursery. There was a little iron bed that had to be a crib. It even had a side that could be raised and lowered. Letty circled it, a look of wonder in her eyes while I imagined the baby lying in it, probably dressed in a handsewn gown covered with tucks and ruffles. A chubby-cheeked infant, cooing and waving her fists, a little girl with a headful of feathery copper curls…

"This is…"

Let me go!

I jerked slightly, hoping the camera didn't catch it.

Behind me, Biff winced and pressed a hand to the earphones, then twisted a knob, but no one else reacted, although I thought Letty looked startled. Perhaps because of the way I glanced around so quickly?

Did I really hear something?

It must have been a bird, or the wind blowing through a partially-clogged chimney, maybe the squeal of a door hinge. Sometimes things like that could almost sound like words.

"…in remarkable shape." I forced myself to finish

the sentence. "...have it sandblasted and repainted... some auto body shop could do it...baked on enamel..." I looked around. "You've got some real treasures here. It's amazing they haven't been stolen."

"I'm lucky," she answered. She glanced around. "Oh, look!"

In the corner, something lay on its side. I could see ears sticking up.

She hurried over, knelt and put her arms around it, lifting and setting the rocking horse on its feet. The rockers were gone and one hoof was missing. In spite of being almost washed clean of paint, it looked pretty good.

"I'm definitely keeping this," she stated, stroking the very lifelike nose.

The horse wobbled on its three legs, staring at her with blank, faded eyes.

"Maybe whoever restores the bed can do something with it, also." Gently, she laid it on the floor again, then simply stood staring at it.

Was she thinking about the child who had slept in the bed, who'd ridden that horse here in the nursery? Her grandfather...or grandmother?

We started out. She looked down.

"What's that?"

There was a large, dark spot on the floor, almost two feet long, an irregular wet-looking splotch with spatters, as if something containing liquid had been dropped, splashing and running before soaking into the wood. All the floors were hardwood and probably had originally been well-varnished. They were still glossy in places. Whatever had been spilled ruined the finish on this one.

I'd swear it hadn't been there when we came in.

Letty knelt, peering at the stain. She touched it, then looked at her finger. There was nothing, of course. The stain had long dried.

"It looks like blood." She shivered.

It did. Now I could see that it was a very dark red, almost black against the wood grain.

"Probably a cat or something caught a bird and dragged it up here. Or rain flooded in from that hole in the roof. Don't worry, we can replace that section if the stain won't come out." I caught her arm, helping her to her feet. "Come on."

She went out with me, looking back at the spot until we were in the hall. Bill and Biff tramped over it without a second glance.

The other rooms held nothing interesting. As did the ones on the right, the bedrooms shared the chimney with the fireplaces on the floor below. There was a small room at the end of the hall, separating the master bedroom from the others. In it was a tin tub and the remains of a cabinet holding a broken pitcher and a shattered basin.

"Now this is definitely unique." I peered into the cabinet.

"What is?" Letty inspected the tub as if trying to imagine bathing in such a small container.

Before I could stop it, my own imagination veered in that direction…Letty crouched inside, up to her neck in suds, hair piled atop her head and tied with a ribbon, perhaps a curl or two falling loose to touch wet, glistening shoulders…

What the hell's wrong with me?

"This commode…" I looked over at Bill, who'd reacted with a lift of eyebrows. I realized, later, it would look as if I were speaking directly to the audience. "Yes, that's where the term came from...a cabinet holding pitcher and basin for morning ablutions."

Again, she grimaced as I used another 'five dollar word.'

"And also, occasionally holding a chamber pot." I grinned. "Don't see one, though. No indoor plumbing, but a place to bathe indoors. Hm."

"Guess they carried water up the stairs," she said.

"Right. Heated in the kitchen, hauled upstairs. Then probably poured out the window afterward." I sighed. "Ah...the Good Old Days."

"I'm beginning to appreciate today's modern conveniences more and more."

We both laughed.

"Are we finished?" she asked as we carefully went back down the stairs.

"Almost."

"What else is there?"

"I want to look around outside, check that well, and such."

She gestured. "Lead on, Macduff."

"That's 'Lay on, Macduff,'" I corrected.

I didn't bother telling her it was bad luck for show-biz folk to quote *the Scottish play*, as it was called. Why ask for trouble? There'd be enough complaints when *DHU* saw the bill for all this.

There had been a garden in back. A low, crumbling brick wall, most of it still standing, made a semicircle around an area that was now nothing but brambles and weeds. Wild blackberry canes and coffeeweed made an almost impenetrable jungle.

"Hey...you've got Cherokee roses."

She looked past my pointing finger at the single-petaled pink roses climbing a nearby pine tree.

"Nice." She sounded barely interested.

Roses? Ho-hum.

"Don't sound so enthusiastic. That's the Georgia State flower, and there are darned few of them left since there's more and more land being cleared for houses."

"Listen who's talking," she shot back. "In that case, you're helping in their decimation, Mr. Construction Man."

I ignored that. "Tell whoever does the landscaping to make certain he spares those. They can be transplanted to the garden." I paused before adding, "It'll give it more ambiance."

I gave the word a contemptuous emphasis. Why? I don't know. Something about her reaction to the roses prompted it. I realized it angered me that she wasn't as enthusiastic as I about that specific treasured flower. For some reason, it resonated a memory…of how some of Jillian's DC friends often ridiculed my accent, though mine wasn't as thick as some Georgians…and Letty's wasn't as pronounced as mine.

City girl, I excused her, trying to ease my own irritation. She simply didn't appreciate that bit of Southern heritage. I wondered where she lived when she wasn't following me around the ruins of her ancestral home.

The outhouse was a wreck. I was surprised the storms through the years hadn't blown it over. It didn't have a crescent moon carved into the door but its use was obvious. The weeds around it were fine and healthy, showing no disturbance. I guessed Biff had probably erred on the side of caution and chosen a nearby tree. I saw no need to fight my way through the briars, so went to the well instead, grateful it was upstream from the privy so there'd be no contamination from that direction.

The top was boarded over and looked to be in good shape, if weathered. I didn't try to remove any of the planks. I'd leave that to whoever did the plumbing.

A creek ran through the back of the property and was actually the boundary line marking where Mercier holdings ended and someone else's began on the opposite bank. It was small, as those kinds of waterways went, deep enough to swim in or float a boat but not big enough to be a threat except during storm season, when a tornado might dump gallons of water into it and make it overflow its banks. The house was far enough away not to be in any danger, though. There would have to be a veritable flood to reach it.

It was called Black Creek, a branch of the far-off Little River, which itself was the largest tributary of the Withlacoochee, one of the few Coastal Plains streams having limestone shoals and white sand bars. I didn't know if the creek had fish. While hunters might trespass, fishermen weren't as daring when there were other places easier to access.

The creek wasn't the interesting thing, however. The small walled-in rectangle of water between it and the well was.

"What the he…" I stopped as I remembered this was going to be aired. No need to get myself bleeped. "What's this?" I gave Letty a sideways glance. "Your great-grandpa didn't have a koi pond, did he?"

"If he did, I doubt if it would've been tucked away back here." She smirked at my ignorance of fishpond placement. "It would've been in the garden or at the front of the house so everyone could see it."

She walked around the wall, trailing a finger across the top of the bricks. They were in surprisingly good condition, probably because the vines and brambles crawling over them and sinking into the water had protected them from the elements.

"I think this is the baptismal pool."

"The…what?"

"Baptismal pool," she repeated, enunciating each word as if I were hard of hearing, instead of merely ignorant. "My father said there were two springs on the property. One was made into a well." She gestured to that structure. "My great-grandfather had the other walled in and allowed the church where he was a member to use it for baptizing. Gilead Harmony Baptist."

The name didn't mean anything. Probably the church no longer existed.

She circled the wall and stopped at one end.

"See?" she pointed. "Here are the steps going into the pool."

I joined her, looking down. Bill leaned over, pointing the camera at the bricks disappearing into the water. There were three steps, neatly mortared into a staircase about a yard wide, though how many might be submerged we couldn't tell. The visible bricks were mossy with algae and looked slippery and none too inviting. I hoped when they were in use someone kept them cleaned.

Like the creek, the water was dark and there was no way to tell how deep it was. Between it and the river, a giant oak leaned protectively, making shadows on the water. I envisioned a line of parishioners in white robes, heads bowed and hands clasped piously in prayer as they waited to descend into those depths, while the preacher floated nearby, maybe wearing rubber waders to protect his clothes.

Involuntarily, I shivered. I certainly wouldn't want to be ducked under something that murky, even for the brief time it took for a baptism.

Letty didn't notice. She leaned forward, about to thrust her hand into the water.

I caught her wrist. "I wouldn't do that."

"Why not?" She looked up at me.

"Snakes." I released her hand and she jerked it back, fingers closing protectively into a fist. "With the river this close, water moccasins might have decided to leave it and slither over here." I glanced back at the water. "Speaking of moccasins, it might be a good idea for us to get back to safer ground."

A bubble floated to the dark surface. It burst with a *pop!* causing a momentary expanding circle.

"What was that?" Letty jumped.

"Just an air bubble." I watched the ripples spread from where the bubble had been. They struck the brick sides of the pool and disappeared. "Sediment in the bottom shifted somehow and released a bit of air trapped under it."

I wondered what had made it shift.

Taking her hand, I pulled her away from the pool and made my way through the weeds back to the house. It was easy to see where we'd walked. The trampled and flattened coffeeweed made a clear path. Some of the little beggar lice seeds clung to the legs of my jeans. Letty's ankles atop the sandals were scratched and sprinkled with blood-dots. Why hadn't she thought to wear boots or some other protective footgear instead of those flimsy gladiators?

We had probably gone a couple of yards before she pulled her hand from mine. Until then, I hadn't realized I was still holding it. Briefly, my palm felt cold as hers left it.

Back at the house, Letty began her closing statements, ending the episode as the host always did. "Well, Dylan, we've seen the property. What's your initial assessment?"

"Ms. Mercier…" I paused, thinking of what I *should* say, and what I was going to. "I imagine this was once a wonderful place, with that ballroom and all, but…"

I paused, shaking my head. She scowled as if she sensed what was coming.

"It needs to be almost completely rebuilt. You're going to have to rewire it, have electrical fixtures installed…the waterlines need to be replaced, not to mention putting in plumbing and facilities for an indoor bathroom…"

I glanced down at the clipboard, its pages now covered with lines and lines of my notes. I hadn't checked the roof. There had been no way to access it, so I'd guessed at the damage.

"It'll take a miracle and a fortune to get all that done. I know this house probably has sentimental memories for you, but…"

The shadow in her expression seemed the wrong reaction to that statement. She looked as if she wanted to deny it.

"…it'd be best if you simply tore the place down and rebuilt it from scratch."

There was a silence after that. I wanted to call it shocked. Letty looked as if she couldn't believe I'd said that. I was wondering why I had, as I realized I'd probably just done Dad out of a project that would net him a sizable fee.

Biff broke the moment by making a twirling gesture with his forefinger, signaling she should say something because he was recording nothing but dead air.

"Well, we aren't going to do that." Letty smiled, and while it was the sweetest I'd ever seen, it also held the glint of a dagger, as if she were daring me to contradict her. "We know where the fortune's coming from. Guess we'll just have to see what miracles Roth Construction can perform, won't we?"

She leaned toward me, seizing my arm and squeezing it.

"…and cut." Bill lowered the camera.

Chapter 7

After another short break, they filmed one more segment.

On instructions from Bill, I told Letty I'd see her on Monday with the estimate and a work schedule. Getting into the truck, I drove away while Bill stood in the center of the track, filming my departure. Once around the bend in the road, I stopped, counted to ten, then maneuvered the truck around and drove back.

"I need to talk to Ms. Mercier a minute," I explained as I got out of the truck. She looked surprised. I didn't say anything else, just glanced at the two technicians and waited.

Bill and Biff took the hint and beat a hasty retreat.

"Got to download the film, give it a scan, and send it on," Bill said. "Besides, we've missed lunch and I'm hungry."

As if to emphasize this, his belly gave a loud growl. I realized I was feeling a little empty, also. We'd worked right through lunch, and it was now fast approaching suppertime.

"Hey, I'm sorry," I apologized. "I didn't realize…you should've said something." I looked at Letty. "When I go into a walk-through, I sometimes get so involved I forget about mundane things like eating, and this place…"

I shook my head.

"It's all right," Letty brushed any problems aside. "Those two can afford to miss a few meals. I'm surprised you didn't have a couple of candy bars to munch on while you held the boom," she said to Biff.

"And have my crunches get picked up by the mike?" Biff shook his head.

He was busy unstrapping himself from the sound case and stowing it and the boom in the van. Bill had already packed the camera and was in the driver's seat.

"Tomorrow's Sunday, so we'll see you on Monday," he said, starting the engine.

This guy was really in a hurry to find somewhere to stuff his face.

"Where are you two staying?" she asked.

He named a motel just outside town. "Company set it up."

She nodded, and raised a hand as Biff climbed in and slammed the passenger door. She waited until they were out of sight before she turned to me.

"Look, Dylan…"

"I was thinking if you're going to have landscaping done…" I didn't give her a chance to say whatever she'd been thinking up while she watched Bill drive away. I had an idea she thought she knew why I wanted to talk to her alone. I guess I hadn't hidden my reactions very well. "…you'd better have someone grade the driveway, too."

"The driveway?" She looked as if she hadn't expected that.

I could almost see the little wheels going around in that beautiful head, revising the speech she'd thought up to turn me down.

"Your car might've escaped today, but sooner or

later one of the bigger weeds is going to take out your muffler or something else." I took a deep breath. "Matter of fact, you shouldn't even be driving this little low-slung car on this road. Are you going to be onsite while we work?"

She nodded. "If we're filming, I have to be."

"Where are you staying? I'll pick you up and you can ride with me to the site." I had promptly forgotten I was going to let Ben take my place.

She frowned.

"I'm not hitting on you," I assured her. "I'm thinking about your car."

Her expression changed. Did she actually look disappointed?

"It'll protect your car and save you gas. Where are you staying?" I repeated.

She looked thoughtful, then said, "Here."

"Here? You mean, in Estonko? With someone who lives here?"

"No, I mean...*here*." She waved her hand at the house.

"You're planning on staying *here*?" I copied her gesture. "In this house?"

"Why not?"

"For obvious reasons."

I wondered if perhaps DHU hadn't bothered to give her an expense account, though Bill and Biff were booked into a motel. That hardly seemed fair, unless the management thought paying for the renovation *et al* was enough money being spent on that particular employee. Or maybe Letty suggested it and they agreed, not realizing what bad shape the house was in.

"This place is a derelict. Where will you sleep?"

She held up a finger. I fell silent, hoping she wasn't going to tell me she'd sleep in the bed in the master bedroom. Besides the fact that it had no mattress, I wasn't certain it would hold even her weight.

Walking to the car, she popped the trunk, and dragged out a bundle. A sleeping bag and a foam mat.

Okay...

"There's no electricity," I reminded her.

She brought out a small propane lantern.

"You've no water..."

She reached in again and pulled out a six-pack, slinging it over her shoulder. "Bottled water."

"That's fine," I said. "But what about bathing? Or..." I managed a delicate pause. "...going to the bathroom?"

"I'll bathe in the baptismal pool," she answered promptly. "As for the other...as you told Biff, there are plenty of trees around. I've toilet paper in the pack, too," she went on before I could ask.

"The pool might not be safe," I argued. "You don't know how deep it is, and there may be..."

"Snakes," she finished for me. "In that case, I'll just reach in and splash, or...I'll drive back to Bill and Biff's motel and use their shower."

I didn't like that idea. At all.

"I don't know, Ms. Mercier. I don't think you should stay here alone."

"That's too bad, Mr. Roth, because I don't see anyone making you my guardian." She softened her next words. "I'll be okay. There's cell phone service if I need it. This isn't some horror movie where the phones never work and I'll be cut off from civilization. Besides, I've my car if something happens."

That did away with all the reasons I could think of.

"Nevertheless, I don't think you should," I made one last, feeble attempt.

"Why? Because I'm a poor, defenseless female?" Her lip curled, coating each word in acid.

"Actually, I...yeah, that's exactly why," I answered, sounding as if I were calling her bluff. "What if some vagrant decides this would be a good place to crash for the night and he blunders in and finds you..."

Again that finger came up. She reached one last time into the trunk and brought out...a pistol, a genuine Colt revolver. She twirled it around her finger gunslinger-style.

I backed away. "Be careful with that."

"Don't worry. I have a permit and I know how to use it." She mimicked blowing smoke from the barrel, then shoved it into her waistband.

"Well. Okay then." I smiled. I couldn't help it. Looked like she could handle anything that happened. "God help the poor tramp who tangles with you." I touched a finger to the bill of my cap. "In that case, good afternoon, Miz Scarlett. I'll be here first thing Monday morning, with your estimate."

With that, I left her standing there, got into the truck, and drove away. For real, this time.

****

Mom didn't see it that way.

"You left that young woman at that old house *alone*?" She couldn't have sounded more horrified if I'd said I tied her stark naked to a telephone pole somewhere. Well, maybe she might've been a little more worried about the *naked* part.

"She said she can handle herself." I shrugged.

"Nevertheless..." As I had, Mom began listing arguments.

I gave her the answers Letty had given me.

"What if some transient shows up?" she countered.

"She has a gun."

"*A gun?*" She shouted that one word. "Good Lord, she might shoot someone."

"I think that's the general idea," Dad put in.

"Dylan, you go right back over there and tell her she can stay here."

"Here?" It was my turn to react.

"Why not? We have space. She can stay in Ben's old room."

Unlike mine, Ben's bedroom had become a guest room.

"Mom..." The last thing I wanted was Miss Argumentative Mercier in this house, especially at night, not with these quirky little nudges my libido was giving me.

"I mean it. Tell her your parents feel it would be best if she stays with us. And safer."

For whom? I wondered.

"Dad?" I looked at my father.

He shook his head. "Don't argue with your mother, son."

"Now get going," Mom said.

"But I haven't had any lunch, and..." I let an adolescent whine creep into my voice.

"Supper should be ready by the time you get back." She gestured to the stove, saying in a wheedling tone, "Pork chops and hashbrowns."

My favorite. That sent me hustling to the door. "I'll be back in a bit."

****

I came back alone.

"She said to tell you thank you very much, but she didn't want to impose." I added, "I think she'd been asleep and didn't like being waked up."

The fact is, she snarled at me, but I think it was more because I'd seen her all frowzy-headed and sleepy-eyed than anything else.

"If she was asleep, that means she didn't eat anything." Mom glanced at the kitchen clock.

It was still pretty early.

Come to think of it, she hadn't mentioned having any food, just water.

"How old is this girl?" Mom asked, looking thoughtful.

"I don't know. Younger than I am. Maybe Ben's age. Why?"

"Is she engaged?" she persisted. "Did she say she had a fiancé or someone…who might be worried about her, I mean," she added as I frowned.

"Not to me." I thought about it. I'd taken her hand as we walked back from the creek. Her left hand. There hadn't been a ring on it. "I don't think so."

"Here."

She thrust something into my hand. A couple of plastic-wrapped somethings in a zip-bag. Biscuits, each filled with a broiled chip chop.

"Thanks." I began to open the bag. Both would be good appetizers before supper.

"Not for you." Her hand came down on mine, pulling the bag from my hand. "Get your sleeping bag, take those biscuits to that girl, and tell her I said you're to stay with her."

"Now, wait a minute."

"Dylan. Do it." She gave me a stern look. The one saying, *Don't you dare talk back*, as intimidating to me at thirty as it had been at three. "I can't in all good conscience let that young lady stay in that house alone."

Grumbling, I went downstairs, got my gear, and came back.

"I haven't had anything to eat, either," I reminded.

"You do now." She handed me a sandwich.

Slices of pork protruded out the edges, while barbeque sauce dripped onto my fingers. I raised my hand, licking off the sauce. I couldn't wait to get to the car and start munching.

"What do I do if she waves that gun at me and tells me to beat it?" I asked, waspishly.

"You tell her what I said…and don't use that tone with me. Now, take these," again the biscuits found their way into my grasp, "and get going."

"I'm going," I muttered. At the door, I looked back. "If she shoots me thinking I'm a burglar, be sure my epitaph reads, 'He always did what his mother told him.'"

I went out.

Behind me, I heard Dad say, "Ella, what are you up to?"

I wished I knew, too.

Chapter 8

Once again, I ate with one hand and drove with the other. The sandwich hit the spot, as Mom's cooking always did, but this time the spot was larger than usual due to my having skipped lunch. I wished I had more. One sandwich wasn't enough for me, but I could almost hear Mom's reply to that.

You can afford to miss a meal or two, Dyl.

Exactly what Letty Mercier said to Bill and Biff. She and my mother thought alike in some areas.

I eyed the biscuits, resting in their little bag on the passenger seat. I could eat them. Letty Mercier would never know.

Right, and if by some unfortunate circumstance, she and Mom meet, and Mom asks her how she liked the chip chops…

I'd have some explaining to do.

It was only as I finished that I realized Mom had the sandwich, as well as those two biscuits, ready pretty quick. Adding that to the questions she'd asked and what Dad said as I left…was Mom trying to orchestrate something here? Maneuver me and Ms. Mercier into some kind of romantic entanglement?

If so, she was going to be disappointed. Scarlett Mercier was the last woman I'd want to be involved with. If we tangled, it'd only be in an argument because she was just too independent and smart-assish. I liked my females a little more…well, not dependent, but at least not smirking and looking as if everything I said amused them in a *one-upmanship* way. I thought of Jilly and how she'd always laughed at everything I said. Every joke I'd told had been hilarious. It was only after the novel came out that it all became so very *not funny,* making me wonder how many of her reactions had been genuine.

I didn't want someone like Jillian again, either, but…I guess the kind of woman I wanted didn't exist…so never mind about that.

"Stop trying to play Cupid, Mom," I muttered, wiping my sauce-smeared mouth, then brushing my fingers on the thigh of my jeans, leaving a dark red smear. "Damn it, I missed the turn-off."

Again.

I'd been so busy trying to figure out what my mother thought she was doing, I drove right past it. Stopping the truck, I backed it a few yards, then rolled across the storm drain.

By this time, it was completely dark. With the lack of light, the trees and pecan grove didn't look as inviting, just a gathered mass lining the road, making the overgrown meadow an ocean of weeds gently billowing in the wind.

I leaned sideways, glancing out the window, trying to see what phase the moon was in tonight. It had the look of a half-dissolved aspirin, floating behind darkly-highlighted clouds, its light barely penetrating the trees. A lopsided nimbus encircled it, the glow seeming to touch the silvery sphere.

Looks like rain, I noted ruefully. *Great.*

Something white flitted from behind a tree, crossing to another.

What the hell...?

I slowed the pickup. Whatever it was moved parallel to the truck, keeping pace. It was too far away for me to see, other than a vague pale thing floating through the shadows of the trees, ducking behind this one, hurrying across to another, as if playing hide-and-seek with me.

Moonlight. That's all, I rationalized.

The truck rounded the curve and I stopped next to Letty's car, looking up at the house.

In the twilight, the old Mercier place looked even more unwelcoming than it did in daylight. Letty had put up the convertible's top, and the little car seemed smaller than ever. It actually appeared to cower before the house, huddled in the weeds as if trying to make itself less noticeable. If it had been a living creature, it probably would've cringed against my bigger truck for protection.

There was no movement from inside. Glancing up, I saw light flickering through the nursery window. As I watched, it disappeared, then reappeared.

What the hell is she doing upstairs at this time of night?

Leaving the headlights sending a bright beam across the porch, I used a heavy hand on the horn, blasting the stillness.

Abruptly, the light disappeared.

"Hey!" Between honks, I added my voice to the noise. "Miz Scarlett!"

A wavering form appeared in the doorway, I was instantly reminded of the hazy thing in the trees. It shaped itself into Scarlett Mercier blinking in the glare of the truck's headlights.

Earlier, when I was here relaying Mom's message, she'd been wearing leggings and a T-shirt. Now, she'd changed into a nightgown. Great…out here in an abandoned house in the dark and she's wearing a *nightgown*. It was sleeveless, white, and ankle-length, and made her look smaller than ever.

"Who is it?" She put a hand to her forehead, shielding her eyes from the brightness. Her hair was tangled and tumbled about her shoulders in a definite bed-head of curls. "I've a gun."

She held up the pistol. She didn't sound scared, but that didn't surprise me.

"Don't shoot." I raised my hands, stepping away from the truck's headlights, between it and the porch so she could see me. "I'm friendly."

"Mr. Roth? Is that you?"

Well now, she recognized my voice. Maybe I wouldn't get shot, at least.

"What are you doing here?" She stamped across the boards of the porch, taking an unerring path to the steps, bare feet making soft slaps on the worn wood.

I hoped she didn't get any splinters.

"My mother sent you this." I came up the steps to meet her, holding out the zip-bag like a peace offering.

"What is it?" She looked down and shied backward as if I were the one holding the gun.

"Supper. She was afraid you might not have thought to pack any food."

"Oh." She paused a single instant longer, then snatched the bag from my hand. "Thank you. Thank *her*, I mean."

Tearing the bag open, she pulled out a biscuit, ripped off the wrapping, and took a bite.

"You shouldn't wander around the house like that." I decided to put in my two-cents' worth while her mouth was full and she couldn't talk back. "I hope you were careful coming down the stairs. I'd hate for you to take a misstep in the dark and fall. At least you had the lantern."

"What are you talking about?" She spoke around a mouthful of biscuit. She'd finished the first in three bites and was attacking the second.

I guess the lady was hungry.

"You know." I gestured upward. "Walking around upstairs. I saw the light."

"If you did, you're seeing things," she retorted. "I was sleeping soundly until I was rudely awakened by you pounding on that horn." She flung a glance in the truck's direction.

"But I saw…"

"…probably moonlight reflecting off a windowpane or something."

I didn't remind her the downstairs windows were the only ones on this side of the house having any glass. Instead, I mumbled, "If you say so."

I wasn't going to get into an argument with her, not at this time of night.

"I do."

By now, she'd finished the second biscuit. Crumpling plastic wrap and bag in one hand and looking as if she didn't know what to do with it, she said, "Thank you," again.

"You're welcome," I muttered.

When I didn't move, she asked, "Was there something else? Besides bringing me supper?"

"As a matter of fact, there is. Since you refused her invitation to use our guest room…" As she started to protest that, I added, "…though very politely, Mom sent me to sleep here tonight. In case you need help."

"Mr. Roth, I assure you…"

"I know you did, and I assured *her*," I didn't give her a chance to finish, "but she said otherwise, so here I am."

"Do you always do what your mother says?" She scowled at me, but I thought I saw another of those smirking smiles hovering.

"Always. Believe me, it's easier than the alternative, and I speak from a lifetime of experience."

She didn't answer, just stood studying me. The headlights made shadows of her cheeks and temples, turning that red hair into a dark mass, giving her a ghostly look. It made me uneasy, though I knew it was merely an illusion brought on by the effect of car lights and darkness. I decided I should probably get back to the truck and turn off the lights before the battery ran down.

"My gear and lantern are in the truck," I went on, adding, "For propriety's sake, I'll sleep in the truck bed and—"

She looked surprised. That I was concerned with what others might think?

"—in the morning, I'll go home and tell Mom 'mission accomplished' and the letter of the law has been carried out. She'll be happy and that's that."

I didn't bother thinking to the next night or the many others before the project would be finished.

"You don't sleepwalk, do you?"

"Never have," I assured her. At least, no one I'd ever slept with, up to and including Jillian, had said so.

"All right, then…" She started back inside, then whirled to add, "Just remember, I've got a…"

"…gun, I know," I finished. "Don't worry, Miz Sharp-Shooter."

At least that made her smile.

"How could I forget, Miz Scarlett?"

"The name's Letty." She turned away.

"And mine's Dylan," I retorted, starting down the steps.

"Good night, Dylan." She disappeared inside.

I heard her footsteps for a few seconds more, then silence as she retreated into the parlor.

"Good night...Letty," I said, so softly she probably didn't hear.

Hurrying back to the truck, I switched off engine and lights, then unlatched the tailgate and clambered into the bed. The sleeping bag, mat, and lantern were where I'd tossed them. Luckily, the lantern wasn't injured by my rough treatment. I'm afraid I hadn't been exactly gentle when I did it because I was angry at coming back here for the third time in one day.

It didn't take me long to arrange everything. The lantern was primed and I lit and set it on the floor against the truck's toolbox just under the rear window. Unlacing my boots and tossing them to one side, I slid into the sleeping bag and wriggled around trying to find a comfortable spot against the grooves in the metal floor. The mat didn't cushion it much.

At last, I settled down.

It was quiet for a late spring night. The lantern hissed softly. From the vicinity of the creek came an occasional froggy croak. Some crickets in the hedge around the steps decided to have a middle-of-the-night jam session and once or twice I thought I heard a faint buzz that might've been a cicada or two, but surely it was the wrong time of year for those. I was thankful it was too early for mosquitoes to be out, what with the water so close by, especially since I hadn't brought any repellant.

A wind sprang up, sweeping from the creek, bringing with it the scent of water and greenery. I hadn't thought I was tired, but abruptly, I gave a deep sigh and fell directly into sleep.

****

I was running...as fast as I could, so fast it hurt to breathe, my heart pounding in my chest. I had a stitch in my side, my stomach knotting with the effort. Someone ran next to me, breath as labored as mine. Man or woman, I didn't know...I didn't look, didn't have time...whoever was following meant us no good and I couldn't stop to speak, much less look.

We had to get away.

Lightning flashed, making everything as clear as day, and I glanced back. A figure stood next to the uncovered well. There was something in its hands, raised to shoulder level.

"Dylan, look out," my companion warned.

There was an explosion, fire streaking from the rifle. I dodged, but too late. Something struck my shoulder, spinning me around and sending me to one knee.

The second shot missed, striking the tree behind me with a sharp ping. *The figure lowered the gun, fumbling to reload.*

"Get up, Dyl. Come on." A hand grasped my uninjured shoulder.

The figure fired again.

There was a sudden sharp thud between my eyes. I didn't feel the trickle of blood dripping down my forehead and into my eyes as my head was knocked backward, nor did I hear the liquid splat! *as bone and*

brain matter spattered the tree…
****

I opened my eyes as a loud *ping* sounded beside me. Something struck my chest, hard and sharp as a pebble launched from a slingshot. Still in the grip of the dream, I threw my arms over my face. There was a second *ping* and a third, and……the bottom fell out.

Those first few drops weren't enough of a warning to fully wake me and give me time to run for the safety of the house. The downpour did that. Sitting up and struggling out of the sleeping bag, I reached for the lantern, then scrambled over the tailgate. Dragging boots and sleeping gear with me, I ran in sock feet across a yard rapidly becoming mud. It took only a few seconds to get up the steps and under the shelter of the porch overhang where I looked at my socks, caked in wet clay reflecting red in the lantern's glow.

"Damn." I threw the sleeping bag to the porch and set down the lantern.

The wind changed, sending the rain at an angle so it doused several inches of the porch. Placing my boots well out of wetting range, I checked the sleeping bag, determining the outside was all that was damp. My clothes hadn't fared as well. My tee was soaked and the legs of my jeans mud-splashed as well as sopping.

"I sure as hell am not going back out in that," I said aloud. Pushing the mat through the open threshold, I kicked the sleeping bag inside and knelt to smooth it. "Gun or not, I'm staying right here." I jabbed a finger at the doorway.

"Dylan?"

The lightning flashed again and I looked up to see Letty doing her ghost imitation in the doorway. She pushed a lock of hair out of her face. "What's the matter?"

"Sorry. Did I wake you?" I stood, explaining unnecessarily, "It's raining,"

"Did you find yourself at high tide?" She glanced at the truck as if expecting to see the bed filled with water.

"Not yet, but I imagined I might soon." I'd left the tailgate down so the water would run off. "I'm sleeping here." I gestured at the porch, my tone brooking no argument.

"You may still get wet. Come on in. You can sleep in the foyer." She turned and went back inside.

That was a surprise. Perhaps the lady had a soft spot for something besides mice.

As I gathered everything, the wind whipped across the porch, bringing a sudden wave of water with it. That reminded me I was standing there in wet clothes. No way was I sleeping in them, possibly adding injury to insult by catching a summer cold.

Letty was nowhere in sight, no doubt snuggled again into her own sleeping bag. Dropping everything in front of the closet where I'd be sheltered from any rain blown through the doorway or falling through the roof, I unzipped the sleeping bag, opening it all the way, using the inner blanket like a sheet. Then I peeled down to my skivvies, wringing out my wet tee and jeans.

The banister to the stairs was barely visible in the lamp's light. From the hole in the roof, I could see rain spattering the upper steps and dripping down them. I hung my clothing over the banister where it angled, in hopes everything would dry during the night. Mud-coated socks followed. Barefoot and clad only in briefs, which were thankfully dry, I settled myself, rolling onto my side. At least here the foam mat gave more support.

Vaguely I noted there was no trickling of light from the parlor, so apparently Letty had turned off her lantern. Squeezing my eyes shut, I stifled a shiver. As the wind blasted through the door again, I willed myself back to sleep, listing to the patter of rain on the steps.

****

Dylan…

The sound was so soothing I didn't want to answer.

Dylan…

The edge of the blanket was pushed aside. A hand slid down my chest, resting momentarily on my stomach before moving lower.

With a mutter, I shifted uncomfortably. "Jillian?"

Fingers began stroking in a familiar caress, making little curling tingles as nails gently scraped the flesh of my thigh. *That's my girl.* I gave a little grunt of enjoyment, then thought, *Wait a minute.*

Jillian was gone, had been for over two years. I was back in Georgia and I'd fallen asleep on the floor of a deserted house with the rain outside and Letty Mercier in the parlor. Who…?

The hand tightened.

"Letty?" I came fully awake. "What the hell are you doing?" It wasn't a yelp but a harsh whisper. I didn't want her to stop doing it, but I had to know *why*? I'd certainly not done or said anything to make her think…

Don't you know?

I didn't answer, because her voice wasn't coming from *above* me. Rather, it seemed to be inside my head, as if I were *thinking* it. I forced my eyes open. She was a blurred shape, hovering. It was almost as if I *sensed* rather than saw her presence.

You want me, Dylan. You know you do…

Her whisper was as harsh as mine had been but also held a hungry sound, almost predatory.

I'm here. Don't hold back.

Her hand slid between my thighs, cupping my jewels, gently squeezing.

Where the hell had my briefs gone? Did I take them off in my sleep? I'm dreaming. I have to be.

Okay, then…if this was a dream, I'd go along with it. No harm in that. I shifted slightly, legs parting so she could grasp me easily.

Her body was so warm it felt feverish, bare skin pressed against mine.

When did she take off her nightgown?

I caught her arms, my own fingers tightening around them, digging into that heated flesh. It should've hurt, but she didn't make a sound. I brushed the hair back from her face. Her eyes were dark in the lantern light, shadows seeming to blend with those of her cheekbones and chin, making her face almost skull-like as it reflected the light.

Damn it, this is no dream. She's real, and she's here. With me.

I felt a surge of lust so deep it hurt, making my body writhe beneath hers. I groaned.

Oh God…all right then, no matter what I'd said before…in that moment, I took it all back. I wanted Letty Mercier more than I'd ever wanted any woman.

"Letty," I whispered. "Are you sure about this?"

Of course, I'm sure. That sibilant whisper came back. *You want me, and I want you. That's all that matters.*

I didn't answer, just placed my hand behind her head and pulled her down to kiss her. Her mouth opened against mine, tongues meeting, flicking… She made a little moaning and pulled away, nipping at my earlobe, pressing her lips against my jaw, trailing a row of butterfly kisses back to my mouth. At the same time, her hands were still busy, roving over my chest, moving in smaller and smaller circles across my belly.

"God, Letty…I didn't realize…"

I wrapped my arms around her, trying to sit up, push her onto the bedroll and get on top. She pinned me down with an arm across my chest.

When did she get so strong?

I didn't care. I fell back, thrusting against her hand, feeling my cock tighten and harden. I knew I should move slower, but I was so damned turned on I didn't want to. It wouldn't be long before I…

The sound of the rain changed, becoming a deluge of water against the roof, gathering speed as if timing itself to my thrusts. It splashed against the upstairs floor, cascading down the steps.

The caress changed to a heavy pumping, her grip tightened, faster…up, down…

"Hey, slow down….I don't want to…"

Too late. I felt it building. I was going to…

I heaved upward.

"Letty!" I screamed against her mouth as my climax gushed over her hand, onto my thighs, spattering the blanket. Her mouth ground against mine. I felt her teeth bite into my lip. I tasted blood, a thick stream trickling down my chin.

Thunder crashed.

"Dylan? What is it?"

I jerked away from the sound of her voice, skittering backward and taking the blanket with me as I crashed my back against the closet door.

Another flash of lightning lit everything, and I came fully awake, seeing Letty, standing in the parlor doorway in that ghostly nightgown.

What the hell?

Why was she standing over there when, moments before, she'd been lying on top of me naked, giving me a half-unwanted hand-job? I could still feel the heat of her tongue against mine, the tightening of her fingers as I came…

Oh God, she bit me. I'm bleeding…

I touched my face, rubbing across my lips, staring frantically at my fingers. Nothing. My skin was unbroken. I ran my tongue across my lip. It didn't hurt.

What about…

My hands searched frantically under shelter of the blanket, brushing over its underside, across my body, finding…nothing. The blanket was dry and so was I, as was my underwear. Underwear? I still had it on?

For God's sake, did I dream the whole thing? I'd swear I was still shaking from the rush of that orgasm.

Letty was staring at me.

"What's the matter?" I caught my breath, inhaled quickly, and tried to sound matter-of-fact. "Can't sleep? I'd think the sound of the rain on the roof would be soothing."

"It would, if it wasn't dripping on my head," she retorted. She took a step closer.

"Think up a better excuse than that." I edged farther away, coming up against the wall, wondering if I was about to repeat in real life what I now realized had been in my mind. "There's no way the roof leaks where you are. There's a solid floor between it and the parlor. It'd happen out here first, and it isn't doing that yet…as you can see."

"Okay, you got me." She gave a shaky laugh. "I confess. I'm terrified of thunderstorms. I know…" She held up a hand as if to stop me from speaking. "…it's a silly thing for a grown woman to admit, but…" She shrugged. "…there it is, and in view of that…"

The thunder from that last lighting jolt cooperatively battered the house. I swear I felt the foundation shake. Letty shuddered.

"…I wondered…" Her voice changed, becoming childlike and tentative. "Could I sleep out here? With you?" She added quickly, "Just to make me feel more secure? After all, that's why you're here, isn't it?"

I hesitated. This was a moment when saying the wrong thing could be a disaster. Should I be flippant, suggestive, or simply nonchalant? I found myself wanting to sleep with her, and by *sleep*, I meant have sex leading to a genuine climax instead of a dream one, but I didn't want to take advantage of her, either.

I made my choice. After all, she was a client and any misbehavior on my part would definitely be a questionable business practice.

"Sure." I gestured. "Don't bother with dragging your bedding out here. Mine's big enough for two. We'll have room so we won't crowd each other."

Amazing how calm I sounded.

I raised the blanket. She saw my bare chest, and took a step backward.

"Don't worry," I said. "I've still got on my underwear. Everything dangerous is covered."

She laughed at that, a silent sound but I saw her mouth curl upward, and an eyebrow follow. *Maybe still slightly dangerous?* that expression said.

Nevertheless, she lay down. I did also, carefully keeping a couple of hands-widths between us. I spread out the blanket. She sighed, wiggled slightly, then lay still. So did I, but I didn't go back to sleep immediately.

I allowed myself the luxury of thinking how nice it felt to have a female lying near me again. She was close enough to touch. If I dared raise my hand, my fingers would brush against that nightgown and the body inside it. I'd be able to feel the warmth of her skin through the thin fabric. Would it hold as much heat as my dream Letty had?

I didn't move.

In spite of my previous denials, I was attracted to Letty Mercier and simply refused to admit it. Now that I was fully awake and convinced what had happened minutes before was a dream, I recognized my subconscious was telling me the obvious, though this was neither the time nor the place to begin anything. Some people might've considered being alone in a darkened house with a pretty girl, both of us as close to naked as possible without actually being so, and a thunderstorm pouring buckets around us...some might've considered that a romantic setting.

Not this boy.

If we'd been upstairs in that monstrosity of a bed, with a feather mattress, perhaps. Down here with a wet wind blowing through an open doorway? No.

Lightning flashed and thunder roared.

She started and rolled over, her eyes meeting mine in the lantern's gleam.

"That was a big one, wasn't it?" I whispered.

She nodded. "I suppose you think I'm a coward."

"If I did, I'd have to call myself a coward, too. I've a healthy respect for lightning. I wouldn't like to be struck by it."

When the next peal crashed, we both jumped.

"Come here." I held out an arm. Abruptly, I wanted her warmth as near me as possible. "Sharing the fear'll help."

She didn't hesitate but wriggled toward me. I tucked the blanket around us and gently curved my arm against her. She burrowed her forehead into my shoulder.

Dylan, what are you doing?

"Goodnight." Her voice was muffled against my chest.

"Goodnight, Letty."

Going to sleep holding a pretty girl, that's what.

****

I don't know how long I slept. All I know is that I was abruptly jolted awake by another explosion of thunder.

Letty was gone.

Please, don't tell me that was another dream.

Raising myself on an elbow, I saw her silhouetted in the doorway. She was sitting on the sill, staring out into the rain. Getting to my feet, I wrapped the blanket around my shoulders and pattered across the dampened floor toward her.

She looked up. She'd drawn up her knees, arms wrapped around them. Surprisingly, she wasn't wet. The wind had changed direction. Again.

"I like to watch it rain, though I don't like the thunder."

"Just another of Life's little contradictions." I eased myself down beside her.

With the wind blowing through the rain, the night had turned cool. She shivered. I slid off the blanket and put it around her.

"You're going to catch a chill." She draped half of it over my shoulders and moved closer. "We'll share."

I didn't hesitate to put an arm around her. She rested her cheek against my shoulder, and we stared out at the rain.

The steps were sodden now, the rim of porch at the edge of the overhang black with water. The car and the truck gleamed with raindrops beading on their hoods and running in rivulets over the bumpers. The little car seemed to huddle nearer the bigger vehicle, just as Letty was pressing against me. Was the soil so wet it had slid closer to the big truck?

"Good thing I decided to put up the top," she murmured. Then she laughed. No, it was more like a giggle.

"What is it?" I whispered.

"I was just thinking. I never expected to be in a situation like this, especially with a Roth."

"What do you mean?"

She straightened, giving me a stare I felt more than saw. "Like you don't know what happened here."

"Letty, I've no idea what you're talking about."

"In that case, forget I said anything." She looked down, cuddling closer and snuggling her head into the little hollow between my shoulder and neck.

After a few moments of silence, she whispered, "I've read your book."

"Please, don't be a critic at this time of night."

"Don't worry, I won't. Was any of it true?"

"I was a high-salaried reporter in Washington, DC.

I lost a libel suit filed by my ex-father-in-law, and now I'm working as a carpenter for my father in Estonko, Georgia. What do you think?"

She didn't answer.

I rested my cheek against the top of her head. Her hair was a warm, soft mass against my chin. It held a lemony fragrance mingled with the fresh scent of rainwater.

****

The next time I awoke, it was morning. I was lying on my back in the doorway with Letty's head resting on my chest and the blanket pulled up over both of us.

Chapter 9

She raised her head, sat up, and stretched languidly with a sleepy mumble, "Mmm."

The movement pulled the nightgown tightly across her breasts, making me swallow loudly. Each rounded globe was plainly outlined, nipples peaked by the cool morning air.

"Sleep well?" I asked, looking away.

"Mmm." Obviously she was monosyllabic first thing in the morning.

"You didn't have any nightmares, did you?"

"Like what?" She stretched again, and shivered slightly.

"Like...I don't know...being chased through the woods by someone with a rifle, or..." I decided to go for it. "...seduced by an incubus?"

"Rifle? Incubus?" She stared at me, then laughed. "You've been watching too many horror movies. That's not what *you* dreamed, is it?"

"Of course not," I scoffed, and lied, "Actually I didn't dream anything. I was too uncomfortable."

"Probably because you were sleeping on a wooden floor in a reputedly haunted house." Her reply was casual, as if it meant nothing. "Anyway, I was snuggled next to you, so no incubus would dare bother me."

She smiled as she said it and I realized she wasn't kidding. She'd just paid me a compliment. That gave me the most stupid, warm, fuzzy feeling, something good to have with the air still cool from the storm and me wearing only my skivvies.

"Thanks for humoring me last night," she went on.

There were any number of replies I could've given to that—joking, sarcastic, serious—instead, I chose to keep it non-threatening.

"It would've been very ungentlemanly of me not to, wouldn't it?" I answered. I forced myself to believe the atmosphere had caused that erotic mental episode. "Besides, that's what I was here for."

Things were still friendly between us, though I'd expected her to awaken, take one look at where she lay, and scramble away as fast as she could.

"Guess it's time to get up and get dressed. What time is it?" She studied the sports watch looking big and out of place on that small wrist. "Eight o'clock?"

She pushed back the blanket and stood up.

I didn't move, except to hastily pull the blanket back into place, trying to look casual as I did it. I'd abruptly become aware I had a massive piss hard-on that more than made up for the imaginary one I'd had the night before.

"I think I'll just wait until you're inside…" I tried to sound casual as I made certain the blanket covered everything. Thankfully, it didn't twitch.

Oh?" Both brows shot up. "…and he's modest, too." Her eyes danced. They flicked quickly to the blanket and back to my face.

She knew why I wasn't moving, damn it.

"Okay, shy guy. I'll leave." She walked, not very fast, into the parlor.

I'd swear there was a deliberate sway to her hips that

wasn't there before.

****

"What now?" Letty asked.

We were standing on the rain-washed porch, the boards so water-logged I was surprised they didn't squish under our feet. We were now dressed and had made separate and unspoken trips into the trees, going by mutual consent in opposite directions.

Letty was wearing the same leggings and sandals but a different shirt, this one a plain tee in a shade of green that did great things to that red hair. I'd swear it matched her eyes exactly.

I'd put back on what I wore the night before. Everything was dry…almost…just damp enough to make me shiver as I slid on the jeans and tee. It took a while to scrape the dried mud off my socks, and I finally had to beat them against the banister. Most of it came off, though they were no longer white but now had an orange tinge. I stuffed them into a pocket. At least my boots were dry.

"I thought I'd get some breakfast," I replied.

I found myself wishing I'd brought a deodorant stick with me. I was certain last night's little dream escapade had made me sweat profusely. Any odor protection had probably been washed away, and I didn't want to offend.

"How about you?"

"Sounds good." She was still agreeable. "Can you recommend a local eatery? Do you have a favorite one?"

"Sure." My answer was so prompt, it might've been rehearsed. "Mom's Place."

"Where's that?"

"Where I live. Come home with me and have breakfast at my parents'."

I actually caught her hand, giving it a gentle tug.

"Oh, I don't know…" The first doubt she'd shown all morning was visible, but she didn't pull her hand from mine.

"I do." We were getting along and I wasn't going to let her fall back into being her old sarcastic self. "My mom's a great cook. Remember those biscuits?" I reminded.

She nodded with a definite expression of enjoyment.

"Besides, I know she'd like to meet you." I released her hand.

"Yeah?" She shook her head. "I think you just want to prove to her you stayed here last night and didn't go off somewhere and spend it drinking with your best buds," she accused, and actually shook her finger at me.

"No, really…"

"Relax." The soothing little pat she gave my shoulder was a surprise. "I'm kidding. Are you always so serious?"

"Frankly, Miz Scarlett…" She grimaced as I called her that. "With you, there are times when I'm not sure how to react," I admitted.

"Nevertheless…"

"Come on, Letty," I coaxed. "Home-cooked meal? As good as your mother's?"

"How do you know?" She laughed. "My mother might be a terrible cook."

"If she's Southern, she can't be," I countered. "We'll be having grits…"

She looked interested, then frowned and turned away, head down.

I moved with her, bending so I could look up into her face. "…bacon and eggs…"

She turned to the other side.

I trotted around so we were still facing each other. "…and cheese toast…"

She sighed. "Cheese toast…all right…you got me."

Baby, I wish I did.

"Great. We'll take the truck and let your car dry out."

"My car *is* dry. I put the top up. Remember?"

She followed me, driving the sports car.

****

"Glad to see you didn't drown last night," Dad said as I came through the kitchen door. When he saw Letty behind me, he went on, without missing a beat, "Good morning, Ms. Mercier, I hope my boy didn't disturb you too much."

I scowled. *Why'd he say that? What are you hinting, Dad?*

"On the contrary, Mr. Roth," she responded, smiling and revealing a dimple that until now I hadn't noticed. Maybe it was because this smile was a genuine one and not her usual sarcastic smirk. "I was glad to have Dylan around."

"Oh?"

"Uh-huh. As much as I hate to admit it, I'm a real scaredy-cat when it comes to electrical storms."

Scaredy-cat? I liked that old-fashioned phrase. *Wish she'd been more scared last night.*

"Dylan has always been a calming presence," Dad lied without blinking, then followed it with, "What can we do for you? I don't have the estimate prepared yet." He obviously thought she'd come for business reasons. "I want Dylan to go to the courthouse tomorrow and see if the plans for the house may have been recorded. After reading his walk-through notes, I think I need to look at the original blueprints if they're available."

"That's fine. I don't think there's much hurry just now," she replied. "Won't the wood have to dry out a bit before you begin?'

He nodded. "While that's happening, we'll have someone check the bricks in the foundation supports. I know a good brick mason."

I'll say he does. My cousin Jerry, Uncle Cliff's son. The electrician we'd hired would be my uncle Rick, and Uncle Cliff would do the plumbing. Too bad Dad didn't have a third brother so we could corner the market on landscaping, too, and make this into an all-inclusive construction company whose motto was *Nepotism at its Best.*

"I'll leave all that in your capable hands," she answered. "Actually, I was invited to breakfast, and…" Voice dropping, she leaned forward as if imparting a secret. "…I'm eager to meet the fearsome lady who inspires such obedience in her son."

"Fearsome, huh?" Dad laughed and nodded into the kitchen. "Well, there she is…the firebreather herself."

Mom was at the stove, almost in the same spot as when I left. If I didn't know better, I'd think she hadn't moved all night.

"Ella, look who's come to breakfast."

"I heard, Charles." She paused, glancing over her shoulder.

Carefully, she removed the pan from the burner, placed each slice of bacon on a sheet of paper toweling, then laid down the tongs and came over to the door.

"Shut the door, Dylan. You're letting in flies."

Obedient as always, I pulled the screen shut,

grimacing as I saw Letty smile, glancing in my direction.

"Mom, this is Letty…Scarlett Mercier," I said, before Dad could do the honors.

"Pleased to meet you, Letty. Come in and sit down, dear." Mom patted her on the shoulder. "Breakfast's just about ready."

It was a pleasant meal, if an odd one. Odd because it was so normal.

I remembered how diffidently polite Mom and Dad always were to Jillian when we came for a visit, as if she were some celebrity and they weren't quite certain how to treat her. There was none of that with Letty. They acted as if she was a relative they were meeting for the first time but were certain they were going to like, much the same way they'd been with Liz when Ben brought her for that get-to-know-the-Roths dinner.

Wait a minute…I swear I felt my hackles rising.

I wasn't certain whether to protest or ride it out and see where this alarming—at least to me—scenario was heading. I decided to adopt a wait-and-see attitude, and was surprised to find, in a very short time, I was laughing along with Letty and we were acting as if she had come often to Mom's kitchen and sat in that same spot at the table.

Mom hadn't stinted on the meal and Letty didn't hesitate while eating it. As my Uncle Cliff would've said, the girl had a healthy appetite. I wondered if she always ate like that, and how she managed to be such a petite little thing if she did. Perhaps she had some kind of exercise program that matched construction work.

As she finished her second piece of cheese toast and leaned back with a sigh, she gave me part of an answer.

"I swear, Mrs. Roth, if I ate like this every day, I

wouldn't fit into my car." She glanced at me. "You were right, Dylan. She's just as good a cook as my mother, but don't tell Mama I said that."

"I doubt I'm ever going to meet your parents" I laughed, gulping down the last of my coffee.

"Don't be too sure," Dad muttered before stuffing his fourth strip of bacon into his mouth.

I gave him a glance, the frown accompanying it asking, *What?*

He'd been making comments like that all during the meal. I glanced from him to Mom, who was studying Letty appraisingly.

Oh, please. That *frisson* of alarm returned. *These two aren't teaming up to be matchmakers, are they? Say it ain't so.*

Letty distracted me by saying, "I want to thank you for offering to let me stay here last night."

"You're welcome, dear," Mom was all smiles. "I'm sorry you refused."

"If I'd known it was going to rain, I might not have." Letty laughed. "And that said, may I ask if the offer's still open?"

"Of course it is." Mom didn't have to think about it.

"Good, because I don't believe I want to spend another night in a sleeping bag." She glanced at me. "Even if Dylan does make a mighty nice pillow."

I'm glad I had already swallowed that mouthful of coffee. Otherwise I might've sprayed the table.

Before I could recover, Mom was on her feet. Thank God she let the comment pass.

"Why don't I show you the room? Then I'll come back and clear the table."

"Let me help." Letty stood also, picking up her

plate.

"You don't need to—" Mom began a token protest.

"After that great breakfast, it's the least I can do."

She reached for my plate, but I held on to it. I still had half my toast and a couple of spoonfuls of grits left. For a moment, we engaged in a ridiculous tug-of-war before she released the plate and looked at Dad's.

"Go ahead," he said.

She picked it up, placing it atop hers, then gathered his knife and fork and her own, laying them on the plate.

Oh, she was racking up points right and left, much to my chagrin and my parents' delight.

With Letty helping, scraping the plates and putting everything into the dishwasher didn't take long. Then she and Mom went through the door into the hall connecting to the upstairs.

"It was my son Ben's room," I heard Mom explain. "It shares a bath with Dylan's old room. I turned that one into a sewing room. I didn't know he was going to come back home."

Letty said something I couldn't understand. Mom replied and their voices faded away.

"A pillow, Dylan?" Dad gave me a stare. He looked as if he wanted to ask for clarification but couldn't figure out how to word it nicely. Finally, he said, "Your mother merely wanted you to make certain the girl didn't come to harm."

I finished my grits, then munched down my toast before I answered.

"She didn't. She's afraid of thunder and needed a little reassuring, was all." I made that my explanation and stood. "You should know by now…"

I stopped as someone came clomping down the

stairs. Letty popped back into the kitchen, snagging the little backpack she'd set by the door.

"I'm going to take a shower. I feel a little grungy."

She ran back to the stairs.

"Good idea." I nodded and took my plate to the dishwasher. "I think I will, too." I gave Dad a direct stare. "Sleeping in my clothes doesn't exactly inspire freshness."

Before Dad could say anything to that, I hurried downstairs.

Reminding myself to bring in the sleeping bag and lantern later, I stripped as I descended. Pulling my socks from my pocket, I shook them over a wastebasket to catch the residual red dirt, then rolled them into a ball and dropped them into the hamper. Jeans, shirt, and briefs followed. In deference to it being Sunday, I decided that when I re-dressed, I'd put on slacks and a shirt.

Letty's presence had nothing to do with my choice of clothing, I swear.

Dad had set up the apartment so the bedroom was the first thing entered after coming down the stairs. There was a wall with the bed pushed against it; on the opposite side, a chest of drawers and a dresser with an old cathode ray tube TV atop it.

Around the wall was the kitchen, with the bath in a nook just off it. The bathroom was as nice as the one I'd previously shared with Ben. It had a shower stall but no tub. I wasn't one to linger and soak, so who needed that? There was a cabinet with a marbleized sink and plenty of shelves below, holding towels and washcloths, shampoo, toilet paper, and soap. A large framed mirror opened to become a recessed chest where my razor, deodorant, toothbrush, and toothpaste were tucked away. The walls and floor were tiled, and it was well lit from two small windows located at the top of the wall on each side of the shower.

Taking the bathmat from where it hung over the shower door, I spread it on the floor, reached in, and gave the faucet a single twirl, sending it as far to the left as it would go. Hot water splashed, cascading billows of steam. I adjusted the knob, got washcloth and towel from the cabinet and plunged in, slinging the towel over the top of the door as I slid it shut.

The water felt good. As I lathered and scrubbed, ridding myself of dirt and grime from the Mercier yard and floorboards, I thought of Letty doing the same thing in the upstairs bath.

Had she taken her worn clothing from the pack and dropped them into the hamper in Ben's room as I had in mine? I envisioned her scampering into the shower, ducking under the flood of droplets.

What color wash cloth and towel did she choose? I glanced at the blue one in my hand as I reached for the bar of soap hanging from its rope over the showerhead. What the hell did it matter what color washcloth she used? Why was I thinking such stupid thoughts?

That didn't stop me from thinking more.

As I rubbed the cloth against the soap, I wondered if she'd used one of the bottles of body wash rather than soap. They certainly lathered more. Maybe she'd chosen a net bath scrubber instead of terrycloth. I could almost see the soap-laden netting rubbing against Letty's arms and throat, lather bubbling as it came into contact with her skin. Suds sliding down her chest, running onto her breasts, dripping from the points of her nipples to the shower floor to spin and gurgle down the drain…

…while I used sudsy fingers to massage her wet gleaming shoulders…

That thought struck me with the force of a fist to the belly. I'd never had sex in a shower, but God, I wished I were with her right then, wet body against wet body, so close not even a soap bubble could've survived between us, while we…

A violent surge of cold water blasted from the shower, sending me staggering under its force. I struck the wall, all ardor and lascivious thoughts wilting in that frigid wave.

Letty had turned on the shower upstairs, and the sudden pressure in the pipes redirected the hot water, leaving me shivering in its absence.

I'd forgotten about the little problem of two people showering at the same time.

Stumbling from the stall and reaching for the towel, I wrapped myself in it and attempted to restore circulation.

Once that was accomplished, I swiped a comb through my hair, dressed, and headed back upstairs.

"Slacks?" Dad's eyebrows shot up. "And a dress shirt, too?"

"It's Sunday," I said.

"So it is," he agreed, glancing to the hallway.

Who are you kidding? It was as plain as if he'd said it.

Mom didn't say anything. They both busied themselves with reading the paper. Dad had the sports section, Mom the Sunday funnies.

"Okay, Dad." I decided to take advantage of Letty's absence to say, "Before she gets down here, I want to know—"

"I feel much better." Letty appeared in the doorway. She was dressed in the green tee and leggings, and the ends of her hair were damp. They made little wet spots on her shoulders. "Thank you, Mrs. Roth."

"Think nothing of it, dear." Mom looked up. "Now then, what do you two have planned for today, since it's Sunday?"

For the first time, she gave my clothes the onceover.

Letty noticed them also but she didn't comment. "I don't know what Dylan's going to do…"

I relaxed slightly as she silently acknowledged how my mother had lumped us together while very skillfully nixing that idea.

"…but while I was showering, I realized if I'm going to stay here, I need more than a tee-shirt and a bottle of roll-on deodorant."

"Like what?" I started to point out I hadn't had either last night, then realized she'd probably have some sharp-edged retort to that.

"Like…a toothbrush and a comb…make-up…some changes of clothing…different shoes…" She shrugged. "I realize now I came very ill-prepared."

"God, Letty, you're only going to be here a few days," I exclaimed. "You're not moving in permanently."

"Dylan!" Mom sounded shocked.

"Sorry," I apologized. "I didn't mean that the way it sounded. I meant…"

"No problem." She seemed to find my verbal stumbles amusing but did nothing to help me pull my foot out of my mouth. "What I'm going to do is drive home and pack a *small*…" She emphasized that one word. "…suitcase and come back."

"Where's home?" Mom asked.

"Aaronton. It's only two and a half hours from here. I'll stay overnight and drive back Monday morning." She hefted the little backpack and smiled at my parents. "Anyway, my dad's going to want a report on how things went." She gave Dad a look seeming to mean something other than she'd said. "He was a little anxious…"

"Will he worry about you staying with the Roths?" Dad asked.

"No reason he should. Not when I tell him what nice people you are, and what well-mannered sons you have." She gave me something that might've been a wink, or maybe she had something in her eye. "I'll see everyone tomorrow."

"Drive safely," Dad said.

With a nod, she went through the kitchen to the back door. I followed.

At the door, she stopped and looked back.

"Don't look so disappointed. I said I'm coming back."

"Who's disappointed?" I said. "I'm merely surprised you'd drive all that way just to get clothes and stuff. Anyway, you don't need makeup." I decided to take a chance and hope she wouldn't think I was shooting her a line. "You're pretty as you are."

"You think so?" She looked surprised.

"Said so, didn't I?" Damn, I sounded so juvenile it wasn't funny. All I needed to do was scuff the toe of my shoe against the floor and say, *Aw, shucks.* "Anyway, you can buy whatever you need here, or drive over to Amesville, for that matter."

"I could," she agreed. "But maybe I want to put a

little distance between you and me. I mean, just because we slept together last night..."

"Not so loud." I put up a silencing hand, glancing back at the door going into the living room.

"...doesn't mean I intend to fall for a guy with curly black hair and sexy blue eyes."

Before I could react, she was out the door and running to her car. I watched as she tossed the pack through the window, opened the door and slid inside and started the engine. Without looking back to see my reaction to that complimentary little bombshell, she spun the car around and drove it out of the yard.

From the get-go we'd grouched at each other like fractious siblings, but a single night in a damp old house made her say I had sexy eyes? While I...face it, I'd been having salacious thoughts about her before we were formally introduced.

Don't question it. In fact, don't even think about it. I wondered if I was going to listen to my own sage advice. Maybe later. Just then, I had something more important I needed to know. Spinning on my heel, I marched back into the living room.

"Okay, now that Letty's gone..."

"...and I'm really surprised about that," Mom said. "But at least she'll be back."

"Mother, whatever you're cooking up, forget it," I said. "Letty Mercier and I are not going to be romantically inclined toward each other any time soon."

"If you say so, dear." She went back to the paper, laying aside the comics and opening the magazine insert.

"Don't do that," I warned. She'd used the same tone she always did when I said something and she refused to argue because she *knew better*. "I...no, never mind. Dad, what's the deal here?"

"What do you mean, son?" Dad looked up from the want ads.

"Quit it. You know exactly what I mean. What's this thing you and Letty keep hinting at? The bygone you two are letting go by. The reason her father might worry about her staying with us?"

Dad didn't answer.

"You may as well tell him." Mom looked around the page she was holding. "It's unfair to keep Dylan in the dark, especially since Letty obviously knows."

Dad didn't answer. Instead, his mouth tightened into a sudden straight line.

"He has a right," Mom went on. "So simply state it plainly…about your great-grandfathers, and the scandal, and everything."

"Scandal?" I looked from him to her and back. "What kind of scandal?"

Dad sighed. "Why bring it up?"

"You already have," she answered. "By not bringing it up."

"So there really is some deep, dark secret?" I asked. "A skeleton in the Roth closet…and the Mercier one, too?"

"I don't know why it has to be dug up at this late date." Dad folded the newspaper and dropped it onto the lamp table in a gesture just short of throwing it. "Everything's going well. Why can't we simply ignore it and—"

"You realize you're only making me more curious," I told him. "What happened?" His expression was so serious I had to laugh. "Come on, Dad. What could be so bad? Did Great-Grandpa Roth run off with Great-

Grandpa Mercier's wife or something?"

Mom drew in a sharp breath.

For a full minute, Dad studied me silently before he answered.

"On the contrary. He ran off with Great-Grandpa Mercier."

****

Excerpt from Dylan Roth's journal, July 12, 1925:

Today, Jules Mercier advertised on the community bulletin board at the hardware store that he wishes to hire workers to build a house. He owns the property on the other side of Black Creek. My work is going well, but I can always use more income, with two little ones now, so I will apply to him as a carpenter.

Chapter 10

I shook my head. "I think I misunderstood. It sounded like you said…"

"That's exactly what I said." Dad didn't give me time to finish.

"You mean he was…gay?" I don't know why I paused like that, as if I were afraid to say the word. I had gay friends, good ones, too, or rather I'd thought they were, before they turned their backs like all the others. But knowing someone gay and being told a family member is…that was different. My liberal attitude crumbled.

"Sit down, Dylan," Dad said. "You don't look too good."

"I imagine he's in shock." Mom's comment sounded so matter-of-fact. "Honestly, Chuck, you could've phrased it a little differently."

I fell rather than sat into the chair that, fortunately, happened to be directly behind me.

"I guess that *would* be considered a scandal," I said quietly. "Back then."

Were my lips really as stiff as they felt? They seemed to have trouble forming the words, and that made me angry. Damn it, this was the twenty-first century. As a reporter, I'd seen and written about things much, much worse than two men forsaking their families because they realized they'd fallen in love.

There's no stigma in being gay.

How often had I defended those friends from the Senator and Jillian's scorn? I felt like a hypocrite. First time I was tested and I failed miserably.

I forced reporter instincts to kick in.

"Tell me."

Once again, Dad hesitated. "Why go into detail?" He spoke to Mom rather than me. "Dylan knows that much. It's enough."

"Hardly."

That one word made him bite his lip.

"*The evil men do lives after them. The good is oft interred with their bones*," he shot at her, defiantly.

She didn't change expression.

"Let's leave Shakespeare out of this," I spoke up. "Tell me, Dad. All the details. If Letty mentions this again, I want to be totally clued in."

He was silent a moment longer. Then I heard, "All right, but…" grudgingly given as he cleared his throat, and sat gathering his thoughts.

This is what he told me:

Dylan Roth came to the States after the First World War. Yes, you're named for him, though that wasn't his real Christian name. Like his last name, it was something unpronounceable and 'Dylan' was the closest English equivalent. I'm surprised no one ever wondered why a Middle European had an Irish first name. He had a sponsor, some soldier he'd met during the fighting, and that soldier had relatives in Georgia so he came here and ended up settling in Estonko. He was an orphan, his parents having died in an influenza epidemic. When he wasn't being a soldier, he was a carpenter, and all he brought with him from the Old Country was a small portmanteau of clothing, a Bible, and his tool kit.

The people here accepted him and he settled in. He spoke English fairly well, thanks to his doughboy friend.

In a couple of years, he began courting a local girl and married her. They had two children, your grandpa and your Aunt Ila.

Jules Mercier arrived a year after Dylan. His people were from Savannah. There's still a small French Creole community there. Unlike Dylan, who had only a couple of dollars his friend could spare, Jules came from a monied family. He didn't throw his weight around, though, and was a generous man.

Anyway, Mercier and his wife, Marianne, lived in a cottage on the property. She was a pretty little thing, from all accounts, but high-strung, and of a slightly nervous disposition.

"Nervous. What does that mean?" I interrupted. "Define 'nervous.'"

He shook his head. "I haven't a clue. That's the way the newspapers described her."

"Newspapers?" My voice went up. "You mean, this got into the papers?" I imagined some hotshot reporter, just like Yours Truly, getting hold of the story and running with it.

Oh, it would've been juicy back then.

He ignored that and kept talking.

Jules became a farmer. He planted corn and soybeans, and was making a good living at it though he didn't really need the money. Eventually, he decided he wanted a bigger house. Later, the story changed...that he liked the cottage fine but his wife felt they should have something better.

Well, anyone in town who could wield a hammer or

a saw wanted the work because it was a chance to make some good money because Jules was offering top wages. One of the men he hired was...

"Don't tell me, let me guess...Great-Grandpa," I finished for him. "Because he was a carpenter."

The words sounded as if they came from the Voice of Doom.

He nodded. "Those fireplace carvings, the doors, and the finials on the stairs...your great-grandpa did all those. He was a master woodcarver as well as a good carpenter."

I remembered the fine workmanship on the mantel in the parlor, and what I'd said to Letty. Dad was right. Dylan Roth, my namesake, had definitely been a talented man.

Dad picked up his story again.

During that time, Jules discovered Dylan wasn't the typical foreigner who didn't speak English and was ignorant of American ways. He was quick-witted, good-natured, and well-educated. He also was the closest neighbor...

"Wait a minute!" Again, I interrupted. "We don't live anywhere near the Mercier place."

"Once we did," Dad replied. "The original Roth home place is the land on the other side of Black Creek," he explained. "Still is, for that matter, all three hundred acres of it. It was abandoned after they... Afterward."

"If it was abandoned, wouldn't it have been sold for taxes or something?" I persisted.

"Son," he spoke gently as if afraid he might upset me.

Too late, Dad, I wanted to say.

"The family's paid the taxes on that property for

118

years. It's still ours."

The two became friends, and often they'd drive into town in Dylan's Model T truck to the local tavern for a drink or two. Even after the construction was finished, the friendship continued. It seemed harmless. Later, after their real relationship was learned, it was remarked how well they kept it hidden, that only one incident was remembered that hinted at anything different about it.

That was after the house was completed, when Jules threw a housewarming party. Dylan and his wife were there, but they stayed only a short time. He was seen having what looked like an argument with a tearful Marianne Mercier. He then spoke to Jules just as heatedly, collected his own wife, and left. After that he never came back to the Mercier place again.

Eventually, Dylan and Jules again met in the tavern, Jules looking bruised and battered as if he'd been in a brawl somewhere. They were seen in what appeared to be very serious conversation, with Jules doing most of the talking and Dylan looking sympathetic. One night a few months later, there was a bad electrical storm and a warning that a tornado was expected. Dylan got a phone call. He and Jules were two of the first to take out a subscription when the telephone exchange was installed. He told his wife Jules Mercier needed his help. He kissed her, sent her and the children to the root cellar where they'd be safe, told her he'd be back 'in a while' and left.

He never came back.

Dad paused.

"He never came back?" I looked up. "That's it? Where did he go? What happened?"

"No one knows exactly. The next morning, after the

storm had passed and everyone emerged to check the damage, Marianne Mercier appeared at the sheriff's office. Her face was bruised and scraped as if someone had manhandled her terribly. According to the sheriff's report, Jules told her he had fallen in love with Dylan Roth and they were leaving and taking the children with him. When she protested, he struck her and locked the children in the nursery, pocketing the key. Dylan arrived and they left in his truck. She tried to get the door open by hacking at it with an ax, but she wasn't strong enough so she came to town for help. Jules' truck was still there but he'd taken the keys, and she didn't know how to drive, and the horses had been let out because of the storm, so she walked into town."

I thought of the distance from the Mercier place to downtown Estonko. If the police station was in the same place then as now, that was a long way for a lone woman to walk in the early hours, especially with the roads muddied and probably cluttered with debris after a storm.

I imagined her leaving two children behind a locked door and forcing herself to make that trip.

"The sheriff took her back home," Dad continued. "They could hear the children crying as soon as they reached the turn-off to the property. The sheriff ended up shooting off the lock and getting out the two kids, who were hysterical. The oldest, who was about five, couldn't tell them anything, except that 'Mama and Daddy had a fight.'

"Inside the nursery on the floor, there was a bloody puddle. Marianne said it was where she fell when Jules hit her. She refused to be taken to the hospital in Amesville. That afternoon, Dylan's truck was found parked in the alley behind the train depot in Amesville, but neither he nor Jules were heard from again."

"What happened to her? Mrs. Mercier, I mean?" I asked.

"She stayed at the farm two more years. Some of the neighboring men offered to harvest the crops but she refused, letting them go to waste. The second year, she packed up the kids and moved back to Savannah where Jules' family took her in. A few months later, she ended up in the state mental hospital."

I shuddered to think how the facilities were back then. Even now, the place wasn't all that inviting, mainly because most of the patients were moved to community facilities and the hospital had stopped taking new patients.

"Her brother-in-law had her committed. Ironically, it was on the anniversary of her husband's disappearance. Guess the emotional strain was too much. She died there. The brother-in-law adopted the kids and raised them."

"What about Great-Grandma?"

"She never believed what she was told, insisting Dylan would eventually come back with a reasonable explanation. He didn't, of course."

"Did the Merciers think we were holding a grudge or something? Is that what Letty meant?"

"Probably," he agreed. "Though we never did." He went back to the story. "Anyway, ten years later, Great-Grandma met someone who persuaded her to have Dylan declared legally dead. They married, and that's why your great-uncles Jim and Rob have different last names. And there you have it."

He stopped, waiting.

All I said was, "If Jules planned to take the children with him, why did he lock them in the nursery and leave them?" My reporter's' mind concentrated on that one statement, ignoring everything else.

"Who knows?" Dad looked a little disappointed at my question, as well as my lack of reaction.

I guess he was expecting explosions of anger or something.

"Maybe he realized two men couldn't care for them like their mother could. Or he decided they'd be in the way. Or…I don't know." He gave me an odd stare. "No one's ever brought up that before, and I imagine there were a lot of other questions asked back then."

He shrugged.

"Suffice it to say, the kids were left behind and ended up better off with their uncle in Savannah."

"Her commitment. That's where the 'high-strung, nervous disposition' verdict came from, I suppose?"

"Guess so," he acknowledged.

"Why haven't I heard about this before?" I knew I sounded as if I were trying to disprove everything he'd said, but it didn't seem possible something like this could be buried so deeply. "You know how small towns gossip. This would've been grist for the mill. How come there's never been a whisper of it?"

"Mainly because the sheriff was a 'southern lawman' and not the caricature kind. He was also your great-grandmother's second cousin, and he let it be known right quick what might happen to anyone with loose lips. He couldn't keep the story out of the papers or a report from being filed, but he sure kept the townsfolk from talking about it, from his deputy to the operator at the telephone exchange."

I remembered…back then, operators could listen in on calls and generally did.

Dad sighed.

From his expression, I couldn't tell if he was proud or ashamed of the sheriff's power.

"The town just wanted it to go away, so they helped the sheriff by staying quiet."

"I need to think about this." I lay back in the chair, an arm across my eyes.

After that, I didn't say much. In fact, I didn't speak for quite some time. I really didn't know what to say, so I just sat, eyes shut. I guess Mom and Dad thought I'd fallen asleep, though I was vaguely aware of them getting up and moving around, leaving the room, coming back…

I re-emerged when I heard the screen door open.

"Where are you two going?" I got up, hurrying into the kitchen.

They were standing in the doorway. Dad was now wearing a suit. I had to admit he looked handsome when he put on something other than his work jeans and a chambray shirt. Mom had changed from the jeans and tank top she'd had on at breakfast and was now wearing a dress…and a hat.

My mother loves hats, the big-brimmed, Southern barbeque party kind. This one was straw with flowers around the crown. On her, it looked good. She was one of those women who could wear such a thing and not appear ridiculous.

"To church. Eleven o'clock service," Mom answered, then asked, "Would you like to come with us? It's been some time."

I was thankful she didn't try to make me feel guilty

but made it a simple statement.

"No, thanks." My reply was a little curt. "I'm afraid God and I aren't exactly on an even keel just now."

I wasn't about to subject myself to a monotonous droning, punctuated by sudden bursts of fire and brimstone, telling me how wicked and evil I was when I knew I wasn't.

The fact was, the Supreme Being and I were presently at a contretemps. To be blunt, I'd lost my faith. I couldn't understand why all this had happened to me. I truly wanted to believe there was a Plan to it all, a reason why. That losing my wife, and my job, and being forced to partially become a child again by living with my parents and working for my dad, was piece of some larger whole. Beginning with the moment Mom opened the door and found me standing there, suitcase in hand…when I blurted out that I had nowhere else to go, and she put her arms around me, murmuring, "It's for the best," that it *meant* something.

I truly wanted to believe that, but I couldn't.

I mean, I thought I was a good person. I'd never stolen or killed. As I said, I was faithful to Jill from the moment I decided she was the one. Even in my reporting, I made certain the innocent were never harmed, and yet…

Why me?

I still had no answer, so I continued struggling to figure it out, ignoring the hometown solace of religion.

"I think I may take a nap, to make up for last night."

They didn't argue, merely nodded as if expecting exactly that answer. Mom pushed open the screen and went down the steps. Dad looked back.

"The pastor's been asking about you. I've been

putting offering envelopes in the collection plate in your name so he's not certain whether you're absent or he simply hasn't seen you."

"Thanks, Dad."

I hoped that bit of sleight-of-hand didn't get him in bad with the Deity. The last thing I wanted was for my father to be on God's bad side because he'd lied for me.

He nodded and went down the steps.

Now that I was alone, I didn't know what to do. The nap I'd said I might take sounded pretty good, though I wasn't really tired. I still didn't know how Letty managed to look so bright and rested after sleeping on a wooden floor. Maybe it was a female thing. Of course, she'd had my chest as a pillow.

Nevertheless, though I went downstairs and lay down, I was too restless to sleep. Five minutes horizontal and I was on my feet again, pacing. I came back upstairs. The newspapers were folded neatly at the end of the sofa, where Mom always put them, but I didn't want to read of current shootings, more statues being ripped down in an attempt to wipe out the past, or another witch-hunt accusation of sexual harassment. My current mental turmoil was depressing enough without sharing the world's.

So there I stood, in a house I'd lived in for twenty-one of my thirty years, and at loose ends.

Idle hands are the devil's workshop. So are idle minds.

I went looking for something to do, and found it. In the living room bookcase, where my pacing eventually took me.

Stopping before it, I found myself staring up at a large book on the top shelf. It was a big volume, nearly twelve inches tall, its leather spine hand-tooled with swirling vines and roses.

Once, when I was about eight, I'd noticed it and asked Dad what that *big book* was. He told me it was the family Bible, and was really old because it had belonged to my great-grandfather, that its extreme age was why no one ever took it off the shelf. That satisfied me and from then on, I ignored it.

Until now.

I remembered what Dad had said.

...all he brought with him from the Old Country was a small portmanteau, a Bible, and his tool kit...

Comfort for his soul and the way to make a living.

I'd never been curious before. After all, great-grandfathers belonged in the past and that's where I'd relegated this one, until now. Suddenly I wanted to know more about him. I *had* to know more about the man behind the scandal. Where better to start than with one of the two things coming with him to this country?

Even standing on tiptoe, I could barely reach the shelf. My scrabbling fingers pulled the book to the edge, where it toppled into my hands.

The family Bible, passed down to the eldest son, from the original Dylan Roth to Grandpa Ted to Dad, and someday...to me, his namesake.

Clutching it tightly, wondering if its weight were partly from any secrets it might hold, I carried it downstairs where I laid it on my desk.

****

Article from the *City News,* June 30, 1926:

Search Continues after Storm for Missing Men

Though Rowen County was left remarkably unharmed by the recent tornado, and there have so far been no casualties reported, sheriff's deputies and townsfolk continue searching for two Estonko residents. Sheriff Ezra Benson of Estonko states that Dylan Roth, 30, a local carpenter, and Jules Mercier, 32, a farmer, were reported missing by their wives. According to Mrs. Roth, her husband received a telephone call from Mr. Mercier asking for his help in securing some farm equipment. Roth left his home just before the storm struck and did not return. Once it was safe to venture out, both women reported their husbands missing. Deputized townspeople are searching the countryside around the two properties.

Chapter 11

For a few moments, I simply studied the book, rationalizing I wasn't delaying opening it but admiring its workmanship.

Apart from its antiquity, it was definitely a work of art. The covering was genuine leather, a deep, glossy brown, though very dusty because it had been on that shelf for a very long time. In fact, I don't ever remember seeing it taken down and opened. Mom and Dad had Bibles of their own, and Ben and I each had a personal King James Version, presented to us at the age of twelve when we were baptized.

That made me wonder where mine was. I hadn't seen it in years.

I brushed that thought aside, studying the one before me. Pulling out my pocket handkerchief—the men in our household always carried a handkerchief, per Mom's orders—I brushed it over the front and sides, wiping away some of the dust. Then I set it on end, looking it over.

The spine had three raised bands, curved to look like vines with tiny leaves. These continued onto the front cover where buds and little roses blossomed. Gently, I ran my fingers over them, feeling the embossing and indentations. There was writing on the cover, in gilded Old English lettering encircled by more vines and roses, but instead of the words *Holy Bible,* it read *Sfânta Biblie, cu Deuterocanonicals și Apocrypha.*

Obviously it was printed in whatever original language Great-Grandpa had spoken, so no mystery there. For now, I was more interested in what might be written inside.

Laying the book flat, I very carefully opened the front board. I wasn't certain how fragile the pages were, but I didn't want to tear anything by forcing it open. It turned easily, a bit of gold-tinged powder flaking off the gilded edges, revealing an end paper with an inscription written in ink so faded I had to squint to read it.

Dat fiului nostru pe occasiona de ziua lui de naștere al optsprezecelea.

It looked to be the same language as that on the cover, but I had no idea what it meant.

"Okay. Let's find out."

I straightened, reaching for my laptop, the only thing I'd brought back from the hostile D of C. Booting it, I typed in a few words and brought up an internet translator.

"Computer, do your stuff."

I typed in that sentence. Since I had no idea of the language, I clicked on the little magnifying glass icon, *Search this translation.* In a few seconds, I had my answer...the language was Romanian and the translation...?

Given to our son on the occasion of his eighteenth birthday.

That shook me, thinking of my great-grandfather as an eighteen-year-old. Was he touched by his parents' gift, or annoyed because what he'd really wanted was a 1915 French touring car, or...wait a minute, he was from Romania...perhaps a thoroughbred saddle horse?

I typed in the words from the cover.

Holy Bible, I was informed. *With Apocrypha.*

The word *Apocrypha* puzzled me. Why was it there? This wasn't a Catholic Bible, I was certain.

I soon got an answer.

Turning the page, I found the frontispiece was an engraving of the Archangel Michael fighting the Devil in the form of a dragon. The title page contained the same words as the cover, and on the back were more words in Romanian and the date, 1914. Below that was printed, *Imprimi Potest, Nihil Obstat,* and *Imprimatur.* That was in Latin, which I recognized. Under each phrase was a name, and after each, what looked like a title.

I flipped through, looking for the *Table of Contents.* Scanning the lists of titles, I saw there were too many books, fifty-one in the *Old Testament* alone. That confirmed what I suspected.

"Shit…this is…" I stopped, guilt rushing in at the profanity I'd just used about the Good Book. "…an Orthodox Bible."

Remembering how suspicious Southerners back then would've been of Catholics, I wondered how the good Primitive Baptists of south Georgia had reacted to a new arrival professing to be Orthodox, something probably few of them had ever heard of. Great-Grandpa must've had a way about him. Hadn't they allowed him to marry one of their native daughters?

"Probably didn't let her forget it, either, after the scandal," I muttered.

I wondered if he'd converted.

I looked back at the leaves I'd skipped.

More Romanian leaped out at me, but I guessed what it meant, for underneath were lines upon lines holding names. This was what I wanted to see.

The first name was *Dlăndru Mihai Rthleăniu.*

My great-grandfather's actual name. *No wonder that clerk at Ellis Island changed it.*

That didn't make the sudden shiver running down my spine any less real.

It was written in ink that was still dark after all this time. I studied my great-grandfather's writing. He'd had a bold but legible masculine hand with a visible flourish. Behind his name in ink of a different shade of blue was another one in parenthesis, *Dylan Michael Roth.*

Under that was his birthdate, March 22, 1896. That gave me another shiver, more of a shudder this time. Why? Because March 22 was the day I'd been born nearly thirty years ago.

So we shared more than our names. I wondered if that was the reason Dad named me after him, because we were born on the same day.

Next to his name was another date, June 30, 1936. It had been written by someone else, in a very feminine and delicate script. Great-Grandma?

Once again, my body trembled. That must've been the date he was declared legally dead. That wasn't the reason I was bothered, however. Today was May 4. In a little over a month, it would be the eighty-seventh anniversary of that day.

To shake the feeling that the arrival of that date meant something, I forced myself to continue reading.

Across from his name on the same line was written, "Married Anna Belle Rowen, June 10, 1922."

Rowen? Was she somehow connected to whoever the county was named after?

"…at Mount Gilead Harmony Baptist Church."

Below that was her birthdate and after it, someone else, perhaps Grandpa Ted, had scribbled her death date. The next line held their children's names, once again written in Dylan's bold script. Theodore Michael and Ila Mae. They had been born two years apart, Grandpa eleven months after their wedding.

Damn, I didn't realize Grandpa was so old. He had nearly a century behind him, but he was still going strong, though he now walked with a cane and complained about it. Grandma pacified him by saying it made him look "distinguished." She was ten years younger than he and occasionally teased him about robbing the cradle.

To the side of Anna Belle's name was another…James Alexander Troup, her second husband and father of the two men whose names followed: James Junior, and Robert. Their wives, offspring, and descendants were written in the margin. Guess whoever formatted this particular version of the family history record didn't allow for second marriages.

The names under theirs had been written in by Grandma: Dad's name, when he married Mom, and my and Ben's births. Uncle Cliff and Rick and their wives and our cousins. Liz's name was there also, attached to Ben's name with the "M" for Married notation, as was Jillian's. After her name was written, "Divorced March 3, 2020," a day that would live forever in infamy, as far as I was concerned. Right up there with Pearl Harbor and 9/11.

I assessed what I'd learned. My great-grandfather's nationality and true name, and that was about all. What good had that done me, except to make him a little more real and not the shadowy figure he'd always been, but now one with a sinister connotation?

As I shut the book, I noticed something was stuck between the Table of Contents and the next page. When I turned it, I found two photographs, pushed so close to the inner hinge I had trouble extracting them. I finally managed to work them loose. The pictures were very old, though in great shape, probably because they'd been inside the book and away from light and dust. The only damage was that they were bent at the corners a little. They were black and white, the edges slightly deckled as a good many photos were cut back then. The first was...

I stared...

...at myself...

How the hell...?

A closer look told me I wasn't the subject of the photo, though there was an uncomfortable resemblance...the same dark curly hair, though it was shorn extremely short in the style of the early twentieth century, so the curls were a mere rug-like mass on top. Do I need to say that I *really* experienced a shiver then?

He was also tall and slim but muscular.

So that's how you looked. I had to admit I hadn't pictured him that way. I'd envisioned him as short and stocky with a broad, high-cheeked face. I don't know why. Looking at Dad or Grandpa, I should've known he wouldn't look that way.

It was a wedding picture. He was holding a girl in his arms, the typical *carry-the-bride-across-the-threshold* pose. She was wearing a dress made of some shiny fabric, satin perhaps, a swath of lace wrapped around her head and trialing over his arm. In one hand she held a bouquet of flowers, the other caressed his cheek. They were looking at each other and smiling.

He loved her, I thought. There's no way the look he gave my great-grandmother could've been anything but genuine. Even if later he'd loved Jules Mercier more, I knew he'd truly worshipped Anna Belle Rowen in that photographed moment.

I turned the picture over. On the back, written in that same bold hand, *The happiest day of my life, the day I married my Annie. June 10, 1922.*

That should've made me feel better. Instead it made me sad.

I looked at the second photo.

Dylan sitting on a porch step.

He was in work clothes, flannel shirt and dungarees, and held a blanket-wrapped bundle, tilting it slightly so a little hand and a bit of a chubby cheek were visible. The inscription on the back read, *"The second happiest day of my life, the birth of my son Theodore. May 3, 1923.*

"If you loved them so much…if you were so damned happy…why did you abandon them?"

I didn't realize I'd spoken aloud until I heard my words echoing through the room.

Shoving the photos back between the pages, I slammed the book shut. I slid it off the table and ran up the stairs to the bookcase, where I struggled to lift it and shove it back into place. Then I stood there, staring up at it, fighting to control my breathing.

Why am I so angry? It happened almost a hundred years ago. The town's kept it quiet. No one today cares. It doesn't affect how I feel about Letty—and I readily admitted to myself that I liked her, a lot—*so what does it matter?*

I couldn't answer that. All I knew was that it did.

Maybe it was because I was named for a man who'd

deserted his family...or because we were born on the same day and the date of his "death" was rapidly approaching. I don't know.

All I did know was that the man who'd been in that photo with Anna Belle had loved her, and if Jules Mercier hadn't come along, he'd probably have stayed married to her. He might never have recognized his dual nature if Jules Mercier hadn't wanted a bigger house to please his "nervous" wife. I wondered if Mercier had known of his own tendencies before then. Had they struggled against it? Was that what the meeting had been about, where Jules talked and Dylan listened? Of whether to fight or give in? When had they succumbed? Had they ever actually physically come together or was it merely admitting the attraction? After they ran away, did either think of what they'd left behind?

"What the hell am I doing?" I said aloud, looking around, glad I was alone.

I couldn't understand why I was becoming so emotional. All I knew was that the next time I saw Letty, I was going to ask her exactly what she'd been told. We'd compare notes, and then...

...if she was willing, I was going to find out more. The fact that Jules wanted to take his children with him but locked them in the nursery instead still bothered me.

Something else didn't sit well. Both Jules and Dylan were apparently religious men. Jules' offer of the baptismal pool proved that, as did one of Dylan's two possessions being a Bible. Forsaking his family, and engaging in a homosexual relationship would've been considered an ultimate sin back then. How long did it take for him to consider Jules Mercier worth eternal damnation? To disappear like that and never, ever, try to communicate with his wife…to find out how his children were, especially his son, the reason for the *second happiest day of his life?*

It didn't add up, and those reporter's instincts I'd thought dead and buried, after all that had happened, were stirring into life and asking questions.

When Mom and Dad came back from church, I was sitting in a chair in the den, working the crossword puzzle in the paper.

"Good sermon?" I looked up.

"The usual." Dad shrugged. "We're all going to Hell in a hand basket and the End Times is on a collision course."

"Chuck," Mom admonished, though she laughed.

"Pastor asked about you," he said. "I told him you'd just left."

"Thanks." I studied the crossword, trying to sound casual because I'd decided I wasn't going to tell either him or Mom what I planned to do. "Want to watch the telecast of the Preakness after dinner?"

We had horses at my uncle Rick's farm, and Ben and I had gone that route as teenagers, wanting saddle horses instead of motorcycles. Dad wasn't much of a horseman but he liked to watch them run.

He nodded. "Sure."

"Dinner's in the crock pot," Mom said. She'd rid herself of hat and purse and was tying on an apron. "I'll dish it up and we'll eat."

Chapter 12

The next morning, the sharp blast of a horn announced Letty's arrival. As Dad ushered her into the kitchen, I saw she'd brought Bill and Biff with her. Bill immediately swung his camera into position while Biff hovered behind with the boom.

"Hey…" I was so glad to see her I made my greeting into a rude remark. "Come in and invade our privacy!" Before she could answer, I caught her arm, giving it a quick squeeze to let her know I didn't mean to be so abrupt. "Hello, Letty."

Her brows went up as she glanced at my hand. "Hi, Dylan," she said softly, as if she didn't want the mike to pick up her voice.

With a smile, I released her and she smiled back.

"Have a good trip? How are your folks?" I continued, making small talk for the camera while actually wanting to know her father's reaction.

"Pretty good," she answered. "My dad was glad to see me."

Meaning he accepted whatever she'd told him?

"Mr. and Mrs. Roth, this is Bill, my cameraman, and Biff, who handles the sound." She got back to business, introducing them with a wave.

Mom and Dad responded with nods. As Letty said 'camera,' Mom's hand had gone to her hair, smoothing it, while the other touched her apron. Dad didn't say anything, watching bemusedly as Bill panned the camcorder, taking in the scene.

There was a momentary span of dead air, filled in when Mom asked, "What do you have there, dear?"

It was then I saw that Letty was carrying a paper grocery bag.

"Just some groceries." She smiled. "Since you've been good enough to invite me to stay here…" She was apparently wording it formally for the camera. "…it's only fair I contribute to the meals I'm going to eat."

She set the bag on the table.

"I stopped at Chauncey's Grocery and picked up a few things."

"Oh, you shouldn't…" Mom immediately began the required refusal, even as she thrust a hand into the bag and drew out a carton of eggs.

"Oh, I should," Letty responded. "You've already seen what an appetite I have."

They both laughed as Letty took three packages of bacon out of the bag—my stomach cheered at that—and a box of stone-ground grits, plus a pound tub of margarine.

Mom responded by opening the fridge and indicating a shelf. "You can put the bacon here."

Letty obediently placed everything where she was told, then again turned back to the bag while Mom put others things on shelves. There was something still in it, a piece of cardboard about three feet long, similar to a mailing tube.

"My dad sent you a gift, Mr. Roth." Pulling the tube from the bag, she swung around, looking at Dad, who was busy refilling his coffee cup.

"For me?" Dad looked surprised.

"Now you won't have to go to the courthouse or wherever to look for the blueprints." She held out the tube.

Dad took it, turning it and looking at one end. There was a plastic cap tightly snapped into place.

"It's a copy of the house plans," she explained. "When I told Dad you wanted to look at them, he said he'd found a set in an old trunk in the attic and decided to keep them…so here they are."

With a little effort, Dad screwed off the cap and tilted the tube. A roll of pale blue paper slid out, along with a flutter of tiny flakes reminding me a bit of the way the mouse's nest had floated into the air from the kitchen island.

He coughed and watched the bits of paper litter the tabletop. There was something written on the outside back of one ragged corner. Dad glanced at it. "'August, 1925.' I should be handling these with cotton gloves. I hope my touching them won't harm them."

Gently, he unrolled the prints, spreading them open on the kitchen table. They immediately tried to curl back into a roll.

"Get something to hold this down, Dylan."

I looked around, gathered a pair of salt and pepper shakers, and took a couple of cups from a cabinet, placing them at each corner of the top sheet once Dad got it fully open. Everyone leaned over the table, peering at the white lines drawn on the faded blue pages, Bill peering along with the rest of us.

"Well now…" Dad studied the top page silently while Bill peeped over his shoulder. He calmly moved sideways so the camera could get a better look.

"Thank your father, Letty. This will be a great help

when they start doing the wiring and plumbing."

Pushing the shakers and cups aside, he began re-rolling the plans, handling them very carefully so no more of the edges broke off. Letty held the tube while he gently stuffed them back inside. Putting the tube under his arm, Dad pulled his cap off one of the coat hooks attached to the back of the door, and looked around.

"Now then, everyone ready to get to work?"

"Let's get started on the dream!" I'd been hovering in the background, and felt it was time I put in at least a penny's worth.

"Let's." Letty caught my arm, wrapping her hands around it.

Surprised at that blatant and very visible display of her interest and hoping it wasn't merely for the camera, I opened the door and escorted her down the steps to my truck.

Bill followed, still filming. When she was inside, I slammed the door. He slid the camera from his shoulder, said, "See you at the house," and he and Biff ran to the van. I was glad they weren't riding with us.

Once we were on the road, heading toward the office where the crews would be waiting for their assignments, I decided to tell Letty I was well aware of our great-grandfathers' decamp and my plan to investigate the family scandal.

"Dad told me what happened," was my opening line.

"And…?" She didn't ask what I meant. For either of us, I could be referring to only one thing.

"And…to say I was shocked would be putting it mildly," I admitted, keeping my attention straight ahead and not looking at her. "I had no idea the Roths were hiding a skeleton. More than that, the whole thing's aroused my curiosity."

"Oh? Curiosity." She arched one of those copper brows. "Is that all that's aroused?"

"Don't, Letty." I looked away from the road long enough to glance at her. Any other time, I might've welcomed a little flirtatious if slightly salacious banter, but not now. "I'm serious."

"I can see that," she said. Her voice changed, became a bit chastened, then matched mine. "Curious in what way?"

"Looking at it from other than a personal point of view, I'm thinking a few things don't add up," I answered.

"No one thought that at the time," she said. "In fact, I'd say they all considered it an open-and-shut case...boy meets boy, boy loves boy, boys leave wives and run away together...pretty cut-and-dried, in fact."

"True enough," I agreed, "on the surface but sit back and think about this so-called 'family scandal' dispassionately..."

"So-called?" she repeated, and pointed out, "Two men abandon their families and leave town together. Back then...no two ways about it...that *was* a scandal."

"I agree, and it offered some immediately stifled gossip fodder, plus a great headline, but..."

"But...?" she prompted.

"Something doesn't add up."

"You've already said that."

The truck's wheels hit a series of potholes in the road. *Bump...bump...bump...*a staccato of sound effects as the chassis bounced, and so did we. Letty winced and braced her hands against the dashboard, regaining her balance.

It was a few moments before she spoke again.

"My great-grandmother didn't seem to think that. Neither did the sheriff."

"Perhaps that's because he was too close to the event. *She* definitely was." I didn't add *my* great-grandmother hadn't believed it. "After all, this was a fairly emotional case, and I imagine everyone involved got pretty psychologically upset. They all knew each other, were neighbors…'*Things like this just don't happen in Estonko.*'" I took one hand from the steering wheel long enough to make air-quotes. "It isn't like it'd be in a big city, where the cops and the victims are generally strangers to each other."

I concentrated on steering around a branch lying in the road, probably blown from a tree during the recent rain.

"Maybe that's why I think something isn't right, because I'm generations removed from what happened and can look at it a little more impersonally."

"All right, then. Let's accept something's out of place." From her tone, I couldn't tell if she was agreeing with what I said or challenging it. "What is it that bothers you? *Impersonally?*"

Okay, she was challenging my argument.

"The kids, for one thing…if your great-grandfather intended to take them with him, why lock them in the nursery?"

She thought a moment. "Because he realized they'd be too much trouble? That was the general opinion."

"That's what Dad told me, but I'm wondering… Did anyone actually ask that question? Or did they simply assume it?"

"They couldn't very well ask Jules. He was long

gone. *Your* great-grandmother wouldn't have known. *My* great-grandmother was the only one present…"

"Right. Marianne. She's the one who said Jules struck her. She bled onto the floor—that's what the stain in the nursery is, by the way."

She winced slightly. I knew she was remembering touching the ancient splotch just inside the nursery door.

"He dragged her out of the nursery, but instead of going back in and getting the kids, he locked the door. Why?"

"Maybe your great-grandfather arrived about then and convinced him to leave them behind. Maybe…" She shrugged and shook her head, more in irritation then defeat, however. "I don't know."

"All we have to go on is what Marianne said. The kids were too small to tell anything. She was the only witness."

"Are you suggesting my great-grandmother lied?"

"I'm not suggesting anything, except that it doesn't feel right."

She didn't answer.

"Look, I was an investigative reporter, remember?" I tried a new argument. "I am…*was* trained to see things others wouldn't notice." I shook my head. "It sounds more like he was trying to keep someone *away* from them. Otherwise, why take the key so no one could open the door?"

"Keep away *who*?"

"I don't know, but the sheriff had to shoot off the lock to get them out."

"I admit you've got a point, but the reason could simply be the one given. He wanted the kids, then thought better of it." I guess the way my face darkened

143

slightly as she brushed aside my argument made her ask, "Anything else?"

"Why abandon the truck? Train tickets were really expensive back then, and there wouldn't be any credit card paper trails to follow. All they'd have to do was keep the truck filled with gas. Why leave it? They wouldn't have to follow a set route like a train would and could make a better getaway."

"People running away don't always think clearly. This sounds like a spur of the moment decision. Maybe at the time it seemed the thing to do. Anyway, they were never heard of again, so I'd say they got away pretty well."

"Right. Where did they get the money to 'never be heard of again?' Apparently neither wrote a check or drew on their bank accounts."

"How should I know? Maybe both carried huge wads of cash."

"Still…" I hated the fact that she had an answer for everything I said.

"Look, you're basing your doubts on two events that have very plausible explanations. Are you certain you're not simply trying to rationalize away the whole thing and downplay it because a relative, even one a hundred years in the past, was involved?"

"Do I need to remind you…*your* relative was, too?"

"Touché." She looked abruptly earnest. "Listen, Dylan. I'm going to say something I hope I won't regret."

I stiffened slightly. "Should I stop the truck? Is it safe to be behind the wheel?"

"Of course it is."

She didn't appreciate my levity. I didn't bother

saying I was only half-kidding.

"Go ahead."

She took a deep breath. "I like you. More than I should at this stage of the game."

I hoped she didn't notice how I relaxed at that, nor the grin I struggled to hide.

"Because of that, I wish we'd met under different circumstances. Without this scandal hanging over us, and…"

"Hey…" I released the wheel long enough to put my hand over hers in a brief touch. "For whatever it's worth, I wish that, too. And the feeling's mutual, don't doubt it. But the scandal *is* there, Letty, old as it is, and something doesn't jibe." Later, I'd want to go into more detail about how I felt about *her*. "Something's not right. I feel it."

"Dylan…"

"Don't try to convince me otherwise. When I'm on the scent of a story, I can't be stopped. Ask my ex-wife. She'll confirm it."

"I hope I never meet your ex-wife," she said.

That definitely made a warm spot in my heart. I leaned back, drove the truck around another pothole, and didn't even feel the jounce.

"Okay, Mr. Reporter, you've planted a seed of doubt," she said, in a tone of resignation. "What do you plan to do about it?"

"I'm going to treat it like I would any other story. Check sources…witnesses…"

"That's going to be difficult. You're talking about something that happened ninety-six years ago. Most of the people involved are dead now, and those who aren't? They probably can't remember."

"Archaeologists have pieced together stories from

longer ago than 1926," I reminded her.

"Most of their work is based on speculation," she shot back.

I ignored that. "I'll check newspaper archives, then…police reports…they're probably stored somewhere."

"Pardon me, but aren't you supposed to be working on my house?"

"Sure am."

"Then, when are you going to do all this investigating?"

"I'll do it after work."

"That may be difficult. By the time you clock out, both the newspaper office and the police department will be closed to visitors."

"On weekends, then. Before I go to work. At night. Online." To show my determination, I named every avenue I could think of. "Almost everything is digitized nowadays. I imagine I can find a good portion of it on the Internet. After all, there's no real hurry, is there?"

"Can I tag along?"

"Why not? You've got a stake in this, too. In the meantime, give me your father's version of the story, and I'll tell you what Dad told me, and we'll see how close they got their facts."

By the time we arrived at the office, we'd determined that our dads' stories pretty much aligned, except for a few personal comments here and there.

At the office, we found everyone clocked in and ready to go. I introduced Ben, who was so damned polite I wondered what he was up to, while Dad introduced my uncles, explaining that Cliff would handle the plumbing and Rick the wiring.

Letty glanced at me. "Relatives?"

"Nepotism, thy name is Roth," I intoned.

There was a third man with them, someone from a company doing water testing. He'd take samples from the well and make certain it didn't contain any toxic elements. I wondered what would happen if it did and hoped nothing had contaminated the well while it lay undisturbed under its wood covering for the past near-century.

Dad and the others went to their respective trucks. I helped Letty back into the Ford and got in. My crew clambered into the back and Ben latched the tailgate, then slid in on the passenger side. With Letty wedged between us, we were on our way.

Chapter 13

We were met by a changed countryside.

Dad had sent one of the landscaping crews ahead with mowers and mini-graders. They'd smoothed the road and cut down the weeds in the mid-track. Letty's sportster would be able to travel in safety now. I hoped she didn't realize that. I liked her sitting next to me in the cab, crowded as it was with Ben's bulk on the other side. That made it even better because she had to lean against me.

They'd also removed a good bit of the weeds and brambles around the house itself, as well as continuing on down the road between the meadow and the trees. The overgrown hedges on either side of the steps had been shorn to the ground but they'd grow again, and be trimmed into a neater shape when they did.

Someone called to me that he'd "left those pink flowers in back as you said to," and I nodded. I'd given orders the Cherokee roses weren't to be cut down. I was determined they were going to grace the garden when it was replanted. I heard one of the other men telling Dad he'd left a batch of cane growing on the other side of the driveway, near the fallen branches I'd warn Biff might be snake-infested.

"Looks like bamboo and sugar cane," he said.

"Sugar cane?" I spun around. "Are you sure?"

Cane plants had to be ratooned after three harvests,

so I was surprised any might've survived after this long.

In answer, he pulled something looking like a greenish five-inch stem from his shirt pocket, holding it out to me. I took it.

"Did I hear someone say 'bamboo?'" Letty asked.

I nodded. "Too bad the baptismal pool isn't in the front. Bamboo…a pool with koi…that'd be a good selling point."

"But it isn't in front," she reminded.

"No prob. You can cut the bamboo and sell it," I suggested. "People around here still like to fish with bamboo poles." I held out the cane. "There's also this."

"Isn't that a piece of old fishing pole?" she said.

"It's something better. *Saccharam officinarum,* the source of molasses, rum, and all that processed white sugar everyone says is so bad for us."

"Sugar cane." Her smile told me we were going back into the one-upmanship game, and she was ready for me. "Oh yes, I remember…Daddy mentioned Great-Grandpa grew sugar cane, along with corn and soybeans." She perked up. "But not commercially, just enough for himself and his neighbors."

Her cheeks pinkened as she remembered who one of the neighbors had been. I wondered if he'd made Dylan a gift of some of the canes, maybe a jug of juice to make into syrup? Then I glanced around, wondering how many of the men here were aware of the story. Had that older generation charitably kept it buried so deep none but our families were now aware? Unless specifically told?

Pulling out my pocket knife, I flipped it open, carefully cutting back the cane's hard outer peel down to the first joint and revealing the fibrous inner core. When I had all the outer coating cut so it looked like the petals of some oddly-shaped flower, I offered it to Letty.

"Here you go, Miz Scarlett."

She accepted the cane, looking at it helplessly. Juice dripped out of the cut fibers, trickling over her hand. "What do I do with it?"

"Chew on the *bagasse*—that's the core—then suck it."

Giving me a look saying she didn't know whether to believe that or not, she obeyed, turning the joint sideways and biting through the fibers with her back teeth. Then she began to suck on the pithy core enthusiastically.

A little too enthusiastically. I had to turn away because I had a sudden wish she was sucking on something else, and was immediately ashamed of that abruptly lewd thought. My cock wasn't, however, urging me to have another.

I ignored it.

"Hey, better slow down." I pulled the stem from her hand as she swallowed. "Cane juice is also a very powerful laxative."

She released it quickly as I said that. I cut off the chewed bit and helped myself to a mouthful of sweet juice. It'd been a long time since I'd had any cane juice and it brought back a swift cavalcade of childhood memories I didn't have time to review or enjoy.

"Okay…let's get to work!"

Dad's call made me tuck away my recollections for later as I stuffed the rest of the cane into a hip pocket. Maybe I'd take it home and plant it and grow my own cane patch.

Chapter 14

The water samples came back A-OK. Drilling and putting in pipes and connecting them to the house began. That involved digging up the ground between the well and the kitchen, but Uncle Cliff promised me they'd put everything back like it was, "which isn't saying much since it's a weed-infested mess at present." He gave me an odd look when I persisted in telling him I didn't want the roses harmed.

"Never knew you to be horticulturally inclined, Dyl."

I was saved from answering by someone calling to me.

Uncle Rick worked with someone from the electric company about running lines to the house. We were going to have to coordinate building the house around what my uncles were doing, so in the meantime, we set to work on the other side of the structure, restoring the porch and steps, while a second crew built a scaffold around the chimneys.

Dad wanted to make certain the chimneys were braced and protected from all the hammering, sawing, drilling, and whatnot as the floors and walls surrounding them were torn away, rebuilt, and re-enforced. After studying the blueprints, he'd decided to leave as much of the original building as possible and simply build around it, encasing it in a new one. He also had someone come out and inspect for termites and other structure-destroying insects and treat as necessary.

Both chimneys were examined from base to top, as well as the fireplaces on each floor. From mortar crown to chimney cap, they seemed stable enough, and remarkably unharmed by so many decades of wind, rain, and sun, as well as marauding hunters who had a predilection for using old chimneys as target practice.

Running something looking like an overgrown drain snake down each chimney cleared them of abandoned birds' nests, spider webs, and a batch of unrecognizable material we threw to one side to load into the back of one of the dump trucks and take to the landfill.

While the scaffolds were being erected, we started on the porch. It was easy to get to, now that the hedges were out of the way. Pretty soon, the smell of freshly sawn wood filled the air, along with the whine of battery-run saws and the rhythmic pounding of hammers, while a pile of sawdust turned the front yard into a golden beach.

****

We were into our second week. The work was going well, everything managed without a hitch.

Letty and I had discussed the porch's reconstruction.

"It'll be nice to walk across it without fear of falling through, won't it?"

She nodded, daring to give me a little hug right in front of Bill's ever-present lens. By now, I'd forgotten he and Biff were around, except for the occasional moment when he'd move past me to take a close-up of something someone pointed out. Generally, he used a *zoom* lens.

"Oh, Dylan, it's going to look so nice."

Her eyes were gleaming as if they quite literally were reflecting stars. In that moment, I thought I'd never seen anyone looking so beautiful.

"You know what would make it perfect?" she went on.

I shook my head. As far as I was concerned, her being there made it perfect. Okay...romantic crap. At least I didn't say it out loud.

"If there was a glider. Right there." She pointed to a spot in front of the parlor window. "Or, even better, a porch swing. We could sit there in the evenings...and swing...and talk..."

"Hey, you make it sound as if you're planning on living here." I'd definitely like that, especially that "we" she'd used.

She looked surprised. "I might. For a bit before DHU sells it...to give it a 'lived-in' look," she conceded.

I looked forward to that.

We'd had some high winds that morning. Another storm was brewing off the coast, trying to decide if it wanted to stay a mere tropical squall or be elevated to hurricane status.

Dad insisted he'd seen some sway from one of the chimneys, so I was on the scaffold, making certain the chimney was well-braced. Doing anything high-rise, meaning over five feet above the ground, was generally my job. Ben, bless his little heart, had acrophobia. If he got on anything higher than a horse's back, he became so dizzy he couldn't walk straight. At the moment, he was firmly on the ground with Dad, inspecting the brick in the foundations and checking for any needing to be replaced or re-mortared before we started on the porch.

****

There was no one on the scaffold but Bill and me. Biff surprised everyone by agreeing with Ben that high places were not his element. Luckily, Bill had a second camera in the van, one with microphone attached. After assuring Dad he had no problem with heights, he climbed up the ladder after me.

I squatted near the edge, resting against the chimney, giving each brick a scrutiny as well as running my hands over them. A couple on the mouth of the chimney had been replaced, but the mortar felt solid enough. The outside was dry, and even if it hadn't completely solidified internally, it would still hold against a strong wind. If a storm came in, we'd stop work and be long gone, so there was no danger either way.

Satisfied everything was good, I straightened.

"Looks A-OK," I said, for the mike's benefit, and turned around, surprised to see Letty standing directly behind me. "Hey, where did you—"

That was all I got out. She rushed me, hands striking my chest. I took a step backward…

…into empty air.

"Dylan!" Bill's shout followed me over the edge as I tumbled, arms flailing.

There's no worse feeling than falling, knowing you can't do anything but wait for the impact. I don't remember tumbling downward, no images flashed before my eyes. There was simply a rush of air, the thought, *I can't stop*, and then that sudden, solid thud as my body struck the ground.

It got very dark…and quiet. For several seconds I couldn't hear, couldn't breathe. Wind knocked out of me, my lungs felt collapsed. Then, I took a deep, rasping breath, my vision cleared, sounds came back in a chaotic babble, and I looked up into my father's anxious face…

"Dylan? Dylan…son…"

…and Letty's, bloodless and strained…

"Get away from me," I managed, voice choked.

"What? What did he say?" She looked at Dad and back at me.

"You…" I struggled to get up. Nothing happened.

What…? My arms and legs wouldn't work. I couldn't feel them. *God, my entire body's numb.* Panic set in. I tried to speak but only a choking sound came out.

"Dad…"

He put a hand on my shoulder. "Don't try to move."

Don't try? I can't. Did I say that aloud? I couldn't tell. No one seemed to be listening to me.

"We've called 911."

"Dad…" I tried to tell him Letty had pushed me, but he turned away, calling to someone.

I looked up, past Letty's white face.

Why, Letty?

Bill was looking over the edge of the scaffolding, camera aimed at me like a big black eye. He lowered it, hurrying to the ladder.

There was a ringing in my ears. The sun bored into my eyes. I shut them, but the light became brighter, cutting through my closed lids with little sparklers twinkling in an ever-shrinking circle. I was falling again, and this time I didn't know when I hit bottom.

Chapter 15

"Dylan?"

"Dad…where…?" I tried to open my eyes. Everything looked as if it were inside a fishbowl, warped and distorted. I closed them again. My head hurt.

"You're in the hospital. Don't you remember? You fell."

I tried to shake my head. That made it hurt more so I stopped. "Fell…Letty…"

"Letty's outside. She's been here since they took you into surgery. Do you want to see her?"

See her? Hell no.

"She…Dad, she push' me…"

"Dylan, you're confused. The only one with you on the platform was Bill. Are you saying Bill pushed you?"

"No…" I disagreed. "No' Bi'…Let'…she…"

I couldn't say what I wanted to. My mouth wouldn't work. I tried to swallow. My throat was too dry.

If I'm in the hospital, isn't someone supposed to be feeding me ice chips?

"…confused…"

That was all I got out before I began falling a third time.

The next time I awoke, I didn't know where I was. My last memory was of lying on the ground with Dad and Letty—why had she done it?—and the others gathered around me, but now?

I realized my eyes were shut, that I was listening rather than seeing. A beeping sound, from far away, the faint rumble of something on wheels, footsteps. I remembered Dad telling me I was in a hospital.

With a moan, I opened my eyes.

Movement to the left made me look that way. Rather, my eyes turned in that direction. I couldn't move my head.

Dad was sitting in a chair under a window whose open blinds let in a stream of brilliant sunlight. He got to his feet, leaning over the bed.

"Welcome back." His voice held that falsely cheerful tone people always use with the seriously ill.

That didn't make me feel a bit better.

"Where...?" I croaked.

I still hadn't gotten my ice chips. My mouth felt like someone had emptied the Sahara into it. I was also aware of a dull but persistent double ache...in my temples and also my right wrist.

"Janssen Memorial." He named the hospital four miles south of Estonko.

"...can't move...head..." I mumbled. "Wha..."

"Don't try," he cautioned. "They put a cervical collar around your neck, to stabilize it."

In spite of that, I gritted my teeth and forced my head to the left so I was looking directly at him. It hurt, like the grinding of a rusted hinge in a gate, but at least my neck wasn't broken. I tried to push myself up, then realized my arms weren't working.

"Dad." Panic hit. I remembered how numb I felt as I lay on the ground, the same as now. "I can't move my arms."

"Just relax, son."

How can he sound so calm? I continued struggling. Wires and tubes jangled.

"Ellie?" His voice changed, sudden helplessness in it.

I turned my head. A hot jolt of pain shot from my neck to the top of my head.

Damn, that hurt.

Mom stood on the other side. I hadn't heard her get up. I also got a brief glimpse of the room…bedside table with tissue box and plastic water pitcher, a small chest against the opposite wall, a vase of brilliant flowers sitting on it.

"You've a broken arm," she said, matter-of-factly but in a way immediately soothing my fear.

How do mothers do that?

"That's why you can't move it."

Something touched my fingertips. That startled me, while at the same time, I was relieved because I *felt* it. I looked down, past a mass of white. It took me a moment to realize the white thing was my arm, encased in plaster and resting on a pillow by my side.

"They've elevated it to keep it in the proper position," she explained as she followed my gaze.

"…only broken?" I asked in relief.

Her fingers pressed against mine. "Oh, Dyllie, we were so worried."

She didn't cry, though. I'm grateful for that. If she had…I probably would've joined in, blubbering enough for both of us.

"Just…broken arm?" I persisted, in a mumble. I didn't even complain about her using that nickname I hated so.

Somehow, Dad understood. "You have a

concussion. That's why you've been unconscious for two days." He gave a shaky laugh. "Guess your head isn't as hard as we thought."

Two days? It was now Thursday?

"Nothing else, thank God. You'll be good as new in no time."

"But not working on this project again," Mom added.

Just great, I consoled myself. Out of commission, for how long?

Dad broke into my thoughts, asking the important question, "Do you remember what happened?"

I'd been waiting for that. "Of course, I do. She pushed me."

"You said that before." He remembered my babbling. "She…who?"

"Letty. Why'd she do it, Dad?" I couldn't hide the hurt as well as the disbelief. "I thought…"

"Dylan, you must be mistaken, Letty was on the ground with me."

"Don't tell me I was mistaken!" I grated at him. God, how I wanted to sit up. "I saw her. She pushed me," I repeated. "Hit me in the chest and knocked me backward."

He shook his head, accepting my outburst without changing expression. "She was standing beside me when you hit the ground."

"Dad, don't defend her." Why was he being this way?

He continued shaking his head.

"Don't do that." I glanced from him to Mom. She was staring at me as if she couldn't believe what she was hearing. "Ask Bill. He got it all on film."

I struggled to sit up. Dad's hand on my shoulders prevented that. Actually, he didn't need to. There was no way I could get up without help.

"Dylan, calm down."

This time, it was an order, his voice still quiet but rock hard, as it used to be when we'd go on a trip and Ben and I would get into a backseat tussle. We always obeyed when Dad sounded that way.

"Letty was with me. Everyone saw her. The minute you hit the ground, I thought she was going to faint. Besides, why would she push you?"

Why, indeed? I didn't answer. I had no answer.

"She didn't do it?" I knew I sounded like an idiot, but I also knew what I'd seen.

"She didn't, son."

Okay, I'd let him think I believed him, until I could confront Letty and find out the truth.

"She's here," Dad went on. "In the waiting room, with Ben. Biff and Bill are here, too. She wants to see you."

Well, I don't want to see her. I didn't say that aloud. I *had* to see her. "Okay."

"Are you sure?"

Guess he was suspicious of my sudden agreement.

"Yes, Dad. I want to see her."

"We'll have to leave." He looked as if he wasn't certain she should be alone with me. Maybe I didn't hide my expression well enough. "You're only supposed to have one visitor at a time…"

"They made an exception for us," Mom whispered.

At that moment, a nurse bustled into the room and hustled both of them out. Apparently, one of those machines to which I was now attached told on me, informing someone I was conscious. She checked a few things, making certain the adhesive pads on my chest were still inserted into the wires leading to the heart/lung monitor making those annoying rhythmic noises, and the respiration clip on my forefinger was still well attached. Tapping some buttons on the machines, she made some notes on my chart and told me she'd inform the doctor his patient was awake, then asked if I'd like to sit up.

I would. Definitely.

She pressed the controls, elevating the head of the bed, then placed the remote and the call button within easy reach of my left hand.

My left hand...oh damn, I'm right-handed...why did that have to be the injured one?

As I came upright, I became aware of extra weight at my thighs. With my free hand, I raised the sheet, sneaking a peek downward.

"Catheter," she said.

"Catheter?" I repeated, dropping the sheet as if caught doing something I shouldn't.

"Isn't that what you were checking? To see why your...apparatus...feels so heavy?"

"Oh. Uh..." That was exactly the reason.

I changed the subject, asking her if she'd tell me how badly my arm was injured. Other than that pain in my neck and the ache in my arm, which was slowly growing stronger, I didn't hurt too much.

She looked surprised. "You mean no one's told you?"

"Only that it's broken. My mother gave me a brief summary. Maybe they think I can't handle the details?" I half-joked, wondering if I was unconsciously stating the truth.

"Considering you fell from a height of over thirty feet," She fiddled with the chart again. "Your injuries are remarkably…I wouldn't call them *minor*, but they were much less serious than expected."

In short order, I learned that besides the concussion and some bruised ribs, I'd suffered an open displaced fracture of the right radius and ulna, confirmed by x-ray. Because both bones in my forearm were broken, I was whisked directly into surgery as soon as I reached the hospital. An orthopedist had been called in, and he set my arm by doing an open reduction and internal fixation. That meant he realigned the broken bones, making certain they stayed in the proper position by holding them together with metal plates attached to the bones by screws.

I was currently on intravenous antibiotics to prevent infection and had also been given a tetanus shot.

"Your parents couldn't tell us if you were current on that."

I shrugged. I was, but I guessed another wouldn't hurt. Would it?

She also told me I'd been on oxygen but they'd removed the inhalers the day before when it was confirmed I was breathing on my own well enough.

"I guess that's the antibiotics?" I gestured to the tube butterflied to the back of my left hand. "What's this?" I nodded to one inserted into the bend of my elbow.

"That's been your breakfast, lunch, and dinner for the past two days."

I glanced up at the little baggie-like sack holding the clear liquid. "I think I'd rather have a bowl of grits."

"Now that you're fully awake, I imagine we can arrange that." She smiled. "I'm certain Dr. Norton will order a post-surgical diet immediately."

"Thanks." I hoped it was something good-tasting, if soft…like the aforementioned grits or mashed potatoes, or a nice, bowl of hot cheese and broccoli soup. "In the meantime, could I have some water?"

She supplied me with a plastic cup, pouring water from the little pitcher on the bedside table, inserting one of those little bent straws into it. As I handed it back, she asked, "Would you like to see your young lady, now?"

"My young…"

It took me a moment to realize she meant Letty, that coy tone indicating she thought there was something more going on between us than there actually was.

I cleared my throat. "Yes, I'd definitely like to see my young lady."

After I saw her, there might be nothing between us. At all.

Immediately the machine registering blood pressure, heart rate and diastolic and systolic levels and whatever, began to beep.

"Oh…someone's getting excited."

What she mistook for eagerness was anger. I forced myself to relax.

"Sorry," I mumbled.

She went to the door, pushing it open and gesturing. "Well, here she is."

She went out and Letty came in, rushed in, as if she were afraid someone would stop her. Bill and Biff were behind her, hovering in the doorway. Bill looked around as if checking that the coast was clear before he took a step forward.

"No," I said quickly, and stared at Letty. "Just you."

She looked back, shaking her head. He nodded and

aimed the camera, taking a shot of her approaching the bed.

"Does everything have to be filmed?" I peered around her. "Turn off that damned thing and get out of here."

"That's what he's paid to do," she said defensively. She managed a lopsided smile as she pulled a chair up to the bed. "You have to admit, your falling from that scaffolding was pretty dramatic."

"Is that why you did it? For the drama?" I hadn't intended to start that way. It just came out.

Her smile faltered. "What?"

"You heard me." I ignored Bill. "Why'd you do it, Letty? Why'd you push me?"

"Push you?" Either she was an Oscar-worthy actress or she hadn't a clue what I was talking about. Guess Dad didn't warn her. "Dylan, why would I…"

She didn't finish, just stopped, staring at me.

"Don't try to think up a lie," I accused. "You've already got Dad doing that, saying you were with him when I fell. I saw you, Letty, plain as day."

"Dylan, that's crazy."

"Is it?" I forced my voice into a quieter tone, gesturing with my free hand, making the tubes bounce and the liquid-filled bags sway.

At that moment, Bill decided to leave. Lowering the camcorder, he turned away.

"Bill?" My voice rapped out so sharply he flinched. "Get in here!"

"Make up your mind." He came in, shutting the door and leaving Biff outside. He rested the camera against his side, waiting for me to say something. "Well?"

"You were up there with me. You got it all on film.

Tell her."

"Tell her what?" Bill looked blank.

"That you saw her push me. You filmed it."

"Dylan…" He didn't say what I expected, what I *wanted*, him to say. "I don't know what you're talking about. You turned around, stepped back, and just…fell."

"You called out," I reminded him.

"Right," he agreed. "That's all I did. It happened so fast. You can't imagine the relief I felt when I saw you were conscious." He glanced at the camcorder. "I think the camera was still filming, but…"

"You didn't see her?" Could I have imagined it?

"Dyl, there was no one up there but you and me."

He was so earnest, I believed him.

"I don't understand." Now I was really confused. They had to be telling the truth. Why would all of them lie? Back to my original question: Why would Letty push me?

"Well, hell…" He shifted the camera. "If you need proof. Look at it."

He fiddled with a couple of buttons, and flipped the camera around. Letty moved so he could hold it in front of me.

"Can you see it okay?"

I nodded. He pressed another button and I saw a figure squatting near the chimney, leaning over, a hand resting on one of the bricks forming the outer rim. It was a weird feeling, watching myself.

****

"Looks A-OK." I turned and jumped slightly. "Hey, where did you—"

A swirl of white cut in front of me, thin and diaphanous as a strip of spider web. I stepped back, disappearing over the platform's edge.

"Dylan!" Bill's shout was clearly recorded, as was the empty platform, blue sky, and visible chimney top. The camera shook as he rushed to the edge, the picture shaky and off-center as he looked down at the figure sprawled in the dirt...me, right arm twisted under me, legs bent. Dad and Letty were visibly recognizable among those crowded around me.

****

All I said was, "Run it back."

He obeyed. I watched the scene three times before falling back onto my pillow.

"I don't understand. I saw you." I looked at Letty.

"Dylan," Bill said, very quietly, and so sympathetically I wanted to deck him. "She wasn't there. It was only you and me, and I swear I didn't push you."

"That flash of white," I persisted. "What was that?"

Before answering, he rewound the scene and watched it again, scowling at that part.

"I don't know," he admitted, shrugging. "A reflection off something? There were plenty of windshields around... sunshine hitting the lens at just the right angle...a bird..."

"Can you run the film slower, see if you can find out *exactly* what it is?" If it wasn't Letty... I was getting an idea I didn't like.

"Sure. I can do a slo-mo, use filters and stuff, but not here. I need my laptop. I'd have to download it."

"Would you do that?"

I must've sounded pitiful because his expression changed.

"If it'll prove to you once and for all you simply lost your balance? Of course," he agreed.

166

"Thanks."

There was a long silence. Both he and Letty stared at me.

"I'd like to talk to Letty. Alone," I said.

"Letty?" He looked at her.

"It's okay. Go on back to the house. You can shoot some of the plumbing and electrical work scenes."

"Right." Clutching the camera, he started to the door, then looked back. "Take care, Dylan."

Was it an expression of concern, or a warning?

He went out, letting the door swing shut behind him. I heard Biff ask, 'How is he?" but didn't hear Bill's answer.

"I'm sorry." I immediately began an apology, not giving Letty time to deliver a scathing denunciation. "I saw… I swear to God I thought I saw you, but if I didn't, if everyone's telling the truth and you were with Dad…"

"I was." The control she'd had in Bill's presence slipped. Her lower lip trembled.

"What the hell did I see?" I blurted. "That's not a rhetorical question. I swear it was a woman…"

"It was probably like Bill said, sunshine or something…and you were thinking of me…"

"Listen, sweetheart…"

A smile flickered at my use of that little endearment.

"…as much as I admit being fixated on you, I didn't imagine…"

"You've been fixated on me?" Briefly, the old teasing Letty was back. "Really?"

"Okay, I admit it." I was glad to have that comfortable, if fractious, feeling surface between us, even momentarily. "You've been in my thoughts a great deal since I saw you at the office. But if you tell anyone

I said that, I'll swear I was raving."

"Oh, Dylan." She caught my good hand.

It was awkward, reaching across my casted one, the tubes keeping her from pulling my left hand toward her. Somehow she managed to squeeze my fingers, and then, she did a really weird thing. She kissed them.

"Hey…if you're going to do any kissing, I want it somewhere besides on my hand."

She looked around, saw the door was firmly shut, then stood and leaned over me, pressing a quick kiss on my lips.

"Damn," I grimaced. "First kiss and I'm flat on my back in a hospital bed. This does not bode well for any kind of romance."

"Oh, I don't know." She tossed her head, making the copper mass sway. "I think it's just fine. I have you exactly where I want you. Completely helpless."

With all these tubes and wires puncturing my skin and sticking in certain orifices? I didn't say that aloud. I felt slightly lightheaded, wondering if I was about to pass out again. My ears weren't ringing and I wasn't seeing bright lights, however.

"Letty, if it's you, I don't mind being helpless."

For some reason, I felt that one sentence, as ridiculous as it sounded, was a commitment of some kind.

She immediately became serious. "Do you believe me now?"

I nodded. "Forgive me?"

"Done." She went from serious to tearful. "If you only knew how I felt when I looked up and saw you falling…"

"Let's not talk about it." I was tempted to tell her it

didn't look too good from my angle, either.

"Your dad's closed down the site. No one really wanted to be there after what happened. Your uncles are the only ones who insisted on continuing to work."

"Good old Cliff and Dave." I shook my head. It would take a total disaster with fire, flood, and earthquake to make those two cease and desist. "Sometimes, I think they've got the American work ethic tattooed on their foreheads."

"They asked that someone let them know how you are," she added, as if that absolved them from familial concern. "By the way, Ben's outside, preparing himself to become an only child."

"You'd better send him in so I can disappoint him."

"Okay." She pushed back the chair.

"Before you do…" I tightened my grip on her fingers before she could pull away. She looked back at me. "We need to talk…about this." I nodded at our hands. "Exactly what it means and where it might go. I swear, Letty, and I'm not shooting you a line or…" A thought occurred to me. "Have they given me any narcotics or anything?"

"I doubt it. You haven't been conscious enough to say you were in pain."

"Good, then I'm not under the influence. We need to discuss *us*."

"We will," she promised. "Once you're home. In private."

Pressing another kiss to my cheek, she left. By now, that dull ache was heading into the acute zone and I had a massive headache. I imagined I'd soon be demanding some painkiller, but just then those two little kisses did more for me than a dose of hydrocodone. In spite of my discomfort, I felt absolutely euphoric.

In a few minutes, Ben came in, falsely hearty. "What some people will do to keep from working!"

I let him think he was cheering me up but I was only half-listening. What I was really doing was wondering, *What the hell did I see?*

****

Excerpt from Dylan Roth's journal, August 19, 1925:

I have been working for Jules Mercier for quite some time and we have become friends. He is an educated, well-spoken man, much like those friends I had when in school in the Old Country. I welcome having someone with whom to converse as I did with them. Not that my friends in Estonko are ignorant, but some of their interests and mine do not converge and my literary references they do not understand. Jules is from an old Savannah family, and while I am middle class, he and I wear well together. I enjoy my work on the Mercier home and, because of our growing friendship, am most careful in the carvings I make for the staircase and the fireplaces. I have also drawn designs for the outside cornices of the dormers and trimmings, what is called here 'gingerbread,' and have assured Jules his home will be something of which he will be proud, without it seeming ostentatious.

Jules is not an ostentatious man. For someone from a well-to-do family, he is very down-to-earth.

I say I enjoy my work, but one thing makes a blot on my pleasure. I will never mention this to Annie nor to Jules lest he misunderstand, but his wife's presence bothers me. I am uncomfortable in her company. She's never said anything to make me feel this way, but occasionally I have seen her watching me as I work. It is hot in Georgia in late August. I would say it is the hottest time of the year, and most of us shed our shirts as we work. When this happens, she always seems to find some excuse to come to the worksite and speak to me.

At first, it appeared innocent enough. She would go to each of us, offering a drink from a bucket filled with water and bits of ice. Whenever she comes to me, however, she lingers, making small talk, which I never see her do with the others. I always quickly take my drink, then get back to work, but she stays, even after I turn away. It is as if I can feel her gaze skimming over my skin.

Once, she actually placed her hand on my shoulder, and when I stiffened and looked around, she merely said, "There was a mosquito. I didn't want it to bite you." I thanked her and turned my attention back to work, ignoring her until she went away. My arm seemed to burn where she touched, and it was some time before the sensation disappeared. Her touch was not a swat as one would make to a mosquito but more of a caress. No woman other than my Annie has touched me that way since three years before our marriage, and that is the way I want it. I wish I had the courage to tell Jules' wife that, but it may be I am mistaken in what I sense, and if I were to say it aloud, it would destroy the friendship I have with him. Instead, I now wear my shirt when I work, no matter how hot the sun.

Chapter 16

That night, Dr. Norton arrived on his evening rounds. He was about Dad's age, and we already were slightly acquainted. He'd treated Ben when he broke his hand catching a fly ball while we were in Little League.

With a greeting, he got to work, checking my chart, taking my temperature, and noting my vitals. Waving a forefinger before my face, he ordered me to follow it, "Look left…right…up…down."

Motioning me to lean forward, he pushed open my gown and examined the bruises across my ribs, pronouncing them "doing fine." Then he removed my cervical collar.

"How are you feeling?"

"Okay, considering." By now, I was in too much pain to be flippant. My head felt as if someone was using it for a drum, and the ache in my arm had increased to a Number Thirteen on a scale of one to ten.

"Only 'okay'?" He looked up from making a notation on the chart he held.

I decided not to be macho. "Actually, I've a headache bordering on a migraine and my arm is giving me fits." I raised the cast, then let it drop to the bed, wincing as my forearm struck the mattress.

"Careful there." He slid his hand under the cast, lifting my arm. "You may have screws holding the fracture in place, but a sudden jolt could still misalign it enough to cause you problems."

He was busy squeezing my fingers and checking their temperature as he spoke.

"Sorry." The last thing I wanted was to disable myself in any way. In *more* ways, I should have said.

"I've put a prescription in my notes and left it with the desk," he continued, gently releasing my arm and replacing it on the pillow. "All you have to do is ask for it."

"Thanks."

"I'm putting you on a regular diet as of now. Have you had a bowel movement or urinated yet?"

The switch from one subject to another was so abrupt I blinked. I reminded him I'd been unconscious for two days and really couldn't say.

"I've also been attached to this," I gestured to the tube running from my hand to the stand, "and that." I nodded to the beeping monitor. "As well as a catheter."

"We can solve those problems fast."

With ease, he pressed the little metal clasps on both lines, cutting off the flow of fluid, then pulled out the needles inserted into my elbow and hand so quickly I didn't feel it, letting the tubes hang free. Next, he removed the respiration clip and pulled down the neck of my gown, peeling off all the adhesive tabs. I winced. In spite of how they'd been placed, a couple still managed to take some hair with them.

Norton didn't stop there. Hand on my chest, he pushed me onto my pillow, flipping up the hem of my gown. I felt myself clasped firmly as, with a sharp tug, he deftly removed the catheter.

"You'll have some burning the first couple of times you have to go," he commented, smoothing my gown and tucking the tube against the little bag attached to the side of the bed under the sheet. "Don't worry. That's normal. It'll go away eventually. Can you walk all right?"

Pushing down one of the metal bed rails, he motioned me to get up. Making certain I was well-covered by the skirt of the gown, I swung my legs over the bed and slid to the floor. He caught me by the arm, a hand supporting my cast. There was a brief moment of dizziness, but then I pushed away from the bed and took a couple of steps.

"Good. You won't need any help getting to and from the bathroom, which is through there..." He gestured to a door on the other side of the room. "By the way, just remember, the first time...don't flush. Get someone in here to check it."

I didn't ask why. This was a conversation I didn't like having. Discussing certain bodily functions with a near-stranger wasn't exactly what I considered usual and proper small talk. I nodded and climbed back into bed.

"I want to keep you a couple more days, observation for that concussion, but if all systems are good to go by Saturday, I'll send you home."

That was what I wanted.

"How long before I can go back to work?" I remembered what Mom had said but hoped that was merely maternal wishful thinking.

"I'm afraid that's something else. Three to six months, depending on how quickly you heal."

"Six months?" That couldn't be. If I were going to figure out what happened, I needed to be mobile, not going stir-crazy while being bedridden and mothered.

Although...suddenly that didn't sound so bad.

"Surely it won't take that long."

"Are you such a glutton for punishment?" He looked amused. "This isn't a greenstick fracture like your brother had." He remembered treating Ben. "This is more serious, and if the break doesn't heal properly, you could be handicapped, as I said," he emphasized.

I guess I looked deflated because he went on, "It won't be so bad. You can lounge around home and be waited on while everyone else is slaving in the hot sun." He made a final notation on the chart before saying briskly, "X-rays in two weeks. Then you can start physical therapy, and if everything goes well..."

"...if it does?" I looked up hopefully.

"We'll see."

****

Everyone came by that night to see me. They must have gotten together and discussed how it was to be done, because they arrived in shifts. As soon as one left, another appeared...Uncle Cliff, Uncle Rick, Dad, then Mom, though I imagine they'd ridden together, then Letty. It may sound disloyal, but she was the one I was most happy to see.

Dad told me he'd ordered everyone back to work now that it was confirmed I wasn't going to die. They'd both spoken to Dr. Norton, and Mom said she had my bed ready and waiting, along with plenty of TLC for the invalid.

Groan.

Letty and I made small talk, but it was obvious we wanted to get to that "serious" one, though neither of us looked forward to having it in the hospital where we might be interrupted by a nurse giving me medication or taking my temperature or something. Mentally, I fumed and fretted, anxious to get home so we could speak in private as she'd promised.

She didn't mention Bill or whether he'd checked the film sequence, so I didn't bring it up either. I was fast coming to the conclusion he had no intention of doing so and had simply said he would to humor me. Okay, fine. I was still going to do my own investigating as soon as I was out of here.

Now that my hand and that other, more personal extremity were freed of their entanglement with tubes and I no longer had wires attaching me to the heart/lung monitor, I could move a little easier. Letty latched on to my fingers and clung as if she thought I was going to be swept away.

I didn't argue about that but thought back to the day we'd stood at the creek and I'd taken her hand and led her back to the overrun garden. Her hand felt good in mine then and it did now, too.

She was in the middle of telling me of Uncle Cliff's progress on digging the trench to run pipes.

"So far, so good. It should be finished—"

The door opened and Ben came in. He stopped.

"Oh, hi, Letty. Thought you had left." He raised an eyebrow, waiting for her to answer.

"I…well, I…I was giving Dylan a progress report. On how things are going. At the site." She spoke in little stops and starts, as if frantically thinking up innocuous excuses. "I thought…he might want to know…"

"Well, darn." Ben looked comically chagrined. "That's what I was going to do."

I wondered if he had any idea what Letty and I were going through. Ben wasn't always the most observant one in the group. He was too absorbed with himself.

A long silence followed. Ben waited. I didn't say anything and neither did Letty. It was obvious he wasn't going to leave, so at last, Letty sighed.

"I guess…I'd better go. I promised your mother I'd help her with supper."

She'd begun doing that as part of her payment for the room. I had a suspicion Letty liked being domestic but didn't want to admit it. Modern woman, and all that.

"Don't hurry out on my account," Ben said. He pulled up a chair, settling into it. "I can wait."

"That's all right. I need to be going." Lettie looked at Ben, then at me. She hesitated. Then she raised her chin, as if accepting a challenge, kissed me on the cheek, and left.

Ben goggled. I don't think I've ever seen his baby blues get so wide.

"Did I just see what I thought I saw?" At least he waited until the door shut before he spoke.

"You did," I affirmed, and managed not to smirk.

"You mean you and…" He gestured to the door.

"I think so. Quite possibly." My reply was cautious. "We need to talk about it."

"Damn, Dyl. When?" He reminded me of a teenage girl who'd just heard a snippet of juicy gossip. If he'd started jumping up and down and squealing I wouldn't have been surprised. "How?"

"I'm not sure." That sounded vague and evasive but was the truth. "That's one of the things we have to talk about."

"So that means you and she haven't…" He made vague gestures, ending with the age-old one of a hand curled into a fist while the other forefinger thrust into it.

"God, Ben!" Generally, his innuendoes merely

irritated me, but this time, it went beyond that. I was angry. Whatever Letty and I had wasn't yet defined, and I didn't like his vulgar insinuations. "I really don't think this is the kind of conversation to have just now. If ever. Or if it's any of your business."

His expression changed. He looked hurt.

Hurt? Ben?

"Dylan, you know I only want you to be happy," he protested, looking so sincere I was immediately ashamed of my outburst.

"Thank you," I replied, adding, "I appreciate that."

Then he spoiled it. "And I think the sooner you get fucked, the happier you'll be."

"Ben…" I protested, struggling to maintain my calm. If I swung at him with my cast and connected, how much would that hurt my arm? I didn't care how much it hurt *him.*

I was glad I was no longer attached to the cardiac monitor. Otherwise the nurses might've thought I was having a heart attack and come running with a crash cart. I was certain Dr. Norton would say getting upset wasn't good for my health. It also wasn't going to be good for Ben's if he kept on.

"Common fact, bro. The sexually satisfied man is a happy man."

"I'm lying here with my right arm in a cast…"

"That's why it's so important for you to have a girlfriend." He was so earnest it was unbelievable. "You don't have to do anything…just lay back and enjoy it…" He took a deep breath. "…and she's so handy…right upstairs in my old room!"

He was fairly shaking with glee, grinning so widely I was certain it must hurt. If he'd gone into one of those little victory dances like a quarterback after a touchdown, running in place and shaking his fists, I wouldn't have been surprised.

"Go." I managed to put a ton of disdain into that one word.

He stopped his celebration, staring at me. "What?"

"Get out of here before I break my other arm."

"How are you going to do that?" He looked genuinely puzzled.

"By hitting you."

He didn't retreat as I'd hoped but stood his ground, asking, "Do Mom and Dad know?"

"No, and you'd better not say anything."

"Hey, I know when to keep the ol' lip buttoned." He made a zipping motion across his mouth. "You want to keep Letty all to yourself for now. I get that. I won't say a word."

"Not even to Liz. I mean it, Ben."

"You know me, bro."

"I certainly do. That's why I'm telling you, you'd better keep quiet about this…and stop calling me 'bro." I finished on a note just short of a shout.

His expression underwent a startling change, to the most solemn demeanor I'd ever seen. He hadn't looked that serious on the day he confided in me he was going to ask Liz to marry him.

"Dyl…" He dared lay a hand on my shoulder.

I looked at it, then back at him, wondering what was coming.

"Pinkie-swear." He held up his right hand, clenched into a fist, little finger extended. "I won't tell a soul. I promise."

He was deadly serious.

I raised my casted arm, "Can't do it with this one," and offered the other. "Left-handed pinkie-swear?"

Grinning, Ben dropped his right hand, holding out his left, and we awkwardly entwined little fingers. As childish a ritual as it was, Ben had never broken a pinkie-swear, so I knew he'd never say anything about Letty and me until we had determined where our relationship, if we had one, was going.

****

The next morning, I visited the bathroom, dutifully called in a nurse to survey the results, and when Dr. Norton arrived for morning rounds, he declared, "Systems A-OK," and told me I could go home on Saturday morning.

Chapter 17

Armed with a child-proof capped bottle of painkillers—and that made me wonder whether that was a dig at my maturity—with my arm in a sling to support it, and a card announcing an appointment in two weeks for x-rays, I was wheeled to the curb by a nurse. I protested I could leave under my own power. She informed me hospital rules decreed otherwise. Mom walked beside me, juggling a plastic bag containing the pitcher, water cup, and emesis basin from my room, along with the vase of flowers, still looking remarkably fresh after a week.

She and Dad had arrived together, with Mom standing discreetly outside while Dad helped me dress.

Today, Dad was driving our family car. The trucks were business vehicles. He stopped the car in the patient loading area and I stood, awkwardly pulled open the door with my left hand, and slid onto the passenger seat.

"Thanks." I looked back through the window at the nurse.

She nodded, spun the wheelchair and headed back inside.

I fumbled with the shoulder harness, then let Dad snap it for me, stifling a bit of resentment as he said, "Be still, Dylan, so I can do this."

I wondered if this was how a baby in a car seat felt.

"Where's Letty?" I swiveled slightly, looking at

Mom, who'd gotten into the back seat. The movement nearly jerked the strap out of Dad's hand. He made an irritated huff.

"She's at the construction site," she answered.

"Oh." I tried not to let my disappointment show as I straightened. "The show must go on, huh?"

"You like her, don't you?" Dad's question was low-pitched, as if he didn't want Mom to hear. There was a loud click as he clipped the belt and turned his attention to the steering wheel.

I nodded.

"You two okay now?"

"Fine. I was confused, that's all."

He looked relieved and gave his attention to driving us home.

As soon as we were there, Mom hurried ahead, disappearing into the house. By the time Dad had me unhooked from my seatbelt and out of the car, she was busy in the kitchen.

"Why don't you lie down and rest while I get dinner ready?"

"I think I will." I was startled to feel fatigued, the walk from car to house ridiculously tiring. I started to the basement door.

"Need any help?" Dad asked.

"No, thanks. I've got it."

My knees felt a little wobbly as I went down the stairs, but I wasn't about to admit it. Mom had fussed and fluttered over me as soon as the car started moving and that got old fast. I knew if I grunted or gave the least indication of pain, she'd probably haul me back to Smith Northview declaring I'd had a relapse.

My plan was to grit my teeth and sneak a

hydrocodone or two when she wasn't looking. I was glad she hadn't taken possession of my prescription. I didn't bother thinking how I was going to manage a child-proof cap using only one hand.

The stair light was on. There was a switch just inside the door so I could see to go down the stairs, then another at the bottom so I could turn off the light once I got there. The bedroom looked much tidier than I'd left it. The sheets had been changed and there was an overstuffed pillow lying beside mine, to support my arm, I guess. As I saw the little plastic pitcher, filled with water, and the cup on the bedside table, I understood the reason Mom had gone inside ahead of us. To rid herself of my hospital 'gifts.'

There was also something that certainly hadn't been there when I left for work Monday morning. It resembled one of the early cell phones, small, with a narrow antenna-like projection on one side, some buttons, and a small perforated plastic square. A faint *white-sound* buzz came through it.

"What the…?"

I snatched it up and stamped back up the stairs, ignoring the jolts running through my body as my feet hit the steps.

"Mom!" I sped past Dad into the kitchen, moving pretty fast for a recuperating invalid. "Is this what I think it is?"

She was at the stove, half-turning toward me as I came through the door. "What do you think it is?"

"It looks like a baby monitor." I raised the thing, shaking it. "Damn it, Mom!"

"Dylan, don't speak that way to your mother," Dad barked.

He'd said that in his "You'd better mind me" voice, one even an adult knew he'd better obey.

"Mom, I'm sorry." I hurried to apologize, then repeated, in a quieter tone, "A baby monitor? Really?"

"I want to be certain I hear you," she said defensively, "if you wake up at night and need me."

"Oh for… I'm perfectly capable of walking up the stairs and knocking on the door if I need you," I snapped. "For crying out loud!"

"Dylan." Dad cut into my rant. He'd followed me into the kitchen. "May I speak to you a moment?"

He caught my injured arm and put his other hand behind my back, a firm but insistent pressure saying if I didn't cooperate, he'd drag me from the room.

I looked from him to Mom, "We're not finished," and walked with him into the dining room.

"Go easy on her, son," he whispered.

"Damn it, Dad, she's treating me like a baby," I complained.

"You *are* her baby," he reminded me. "If you could've seen her face when I told her what happened… I was afraid I was going to have to admit her, too. She worries about you, Dylan. Grown-up as you are. Ben, too. When you have kids of your own, you'll understand."

I was glad he didn't say "if."

"So do I," he admitted. "I just try not to make such a fuss about it. One of us crying is enough."

My parents had always been demonstrative people. They didn't mind showing affection, but Dad had never said anything like that before. Now I was properly ashamed of my outburst.

Muttering under my breath, I went back into the

kitchen.

Mom was standing where I'd left her, looking anxious. From her expression, I figured it wouldn't take much to make her burst into tears.

"Okay, I'll put this back where I found it," I conceded and shook my finger at her, making a mock grimace to show her I wanted her to think I was pretending not to be serious though I really was. "I don't want you staying awake listening, understand? If I need help, I'll make sure you can hear me without this thing."

She didn't answer. I put my arm around her, hugging her awkwardly.

"Sorry, Mom. I appreciate you worrying about me."

"Oh, Dylan." She returned the hug. It was exactly like the one she'd given me the night I came home from DC.

That made me feel even worse. For a minute, I wished I were small enough to crawl into her lap and snuggle my face against her neck as I had when I was three. I was glad she didn't tell me having a broken arm was also "for the best."

After that, I went back downstairs. Replacing the monitor on the table, I lay down and arranged the pillow under my arm. Then, I surprised myself by actually falling asleep.

When I woke again, Mom had dinner ready. Dad and I ate our sandwiches and salads, he went back to work, and I went back to sleep. Abruptly, I was exhausted. Again.

The next time I surfaced, it was suppertime, and Letty and Dad came through the door together.

Letty greeted me with a hand-squeeze that was neutrally friendly. For appearances' sake, I hoped. She asked me how I felt. I responded by telling her about the baby monitor. She laughed and asked Mom how much of a baby she expected me to be. Mom proceeded to relate some anecdote about my behavior when I was two that sent both into giggles. I grinned and bore it.

Women…why do they think it amusing to remind a man of the days when he was a helpless infant?

After supper, I waited impatiently while Letty helped Mom with the cleaning-up. Once the dishes were in the dishwasher, the leftovers in the fridge, and the old folks settled in front of the TV in the den, I said, in an overly casual way that probably fooled no one, "You mentioned you'd like a swing on the front porch. Want to take a look at ours and see how it fits in with your idea?"

At Letty's "I think I'd like that," I took her hand and led her out the front door and onto the porch.

"Dylan?" Mom called, as she heard the front door open.

"Just going outside, Mom. Going to show Letty our porch swing. No climbing trees, I promise." I let the door shut behind me.

We settled into the swing. Letty leaned back.

"I think this is exactly what I want. This is nice."

"For early summer," I agreed. "Nothing beats sitting in a front porch swing watching the sun go down. Later, when the mosquitos come out, it won't be so nice, however."

"No problem. I'll buy some of those mosquito-repelling plants," she replied.

"Mosquito-repelling plants? You're kidding."

She shook her head. "There are plenty of them…peppermint, basil, citrosum. After the house is finished, I'll put planters on the porch and in the garden. I think—"

"Okay, enough small talk." I caught her hand in mine. "Letty, I didn't ask you out here to talk about plants or porch swings. I want to talk about *us*."

"Go ahead, then." She gave me a look I couldn't interpret in the fading light.

Of course, all the little speeches I'd rehearsed fled into the darkness. The cowards. I took a deep breath and decided to wing it.

"Letty…"

"Wait." Her fingers went over my mouth. "Maybe I'd better go first."

"Okay," I mumbled. She removed her hand.

"When I saw you at the construction office, you reminded me of my ex-husband."

"You were married?" The most vicious stab of jealousy went through me.

"Don't look so surprised," she snapped. "You think you have a monopoly on divorce? It happens. Yes, I was married, and you look so much like him, I thought, *No way I'm having anything to do with that guy.* Well, we see how that turned out." She laughed, voice rueful. "The best laid plans of mice and Scarlett Mercier. To quote an old song, *I don't know where or when*…or why, but I fell in love with you, Dylan Roth, and I don't want it to stop."

Then she kissed me, a real kiss, not a peck on the cheek or the lips but a genuine, deep-searching, tongue-against-tongue kiss.

I hadn't said a thing.

The creak of the door made us separate fast. Dad pushed open the screen.

"Your mother and I are going to bed," he

announced. "Everything okay out here?"

Hell, yes! I wanted to shout, jump up, and do a little victory dance of my own that would definitely shake up my healing bones, but I didn't move, except to tighten my grip on Letty's hand and hope he didn't see.

"Couldn't be better, Dad."

"Don't stay up too late. You need your sleep, son."

"Yes, sir."

"Good night, Letty."

"Good night, Mr. Roth," she replied, demurely.

He glanced at her. "Don't let him do anything to jeopardize the healing process."

He disappeared back inside.

"He's right, you know." She slid to her feet, tugging on my hand.

At that moment, a third wave of exhaustion hit like a ton of bricks, so I didn't argue. Nevertheless, I stalled a bit, pretending to have trouble getting out of the swing, giving the parents time to get upstairs. With a grumble at being such a weakling, I let Letty assist me to my feet.

We walked to the door. Letty opened the screen since my good hand was busy hanging onto hers. We went inside and I walked her to the stairs. I released her hand.

As she went up the first step, she turned and looked back at me.

"I nearly forgot…Bill said to tell you he's working on the film. He'll bring it over when he's finished."

"Thanks."

She caught my face in her hands and kissed me, another lover's kiss.

"Good night, Dylan."

I muttered something appropriate and didn't move

until she was out of sight.

Getting ready for bed was a bit of a struggle. That morning, as Dad helped me get dressed, he'd thoughtfully supplied a tank top so I didn't have to force my cast through a sleeve, but I wasn't about to wake him now. I guessed both he and Mom forgot about me getting *out* of my clothes. I found myself wishing Letty had volunteered for that chore. I could think of several ways she could've done it.

Missed opportunity. Damn.

Putting on PJ bottoms was out of the question, so I ended up leaving on the tank top, stripping down to briefs, and wriggling around in bed until I was settled with the pillow under my arm.

By then, I wasn't sleepy, of course, what with snoozing in the afternoon, to say nothing of the fact that the scene on the porch kept replaying itself in my brain…how soft Letty's lips felt, how I'd wanted to do more than kiss her, remembering back to the night in my sleeping bag, her body snuggled against mine. All that did was make me damned horny.

Yes, Dad, I want to do something definitely jeopardizing the healing process.

I lulled myself to sleep thinking about Letty and me…how we'd both been losers at the game of love but were now given a second chance that I, for one, wasn't going to spoil.

Take it slow, Dyl… Nope. I had to get well as fast as possible, so we could…

That's when I fell asleep.

****

Dylan…

My name, whispered into my ear, brought me out of

sleep and aware of the fact that something lay across my chest so heavy I couldn't breathe.

"What…" I managed to wheeze.

Opening my eyes, I struggled to sit up. It was pitch dark, no light from outside coming through the tiny basement windows.

Shhh.

A hand pushed me back onto the bed. The arm across my chest held me immobile. Cold fingers touched my mouth.

"Letty?" My God, she'd thrown caution to the winds and actually gotten into bed with me. *Well, all right!* I brought up my good hand, sliding it around her waist. Her skin was bare, and frigid.

Wait a minute. Frigid? In June? How could that be?

"Get under the covers," I whispered.

The hand left my mouth and she slid under the sheet. I flinched as it touched my bare belly and moved downward inside my waistband. Her fingers were so cold I wondered if I'd have frost tracks on my skin. Her hand didn't stop, and the boys were suddenly encased in an icy grip. I managed not to cry out, but I swear I felt them shrink into themselves.

"Damn! Your hand's like ice."

My entire body began to tremble. I couldn't stop it. By now, I was a mass of goose pimples.

I'm sorry, Dylan. I couldn't wait any longer.

Cold kisses burned their way across my cheek. I was certain I'd have frostbite. The weight left my chest as she moved her arm and settled over me, legs gripping my hips.

Just lie there. I'll do everything. Another kiss touched me, leaving a spot of burning cold.

With a sigh, I closed my eyes again as she guided me inside her. She began to rock against me...

"Dylan?"

Light flooded into brilliance. My mother, wrapped in her pink chenille robe, stood on the stairs.

I blinked, struggling to sit up while I tugged at the sheet, futilely trying to hide Letty from her sight.

It took a minute for me to realize I was alone. Where the hell had Letty gone? I envisioned her sliding over the side of the bed and under it.

"Are you all right?" She put up a hand, shielding her eyes from the light. "I heard you through the monitor. You were talking."

"What did I say?"

"I couldn't understand, but I thought I'd better get down here."

"My arm's hurting a little," I lied. That was better than saying, *I was screwing Letty until you interrupted.*

"Did you take one of your tablets?" She came down the stairs and over to the bed. The hydrocodone bottle lay next to the monitor, its top tightly capped.

I shook my head. "I felt all right when I went to sleep."

"Then take one now." She poured water from the little pitcher and picked up the bottle, shaking a caplet onto her palm.

"Yes'm."

I didn't need a pain pill, didn't want one, but other than say I'd lied, I had to take it. Obediently, I took the tablet and the cup, washed it down, and returned the glass to the table. Then I lay down again. I hoped Letty wasn't too uncomfortable. I pictured her huddled under the bed, peering out from under the edge of the bedspread.

Mom helped me settle my arm, then tucked the sheet around me. "Tomorrow night, ask Dad to help you get into your pajamas."

She'd always disapproved of me sleeping near-naked. She would've taken an even dimmer view of how I slept when I was married, if she'd known about it.

"Okay." I was too shaken to think of anything else to say.

With a kiss to my cheek, she went back up the stairs, asking, "Do you want me to leave the stair light on?"

"No, that's okay." I was still too flustered to be insulted. I yawned elaborately. "Whoa…that stuff works fast. I'm already getting sleepy."

She nodded and disappeared from view. In a moment, the light went out and I heard the door shut.

After a few moments, I dared whisper, "Letty? You can come out now."

No answer.

"Letty? Did you hear?"

I maneuvered to the edge of the bed, waving my good arm over the side, pushing away the bedspread. No way I could roll over and peer under it.

Letty wasn't under the bed. She wasn't anywhere in the basement, and I knew it. Okay, so once again she hadn't been the one climbing into my bed. Whatever invaded my dreams at the Mercier house had followed me home, like a stray puppy. Unlike a homeless canine, however, this wasn't something I wanted to keep.

That thought gave me a chill and a determination not to go back to sleep. If *she*, whoever or whatever she was, showed up again, I wanted to be fully conscious and ready. The medication decided differently, taking hold, and I couldn't fight it, so I hoped it would numb my mind enough that my night visitor wouldn't be able to rouse me. I had a feeling she wouldn't bother me unless I could respond.

I fell asleep with the question buzzing around in my drugged brain: *Who are you?*

****

From the diary of Marianne Mercier, August 30, 1925:

Work on the house is going well. Jules believes it will be finished sooner than expected. I'm glad. I wish a house so grand no one will think we're like the rest of these people, farmers and laborers, though Jules pretends to be one of them. He's even made a friend of our neighbor, a man named Dylan Roth, a foreigner from some country I've never heard of, in the Balkans, wherever that is. He and Dylan often go to the tavern and have a beer and such after the men have finished work.

Though he's a carpenter and should be beneath my notice, I find myself often studying Dylan Roth. Truly, he's a handsome man, much better-looking than Jules. He's noticed me, also. I've made a point to bring the men water while they work, and he often watches me as I go from one to another, offering the dipper. It's very warm and the men often work without their shirts, though they aren't blatant about displaying their sweaty half-nakedness, even Dylan. He's magnificent. I find myself glorying in watching him move, seeing the muscles glide under his skin, damp as it is with perspiration, and shining so tanned in the sun.

I'd hoped to find someone among these men I could love since I don't care for Jules any more. Now I've found him. Dylan is the one I want. Out of them all, that callow boy in Savannah, the one in Brunswick, and those in between, I know now they were mere passing fancies. It is Dylan Roth who feeds my passion.

He pretends shyness when I approach. Once, I dared touch his bare back, and after that, he now wears his shirt as he works and swelters while the others do not. How can I not want a man so reserved and yet so handsome? His smile tells me he senses my interest and encourages me to be bolder while he's discreet to other eyes.

Chapter 18

For the next two weeks…tedium, *ennui*, *longueur*…
look up any word in the thesaurus meaning "boredom"
and you'll know how I felt.

…and so it went…

Each morning, I awoke when everyone else did,
tolerating the embarrassing process of having Dad wrap
my cast in plastic wrap so I could shower. Afterward,
he'd help me get dressed, occasionally reminiscing how
he'd struggled to assist Mom in dressing me when I was
a baby.

"Oh, you were such a little wiggle-worm."

I didn't need that.

It's amazing how getting out of clothes while having
one arm in a cast is much easier than getting into them.
Why does it require two hands to snap a pair of jeans or
tie shoelaces when the twist of two fingers could open a
waistband and shoes can simply be kicked off? Don't get
me started on socks.

Another of the unanswered mysteries of the
universe.

I was grateful it was summer because, at this point,
it looked like I was sentenced to wearing muscle shirts
for the next six months.

After I had breakfast with Mom, Dad, and Letty, I
watched my father and my girl leave for the construction
site. Then it was just Mom and me…and loose ends.

Mom had plenty to keep her occupied, all those housewifely chores she'd been handling for thirty-two years plus various women's groups and who-knows-what. Occasionally, she'd help out in the office if business got too busy.

That was where she and Dad met. She had been Roth Construction's clerk/cashier. Once Ben and I came along, she happily retired. Now, however, I was kind of the fifth wheel, very much in evidence but completely useless, just taking up space. At least she'd abandoned most of the smothering, thank God, but she was still apt to come running if I made the slightest sound of discomfort.

When she wasn't darting in and out, making short trips here and there, but never staying gone for long, she kept the TV running, volume loud enough that she could hear it from whatever room she was in. I, on the other hand, had absolutely no interest in talk shows, game shows, or soap operas. Since Dad stubbornly refused to subscribe to cable, my viewing choices were limited. I'd watch the news but those segments were short compared to all the other stuff clogging the airways during the day…and much too depressing, anyway.

I tried to read, taking refuge downstairs with a novel, but it didn't hold my attention. There was only one book in that bookcase I wanted to look at, and there was no way I could get it off the shelf while I had only one hand to maneuver it. Besides, I didn't want Mom or Dad to get even an inkling of what I planned.

As a result, I slept a lot, assisted by popping pills, but it wouldn't be long before I'd either run out of medicine or become addicted, so I had to be careful there. Besides, the pain wasn't so bad now.

The bright spots came at night. Letty and I played board games, checkers, Scrabble, and such, at the kitchen table. That was fun and managed to distract me. Occasionally, we sat in the swing, talking and stealing kisses, with ears tuned to the sound of footsteps coming toward the door.

It was childlike, harmless, and sweet...but I was rapidly wanting something more adult. Specifically, I wanted to pick up Letty, sling her over my shoulder, and carry her caveman-style to my basement lair, broken arm and cast be damned.

Somehow, I managed to subdue my more Neanderthal tendencies. Probably because I envisioned Mom's face as I raced toward the basement stairs with Letty balanced on my shoulder.

I wasn't the recipient ofany more attempts of spectral seduction, however, probably because I'd self-analyzed myself into believing those two episodes had been some kind of subliminal manifestation of my suppressed libido.

Thank you, Dr. Dylan Freud.

I'd be cured of that once I got out of my cast, I promised myself.

At last, after fourteen days of eternity, the time rolled around for me to return to the hospital for x-rays.

****

Monday, Dad reminded Mom she was needed at the office. Jen had worked her last day before taking maternity leave, in preparation for bringing a new Estonkon into the world.

In the turmoil of my accident, Mom had forgotten. She was now properly panicked.

"How's Dylan going to get to his appointment

tomorrow? He can't drive."

"Don't worry, Mrs. Roth." Letty to the rescue. The girl was definitely fitting herself into our family. "I can take him." She gave me a smile. "There's plenty for Bill to film at the site so I don't have to be in every shot."

It was settled. I mentally clapped with glee. Having someone other than Mom drive me gave me freedom to do what I wanted. I was certain Letty wouldn't throw a monkey wrench into my plans. After all, she was already a co-conspirator.

That morning, Mom, carrying two brown bags filled with sandwiches, chips, and refrigerator dishes of fruit salad, rode with Dad to the office, leaving me in Letty's sarcastically loving care. My appointment was at nine-thirty, and she decided if we left at eight, that would give us plenty of time.

I was so brightly eager she gave me a couple of suspicious glances, but she didn't ask any more questions. Glancing at her watch, all she said was, "We'd better go. You don't want to be late."

The appointment didn't take long as those things go.

Within five minutes of signing in, I was whisked away by the nurse, leaving Letty reading a fairly recent gardening magazine.

My arm was x-rayed. Dr. Norton looked at the films, told me healing was progressing well. If it kept on like this, the cast could come off and a splint would replace it very soon.

When pressed about my return to work, he hedged with another, "We'll see."

I left the hospital with two cards, one informing me he'd see me in two weeks and the other setting up an appointment for physical therapy, beginning that coming

Thursday, for twice a week until he saw me again.

In the car once more, Letty pointed out it was getting close to noon. "I'll make lunch when we get home. Sandwiches okay?"

"Fine," I agreed. "But before that, there's something else I want you to do for me."

"Dylan," she frowned as if she guessed what I was thinking. "I don't believe you're quite ready for..."

"Sweetheart," I met her gaze because she *didn't* know what I was thinking. Not this time. "You'd be surprised what I'm ready for. But that's not what I meant."

"No?" She looked taken aback.

Dare I hope there was disappointment also in her expression? I let a brief moment of pleasure flit through my mind...Letty as a naked nymph teasing a satyr who had my features, only instead of a Pan pipe, he was lugging around a white-casted arm.

"I want to go to the Estonko Historical Preservation Society."

"Estonko Historical Preservation Society? Why?"

"Because, my dear Ms. Mercier." I leaned across the seat, kissing her on the tip of her nose. "I want to see if they have any newspapers for June 1926."

"Oh." She stiffened, glancing around as if to make certain no one had seen. "Why? I mean, why do you have to open that particular can of worms? It doesn't really concern us, and..."

"Letty, it very much concerns us," I retorted. "If it didn't, your father wouldn't have worried about you staying with us, and Dad wouldn't have said he was glad the Merciers were letting bygones be bygones."

"That doesn't mean—"

"Oh yes, it does." I didn't intend for her to argue with me. "What was the first thing you said to Dad when you walked into the construction office?"

I'd been curious about that.

"I…well…" She thought a moment, then sighed in defeat, repeating as if from memory, "*My name's Scarlett Mercier and I hope you're not going to throw me out of here, Mr. Roth.* Okay…I see what you mean. We had no idea whether the Roths might hold a grudge against the Merciers…"

"…though it appears it wasn't vice versa," I interrupted.

"…but that's all over now. *Your* dad likes *me*. *I* love *you*. *My* dad'll like you when you two meet. Anyway, no one around here now seems to know what happened, so why bother?"

"Because something doesn't feel right," I fell back on my original answer, ignoring the tiny niggle of *What if you're wrong and there's nothing?* "I don't know what, but it just isn't right."

"You may find something you won't like," she pointed out. "What if the newspapers say Anna Belle shot Dylan?"

"What if we discover *Marianne* did?" I retorted. "Or maybe she shot both Dylan and Jules and buried them in the cellar?"

"The house doesn't have a cellar. Remember?" She shook her head, giving me a pert smile. "Anyway, they would've found the bodies when your uncle put in the plumbing. The only thing they dug up were some old rifle casings."

I shrugged, acknowledging that fact. "Dad said the sheriff tried to suppress the story. Maybe I just want to see how much actually got out."

"Okay, don't listen to me," she straightened, sighing in defeat. "But if you find out something you don't want to know, be warned. I'm going to say, 'I told you so,' and really rub it in. Now then…" She started the engine. "How do we get there?"

"It's on East Lawrence," I said. "In the old Physicians' Office Building."

Chapter 19

The Estonko website said the Historical Preservation Society met on the first Tuesday of every month at 7:00 pm. Since today was the second Tuesday, I hoped someone would be there, perhaps tidying up after last night's meeting or something.

She was. A bright and polite lady about Mom's age, who introduced herself as Betty Atwood and immediately exclaimed, "My goodness, what happened to you, sugah? Not a car accident, I hope?"

"Construction," I explained and didn't go into detail, though I added, "Doctor says I'm doing fine," so I wouldn't sound too curt.

"Well, thank goodness." She gave me a bright smile. "How can I help you two youngsters?"

"I was wondering if you have copies of old newspapers?"

Other than aware Grandma gave them her kitchen work island, I'm sorry to say I'd never been curious about what the Preservation Society contained. I'd always envisioned it as kind of a museum filled with dusty old stuff people didn't want but refused to throw away, so it got donated.

"We've a few of the *Daily Courier*," she acknowledged. "That's the one most people subscribe to. What dates were you interested in?"

"June of 1926," I replied, thinking the story of the

storm would be the headline the day afterward, "and July, 1936."

"Hmm." She pursed her mouth, thinking. "I don't know… Let me check." She disappeared into another room.

I realized Letty wasn't standing with me. She had wandered to a group of photographs arranged on the wall near the door. She leaned forward, peering at a small one, a group of school kids in knickers and pinafores.

"Here we are." The lady was back, bringing with her some small stiff sheets. She placed them on the desk. "You're halfway lucky."

"How's that?"

"I've a couple of issues from the Twenties. Nothing from '36, though. That's unusual. Usually it's the other way around. The farther back one goes, the rarer they are. Sorry." She looked as if she hated disappointing me.

"Oh, well." I studied what she'd placed on the desk as she very politely left me and walked over to Letty, speaking to her in a low voice.

They'd had the papers laminated, encasing each one forever between protective sheets of plastic. It was a good thing. The edges of the top sheet had already started falling apart. The entire page was dark tan in color, and very brittle-looking. It must've been old when it was donated, for the paper to have turned that particular shade of yellow. A border of tiny flecks of paper surrounded the page. It had probably begun flaking away as it was being prepared, in spite of the handler's caution. A couple of the others were mere fragments…part of a headline, the beginning of a story with the rest crumbled away. The pieces had been placed where they might've appeared on the page. One had been ripped in half, its other section completely gone.

The newspaper was small. Only about eleven by fifteen inches, a bifold with a single sheet forming front and last pages laminated as one piece. There were only two issues in the stack, June 30 and July 2. The three editions preceding them were absent. I picked up the plastic-coated sheet.

The story took up a good portion of the front page, and I skimmed it impatiently, before stopping to glance at the rest of the page. It seemed simply the usual story of a weather disaster. There was a description of the strength of the storm and the course it had taken, with a damage report. No other headlines worth bothering with, certainly nothing stating, *Neighbors Desert Wives and Run Away Together.* I doubted if it would've been phrased like that anyway.

Disappointed, I went on to the July 1 issue.

Tornado Touches Down in Estonko, the headline read, *by Robert Bascom*, the byline credited. In the center of the first column was a bold black box, noting: *"...for other information on storm damage in Estonko and surrounds, see our June 30 edition."*

This one was a probable rehash of June 30th's headliner. Nevertheless, I read through it, hoping it would yield some information. At the very end, I found it. "...related story on area fatalities, Page 2."

I flipped the sheet, glancing down.

Search Continues for Two Men Missing After Storm.

Now we're getting somewhere.

It was a one paragraph article, stating the bare facts: My great-grandfather went to help Letty's great-grandfather put away his farm machinery before the storm hit. Neither were seen again. A search party was organized.

That's all? I looked up, dropping the paper to the desk. The plastic laminate made a dull thump.

Mrs. Atwood looked away from the picture she was discussing. "Didn't find what you wanted, dear?"

I shook my head. "The ones I need are missing. Are you sure you don't have any more?"

"I'm certain. The others are from the forties and later. Back then, people didn't think of saving newspapers for future generations, I'm afraid."

I must've looked extremely disappointed, because she walked over to the desk, placing a hand on my shoulder.

"You might try the *Daily Courier* archives in Amesville. What do they call it...something gruesome...the morgue?" She shuddered delicately. "I'm sure they'll have copies of *all* their papers from the first one printed." She smiled. "They should."

"Thanks." I restacked the plastic sheets and handed them to her. "I wonder..."

She turned to look back at me.

"Can you make a copy of a story from a laminated sheet?"

"I'm sorry. The plastic makes a glare and it doesn't reproduce well." She shrugged. "That's the bad thing about lamination, but it's the only way to preserve the pages."

"Well, thanks, then. I appreciate your help." I looked over my shoulder. "Come on, Letty."

"Take care of your arm, dear." Mrs. Atwood called as we left.

I raised my good hand in farewell.

"I heard what she said. We are *not* going to

Amesville," Letty informed me, once we were in the car again.

"Beg to differ," I replied. "The June 29 issue wasn't there. All I found was an article three days later, stating Jules and Dylan were missing and making it sound as if they were storm casualties."

"The sheriff managed his cover-up. You knew that already. They'll have the same paper in the archives and it won't say anything different," she pointed out, tapping her fingers impatiently against the steering wheel. "Why bother?"

"Because I want to see the paper coming out the day *after* the storm. I also want to look for any follow-ups."

She was silent for nearly a minute, biting her lip before she said, "Okay, but we're stopping for something to eat. I'm hungry and you need to keep up your strength."

"You're being sarcastic, aren't you?" I gave her a half-angry glare. "What do I need strength for?"

"You're damned right I am." She ignored my question, saying, "I think you should go home and go to bed…"

"Why, Miz Scarlett, is that an invitation?" I gave her a definite leer. "In that case, I think we'd better stop at one of the pizzerias. I do believe I'll need a great deal of strength."

She didn't answer, just shook her head. Her stomach chose that moment to growl loudly.

"Don't worry. They also serve burgers," I said. I was beginning to feel a little hungry, too.

I pressed my luck by chucking her under the chin. She slapped away my hand but there wasn't any anger in the movement. It was a very playful slap. I barely felt it.

"My treat."

"You wish," she muttered as she pressed the starter.

Chapter 20

Letty didn't talk much as we ate. I blamed it on the fact that her mouth was full of pepperoni burger and spaghetti fries, so-called because they were cut in a corkscrew pattern. She did come up for air long enough to say, "This is delicious," but that was all.

Once in the car again, I leaned back, slapped my belt buckle, and sighed. "Ahhh...the Inner Man has been satisfied."

"Inner *Child*, you mean," she corrected. "I don't think I've seen anyone, outside of my fifteen-year-old brother, put away so much food. You'd better watch it. One day you're going to wake up and find yourself transformed into a blimp...if a heart attack doesn't get you first."

"Never happen," I didn't tell her my usual strenuous workday kept the pounds off. "However, if you're worried about my health..."

"Me? Worried? Hah." Her denial was delivered with a sneer.

Good thing I knew she cared or her tone might've made me worry.

"...I'll have a large salad tonight."

"Don't think I won't hold you to that," she said, and startled me by seizing my left hand and squeezing it. "You don't usually eat like that, do you?"

"Are you kidding? You've seen how Mom cooks."

Mom might be a Southern cook, but, with the exception of breakfast, which she considered was a fuel-up for the rest of the day, she was definitely calorie-conscious. Even her fried chicken was oven-broiled.

"And it's going to stay that way." She released my hand and started the engine.

"Hey."

She looked at me. "What?"

"Thanks."

"For what?"

"For caring." I didn't say more, otherwise this might get overly sentimental.

"Someone's got to look out for you when your mother's not around." She released the hand brake.

At the newspaper office, I had much better luck than in Estonko. Explaining at the front desk what I wanted, I was referred to a couple of people, ending with a lady as nice and helpful as Mrs. Atwood. Setting aside her keyboard and introducing herself as Joan Ellis, she answered that yes, they did have copies of the newspaper, from the very first one issued in 1867.

She went on to explain that originally they'd kept three copies of each paper in their morgue—now called the *Information Archive*—and when microfilm and then microfiche came into common use, transferred the data onto film, thus saving a great deal of space and preventing all that ageing, brittle paper from becoming a fire hazard. Microfiche, however, had a limited existence rate, so with the intrusion of computers into our lives, all the information was again converted.

I told her what I was looking for. While Letty settled at a small reading nook and pulled a copy of today's paper from a hanging file stand next to her chair, I was led to a carrel where a machine called a digital microfilm reader was located. When she began an abbreviated tutorial on how to use the machine, I pointed out my very obvious handicap.

"Oh, that was inconsiderate of me, wasn't it?" She looked slightly embarrassed. "How could I have ignored something so obvious?"

While I assured her I wasn't insulted, she offered to stay and help me.

"This is usually when I take my break, so I'm free for a bit."

"That'd be great. I could ask my chauffeur for help, but…" I glanced through the door to the chair where Letty sat with her pert little nose studiously buried in the local news. "I'm afraid she's a bit put out just now because she had to drive me here from Estonko."

She laughed at that, and asked me what dates I was interested in.

I was disappointed when she brought up the June 30, 1926 edition, however. The story was exactly like the one I'd seen at the Preservation Society, about the storm and nothing else. Hadn't Letty said it wouldn't be different?

Undaunted, I asked her for the June 29 issue, adding, "I think you went past it."

"Oh no," she said. "That was the day after a tornado touched down. They didn't put out a paper that day."

"Oh? I'm surprised there wasn't a special edition, in that case."

"Generally, I suppose they might've, but it struck late in the evening on Monday, and the next day was completely chaotic. I think that was the only time the *Daily News* missed an issue. They simply made it the lead story for the Wednesday paper."

Damn. That didn't sound right. I'd think the editor would've sent reporters out as soon as it was safe, perhaps even before, to get reactions, survey the damage then and there, so people would know what had happened, not wait two days when everyone would probably already be half-aware.

Was that evidence of Sheriff Benson's *influence*?

"May I get a copy of this one?" I asked.

She nodded and went to work, highlighting the article and creating a high resolution image which she saved as a pdf and sent to a printer.

We scanned the other pages.

Nothing.

I would've liked to simply have gone through each day from then to the date Great-Grandma had her husband declared legally dead, but that would've taken more time than Ms. Ellis could spare. Her break would be over soon, and I didn't want to keep her from whatever task I'd interrupted.

Instead, I asked to see the issue for July 2, then the corresponding edition of the following year, and the year after that, then the date written after Dylan's name in the Bible.

In the end, I came away with hardcopies for which I paid the royal sum of one quarter each.

"Well!" Ms. Ellis glanced at her watch as she wrote me out a receipt for the three dollars I'd spent. "That was well-timed. My break's now officially over."

"I appreciate your taking time out to help me." I meant it.

"Think nothing of it," she replied, and glanced at Letty, who returned the folded newspaper to the hanging file and got to her feet, looking impatient. "Looks like your driver's waiting."

****

"Did you find anything worthwhile?" Letty glanced at the sheets I held as she locked me safely into my shoulder harness.

She started the car and pulled away from the curb.

"I think I found quite a bit." I knew I sounded smug, and I was raring to be the one to say, *I told you so,* but I managed not to.

"Oh? What?" She craned her neck, glancing down as if trying to read the top page.

"Keep your eyes on the road," I cautioned severely. "I don't want you running into a ditch and breaking my other arm or something worse. You can see when we get home."

She gave me a grimace of irritation but obediently turned her attention back to the highway and didn't speak again until we reached our driveway.

Chapter 21

"I don't know about you," Letty said as we came through the kitchen door, "but my burger is long gone. What is there around here we can snack on to tide us over until your mom gets home and I help her with supper?"

She swung her purse off her shoulder, looping the straps over the knob of the back door. That startled me. It was exactly what Mom always did, so she wouldn't have to hunt for her bag whenever she went out. It was a familiar gesture, and she made it seem such an unconscious one that it came to me...*she feels at home here*. That engendered some not necessarily disturbing but definitely acute emotions begging to be explored.

"First, come downstairs," I answered, and caught her hand, tugging on it as I continued toward the basement door. "I've something to show you."

"I'm certain you do." Laughing, she took a step, then halted before taking another, not pulling away but not in any hurry to follow. "I imagine it's a sight to behold, but I still don't think you're in any condition—"

"Why do you always assume the worst?" Releasing her hand, I awkwardly put my casted arm around her waist. "Or maybe it's the best?" I pulled her in for a quick kiss. "That'll come later, I promise. Right now, I want to show you something else."

"We-e-el-l." She looked thoughtful, rolling her eyes and tapping her cheek with a forefinger. "Later? You promise? How much later?"

"God, you *are* a tease!"

"Never said I wasn't." She gave me a kiss as quick as mine had been. "Isn't that why you love me?"

Oh no, I wasn't going to fall into that trap, not just now. We'd already established neither of us knew why we loved each other, and now wasn't the time to dissect that particular problem.

"Come on." This time she followed meekly as I went down the stairs.

Once downstairs, she looked around with approval.

"Not exactly the caveman's lair I expected. I like it."

"I knew sweeping all the half-gnawed bones into the trash was the right thing to do." Secretly, I was thankful I hadn't left my PJ bottoms lying across the end of the bed as I usually did, or my underwear draped over a chair, and had decided that morning to at least smooth the bedspread before I went upstairs.

"Okay, I'm here. What is it I'm supposed to be seeing?" She spun in a circle, waving her hands.

"Over here," I led the way to the kitchenette.

The night before, I'd waited until everything was quiet, then tiptoed back upstairs.

Dragging a stepstool from the kitchen into the den, and hoping Mom had the bedroom door shut and wouldn't hear, I stood on it and maneuvered the Bible off the top shelf, somehow managing not to drop it as I balanced it against my cast. Opening it, I took out the picture of Dylan, struggled the Bible back into its place, and put the stool back in the kitchen. Then I hurried back downstairs and into the kitchenette.

On the wall next to the apartment-sized fridge, Dad had affixed a three-by-two-foot corkboard, much like the one upstairs in Mom's kitchen. Hers was littered with recipes, birthday cards, grocery coupons and other things she wanted to keep handy. Under it all, I think there might still be copies of Ben's and my college graduation invitations and a couple of ancient elementary school programs.

My board was bare. I'd had a calendar thumb-tacked to it, but I'd removed that, sticking the photograph in the upper left corner. My plan was to make a board like those I constructed when I was working on a story. It helped with continuity, and also was visible evidence to my editor of what I was working on.

"*Voilà.*" I stopped before the board, gesturing to it.

Letty stared at the single photograph, then slowly approached, leaning forward to peer at it. When she looked at me, I couldn't exactly interpret her expression. Then I realized…it was surprise. She'd never seen a picture of Dylan Roth. She was slightly shocked by her first sight of the man who was one of the skeletons in our mutual family closet.

"I didn't think he looked like that. Dylan…you resemble him."

"I guess I do. A little." I decided not to bring up the coincidence of also sharing birthdays.

"*A lot.* Where did you get the picture?"

"I found it in the family Bible. *His* Bible, one of the two things he brought with him from Romania."

"And you're…" She glanced at the papers I held. "…you're making a crime board?" she guessed, voice rising slightly as she understood. "That's why you wanted those newspaper stories. You're going to plot it all out, and see…what?"

"I don't know," I admitted. "When I was a reporter,

when I worked on a story, it always helped to do this. Looking at photos of people involved, reading impressions I'd written and facts I'd discovered…occasionally that made me think of things I didn't realize I knew, and raised other questions…"

"A good idea. Maybe it'll convince you there's nothing to discover." She pulled the papers from my hand. "Don't just stand there, let's get this up. Got thumbtacks?"

I pointed to the little box I'd left on the counter.

****

"Okay." I stepped back, staring at the corkboard.

At the top left was Dylan's picture. Next to it was a piece of paper with *Jules Mercier* written on it in marker. Beneath, we'd attached the copies of the newspaper stories, neatly trimmed so they fit better.

"Dylan Roth, age thirty," I gestured as I spoke, "and Jules Mercier, age thirty-two. One from Romania, the other a former resident of Savannah. Wonder why he came to Estonko? Why would someone from a fairly wealthy Creole family move to such a small town?" I studied the paper with his name. "Is there any chance you can get a picture of your great-grandfather?"

"You want to add Jules to the Rogues Gallery?"

We'd both begun calling our ancestors by their first names, making it more personal.

"It'd help to see him and not this piece of paper."

"We've got scads of family albums, but if I go asking Daddy for something like that, he's going to get suspicious and want to know why. What do I tell him? *Oh, nothing much…Dylan just wants to shake the family tree and see how many skeletons fall out*?"

"Can't you get it without his knowing?" I didn't

216

point out how I'd managed to get Dylan's that way. I doubt if Mom or Dad even knew it existed. Probably, neither had ever looked past the 'Family Tree' page. "When do you plan on going home again?"

"Weekend after next, I guess."

"Think about it."

I tried to soften my tone so it didn't sound so much like an order, and turned my attention back to the board. I'd miss her while she was gone.

I resumed my narrative.

"What did they have in common?" Holding up my left hand, I ticked off answers on my fingers. "They were neighbors. They disappeared on the same day. Nothing else. They officially met when Jules decided to build a new house." I looked at Letty, adding, "Dylan did the scroll work on the fireplaces, by the way, as well as the door surrounds, and the banisters."

Letty nodded, obviously remembering what I'd said about the mantel scrolls.

"We know the real story and we know what the newspapers say, thanks to Sheriff Benson's cover-up, but what else can the news stories add?"

"You tell me, Mr. Investigative Reporter," Letty replied. "This is *your* show."

"Yours, too, Ms. Letty Mercier," I retorted. "Okay, the newspapers…" I gestured again to the corkboard. "This first story doesn't offer much. It's merely about the storm. The July follow-up about the search party doesn't really go into detail. Sheriff Benson strikes again. But this one…" I tapped the year-later story. "It definitely says something."

"Like what, exactly?" Letty squinted at it. The print was slightly blurred.

"Allow me." I read it aloud:

Anniversary of Disappearance Brings No News
by Robert Bascom

It was a year ago on this date that a summer storm came off the Atlantic Ocean, transformed itself into a tornado, and swept across Rowen County. Most towns suffered property damages but no loss of life. For two Estonko families, however, the aftermath of the storm still remains.

Both Marianne Mercier and Anna Belle Roth lost their husbands that night. On the anniversary of the event, this reporter decided to visit them and see how they fared.

Mrs. Mercier is a small woman, delicate-looking, with a definite nervousness of disposition. She lives with her two children on a farm now lying fallow since her husband's disappearance. A small pool Mr. Mercier allowed Gilead Harmony Baptist Church to use for its baptisms had also been closed from use. It is perhaps because of this isolation that she greeted me at the door with a loaded rifle and refused to allow me entry to the house. After much explanation, we sat on the porch, the weapon resting across her lap as we talked.

She's heard nothing from her husband, she claims, and doesn't expect to. Marianne Mercier has accepted that he was killed during the storm and his body swept away to some place where it may never be found. She has plans to sell the farm and move her children back to Savannah to stay with her husband's family.

Though I wished to ask questions about the night her husband disappeared, she fielded them away, refusing to answer. One thing she did say was puzzling, however: "What happened was all Dylan Roth's fault. If he'd..."

Immediately, she stopped, putting a hand to her mouth.

"If he'd what?" I asked. "What was his fault?"

"Nothing." She shook her head.

I tried another angle. "It's been reported that when you arrived at the sheriff's office after the storm, you were extremely bruised. As if you'd been beaten. Would you care to comment on that?"

She refused to elaborate, declaring she'd fallen while walking to town.

"I'd heard otherwise, Mrs. Mercier. Didn't you have an argument with your

husband that night? It's said he'd also been in an altercation at a local tavern. Was Jules Mercier abusive? Did he beat, then abandon you? Where did Dylan Roth fit into this?"

At that she became very agitated, and before I could say more, got to her feet, brandishing the rifle. "My husband was killed in the storm. As for Dylan Roth...he got what he deserved, and you will, too, if you keep asking questions."

I beat a hasty retreat. She didn't move until I was in my automobile and going down the drive...a most unhappy lady, and very unsettled by that year-old tragedy.

Mrs. Roth, however, was more welcoming and very gracious in answering. She too has suffered a great loss, but unlike Mrs. Mercier, she believes her husband will someday return.

"These storms can scoop up things and carry them miles away. I thinkthat's what happened to Dylan. Even now, he could be wandering around in a daze, not knowing who or where he is. Perhaps he's in a hospital somewhere. Jules Mercier also. My husband loves me,

and one day, he'll remember and then he'll come back to me."

When asked about the friendship between her husband and Jules Mercier, and Mrs. Mercier's hostility, she had this to say: "Jules and Dylan were good neighbors. It was only natural for him to call and ask for help in putting away his farm equipment before the storm hit. As for those stories Marianne Mercier is telling...she's a grieving woman with a highly excitable temperament, and the less said, the better."

These two women, for all intents and purposes widowed by a tropical storm, view the incident through different eyes. One is hopeful as she cares for her children. The other is resentful and hostile to the world. It will be interesting to see what the future holds for each and which one is correct.

"She was going to sell the farm. That certainly didn't happen." Letty looked thoughtful. "I'm glad she didn't."

"So am I." I squeezed her hand, then straightened to tap the clipping with a forefinger. "Seems Anna Belle never believed the story that Jules and Dylan ran off together, which is what the reporter is obviously hinting at. Guess he heard a rumor Sheriff Benson couldn't stop. He couldn't come straight out and ask her, though. Not like we might today."

"Nevertheless, he reminds me of someone I know," Letty said. "Who shall remain nameless."

I ignored that. "'As for those stories Marianne Mercier is telling...' That hints at a bit of animosity. And there's Marianne getting so upset."

"Maybe she realized what he was getting at but didn't want to be reminded."

"Anna Belle didn't get upset. In fact, the reporter described her as, and I quote, 'welcoming and gracious.'"

"So she was of stronger stuff than Marianne. It takes some people a long time to get over losing someone, no matter how it happens. Losing a husband to another man would be a huge blow to the ego. Anyway, people mourn in different ways, you know." Letty defended her great-grandmother a little heatedly. "The reporter said she was of a nervous and delicate disposition, didn't he?"

"Wasn't that an early twentieth-century euphemism for *a bit off her rocker*?" I asked.

She glared at me.

"I'm sorry, Letty, but she *did* end up in the state hospital a few months later."

She acknowledged that with a sigh. "You think the disappearance drove her insane? That she loved her husband so she couldn't accept the fact he loved Dylan more? And was ready to shoot anyone who even hinted at it?"

"I swear I don't know," I admitted. "All this story tells us for certain us is that Marianne wouldn't talk about her husband, while Anna Belle was very forthcoming. It could be as you say. What really interests me is that she didn't become upset until he pressed her about the bruises she supposedly received while walking into town. Dad said she told the sheriff they were received in a fight with Jules when he tried to take the children. When he supposedly knocked her down and she bled onto the floor. That spot we saw in the nursery… Remember?"

She shivered and glanced at her fingers. "Don't remind me."

"That's another thing." Again, I brought up the argument I'd said to Dad, though I admit I was beating a dead horse by repeating it so much. "Why tell her he was taking the kids, then lock them in and leave? The idea that Dylan's arrival made him change his mind doesn't fly. I think he did it for some other reason."

"Like what?" Letty nibbled on a fingernail, studying Dylan's picture. He smiled out at her, embracing his bride.

"That's what I don't know." I shrugged and looked at the next article. "Moving on…Two days later, there's a retraction." Again, I read from the board:

Publisher's Note: Retraction on A Story Published on June 28, 1927

It has been brought to this paper's attention that the article "Anniversary of Disappearance Brings No News" *published in our June 28 edition contained opinions and statements bringing undue stress and perhaps public discomfort to the persons with whom the story was concerned.*

The editor wishes it known that these expressions were those of Robert Bascom, the reporter involved, and not of this newspaper. We apologize to the public in general and Mrs. Mercier and Mrs. Roth in particular for any embarrassment caused by our employee's thoughtlessness. Mr. Bascom has been severely chastised for his lack of judgment.

"Sheriff Benson back in control. He goes back to the editor, breathes a little fire and brimstone about his reporter harassing the ladies. Result: Mr…." I peered at the byline. "…Robert Bascom gets a reprimand and the paper makes a public apology. There's nothing afterward until the declaration of Dylan's death, with the so-called obituary, and then the announcement of Anna Belle's second marriage."

We both looked at those very short articles, neither taking up more than an inch of news space.

"She was officially a widow for all of a week," Letty said softly. She looked up at me. "If it had been you, I'd have waited longer than that, Dyl."

"Thanks, sweetheart, but she'd really been a widow for ten years, even if she didn't admit it."

That stopped me for a minute. I didn't want to think of Letty losing me or my losing her. We hadn't even gotten started yet.

I picked up the thread again, a little forcefully, to dispel a sudden sickening twinge. "So, to sum up and do a bit of extrapolation... Two men meet, become friends, realize they want to be more than friends. Did they wonder what to do about it? Is that why they didn't see each other for a while, hoping maybe the attraction would wear off?"

"That doesn't explain Jules' fight," Letty put in.

"That was later. First came the housewarming party, when Dylan and Marianne had their argument. *That* was when they stopped seeing each other. Why? What did he say to her or she to him? Enough to make him leave the party and never go back to the Mercier farmstead until the night of the storm. Then Jules turned up looking as if he'd been in a brawl."

"Maybe he was sublimating his passion by getting into fights?"

"Perhaps, but where? It wasn't at the tavern where they usually met or Dad would've mentioned it. Bet if I check police records, I won't find any arrests for disorderly conduct, either. Whatever, it brings them together again. Then, the storm comes along and Jules sees it as the perfect cover to run away. Maybe he springs it on Dylan when he arrives at the farm but Dylan does convince him to leave the children. *They're better off with their mother*, that sort of thing." I thought of the inscription on the back of the photograph of Dylan holding his newborn son. "The next morning, Marianne walks into town and reports her husband missing, and soon after, so does Anna Belle. I wonder how she reacted to what Marianne said? A search party is formed and Benson, who's Anna Belle's second cousin, decides for propriety's sake to squelch the story, making it seem the two are merely storm casualties. Did I miss anything?"

"It sounds very feasible," Letty said grudgingly, after a moment's silence.

I'd been watching her face as I spoke. She seemed genuinely disturbed by my synopsis of how I thought it happened.

"But we know better." I held up a finger.

"No, *you* know better," Letty corrected, "or you think you do." She heaved a heavy sigh. "Frankly, I can't see anything sinister in any of this. On the surface, it simply looks like a very tragic set of circumstances, no matter how it happened. Two men probably got killed in a storm."

"There are too many unanswered questions," I complained. "About the kids…Jules' fighting…the argument at the party…Marianne's insistence that her husband is dead. Why is she so certain? Did she see them swept away by the tornado? What did she mean by, 'Dylan got what he deserved?' Did she see their deaths as divine retribution?"

"Even knowing the *real* background facts, I don't

see anything out of place. What do you want, Dylan? Some piece of evidence that'll point to Jules and your great-grandfather as residents of some out-of-the-way nursing home in Florida or some place?"

"It should happen," I answered.

"Are you sure you're not simply trying to make something where there's nothing because you're bored?"

"Bored?" I pretended disbelief. "How can I be bored with you here?"

I caught her in an awkward embrace and gave her a kiss. She laughed and returned the favor for several heart-pounding moments before pushing away.

"I swear, Letty," I went on earnestly. "I *know* something happened that makes this into more than a *tragic set of circumstances*, no matter how we look at it. I simply need to find the key to make it all clear."

"How do you plan to do that?"

She was obviously tiring of the repetition.

I already had an answer, and I knew she wasn't going to like it. "It's too late to do any more today, but tomorrow, I think we should see if Mr. Robert Bascom is still with us."

"Oh for goodness' sake!" That made her laugh and shake her head pityingly. "If he is, he'd be well over a hundred. How much information do you think you'd get out of a centenarian?"

"Enough." I figured I may as well go for broke. "I'd like to talk to Marianne Mercier's doctor at the state hospital, too."

"Don't expect me to drive you to the state mental hospital. That's a hundred and eighty-two miles, and a whole tank of gas, one way."

"Not even if I ask you nicely?"

"How nicely?" I could tell by her smile she already knew the answer.

"Like this." Awkwardly, I swung her into my arms and kissed her, then began to nuzzle against her neck, just under her ear.

She pushed me away. "Do you always use sex to get what you want? Should I make a note of that?"

"This isn't sex. This is kissing." I pressed my lips against her earlobe, then nipped lightly.

"It definitely *is* sex...foreplay, at least." She shook her head.

"That's the way Jillian always got me to do anything," I confessed. "Can't it work in reverse?"

"I'm not Jillian."

"For which I thank God every day." I released her with a final peck on the cheek. "Let's discuss it later. Right now, let's take a break and talk about something more pleasant...namely us."

I caught her hand, leading her from the kitchenette.

"Or better yet, not talk at all." I kissed her. She didn't seem exactly averse to that, so I did it again. "Damn, I want to get you horizontal."

"You sweet talker you," she murmured.

"Why don't we get into something a little more comfortable?" Encouraged, I maneuvered her toward the bedroom. "Like a bed?"

"Dylan..."

"Don't worry." We rounded the wall. "I promise I won't do anything to hurt my arm."

"It's not your arm I'm worried about."

"Shhh..." I pushed her onto the bed. She didn't protest but went with the flow and lay back as I leaned over her.

Okay, we didn't do much of anything we couldn't have done in the porch swing, but it felt so good after so long, just to have Letty's lovely body against mine. I swear I was experiencing sensations I hadn't felt in over fifteen years. Hot and cold, burning, pounding lust, and timid hesitancy. It was like I was a teenager again, eager, impatient, with my adult self forcing me to exercise caution, not simply because of my injury but also because we were in my parents' home and I didn't want to do anything that might cause Letty the least amount of embarrassment.

I let the teenager take over momentarily, telling myself it was hours yet before the old folks would be home. That encouraged me to maneuver my uninjured hand under her tank top, sliding it upward and discovering today she wasn't wearing a bra. I cupped and caressed a warm, full breast. As I carefully caught the nipple between my fingers and gently tweaked it, she gave a little moan against my mouth.

That was music to my ears and encouragement to my cock.

Letty wasn't lying there passive, however. Her hands worked under the hem of my muscle shirt. When they both brushed their way across my chest, I nearly flinched it felt so good. Then she discovered an erotic zone. From my first sexual encounter, it'd been a secret source of embarrassment that my nips were extra sensitive. I'd always thought arousal through nipple stimulation should be a female thing, but—damn!—it felt good as her fingers began a little swirling movement across each one.

Then she slid her hand down to my zipper, fumbling with it.

Yes... I thrust upward slightly.

Get away from him!

"What was that?" Letty jumped, pulling away so quickly she didn't notice my own startled reaction.

"What?" Had I really heard it? A whisper as sharp as the one I'd imagined in the nursery that day as I bent over the crib?

"I thought I heard someone."

"A bird...." I resumed kissing her ear, nibbling across her jaw to her chin.

"Could we hear a bird down here?" She was so distracted I doubt she even felt the caress I gave her breast. "It sounded like a voice."

"The wind." I paused long enough to elaborate. "One summer when I was a kid, I kept running to the house because I thought I heard Mom calling me. Turns out it was the wind blowing the door on the garage. The hinges were rusty and they squeaked, and it sounded exactly like someone calling my name."

"This wasn't a rusty hinge." She looked toward the stairs.

I caught her chin, turned her head and kissed her again...as I heard the back door open.

"Dylan? We're home."

Letty stiffened. "Your mother...do you suppose she..." She hastily pulled down her tank top, covering those luscious breasts.

I sighed. "Guess play time's over." I stood, adjusted my own shirt, checked my jeans to make certain they were zipped, and offered my good arm. "Shall we?"

She hung back, whispering. "If she saw us, how can I face her?"

"She didn't see anything." My own answer was just

as low. Why were we whispering? "You imagined it."

She looked unconvinced.

"Listen, if it was Mom—and I tell you it wasn't—she won't look at you. She always avoids eye contact when she's embarrassed."

She looked up at the stairs again, then back at my arm, which was still extended. Gently, she hooked her own through it, pressing against me as if for more than mere support going up the stairs.

I liked it, though I hated the reason why.

Mom was her usual bright self, greeting Letty and asking if she'd had any trouble finding the hospital.

Letty gave me a glance as she answered, silently accepting the fact that Mom wasn't acting as if she'd peeked down the stairs and seen her son and houseguest *in flagrante delicto*.

There was a sudden tense moment when she asked, "Where were you? I called as we came in, but…"

"We were downstairs," I cut in before Letty could say something incriminating.

"Oh?" She set the bag of groceries she held on the table. "Put that one over there, Chuck."

Dad obediently set the other on the counter.

"Yeah, Letty was curious about how my apartment looked, so I gave her the grand tour."

"Did you show her your etchings?" Dad put in, mischief in his blue eyes.

Shut up, Dad. I gave him a quick glare. He shrugged.

"No etchings," Letty cut in. "Though he has a nice calendar on the bulletin board. I think it's a lovely place. Did you do all the work yourself, Mr. Roth?"

That's right. Distract him. That's my girl.

"It was a family affair," Dad replied. "My brothers

helped."

"I especially like the bathroom, and the way the kitchen's set up."

Dad murmured his thanks and Mom interrupted, asking me about the doctor's visit and made a great show of reacting to the fact that I was healing well.

"You mean, I may not have you underfoot for much longer?"

"Hey," I protested. "That's a different song from the one you were singing earlier." I pretended to be hurt.

"Oh hush. You know I love you." Mom patted my shoulder. "I was thinking how bored you've been. I know not being able to drive has really—"

"No problem, Mrs. Roth," Letty spoke up. "I'll keep Dylan busy. He's going to show me around South Georgia and I'm going to drive while he does it."

"Letty, that's so sweet of you."

"Yeah, I think it is, too," I said, realizing she'd just given us an alibi for being out of the house all day.

Dad interrupted things by dropping some papers onto the table along with a pen.

"Sign these," he said, in his usual abbreviated way.

I picked up the pen, studying the paper. "What am I signing?"

"Application to receive disability benefits while you're out of commission. Don't think I'm going to pay you while you're being waited on hand and foot and chauffeured around the countryside. Already got the workman's comp papers sent in and the wheels in motion on that." His eyes twinkled as he glanced at Letty, who was now talking animatedly to Mom but loud enough for us to hear.

"What are we having tonight?"

"Brunswick stew and barbeque with chips. That's why we stopped at the store."

My favorite, after pork chops and hashbrowns.

I maneuvered the pen into the fingers of my right hand and signed the papers, folded them, and handed them and the pen back to Dad.

He nodded, put them in a pocket, did a quick head-jerk at the door and went into the den.

I followed.

"Everything all right, son? You look a little flushed."

"Sure." Damn, if I looked flushed now, how had I looked when Letty and I came upstairs?

He glanced back toward the kitchen. "You really like this girl, don't you?"

"Yes, Dad." My eyes followed his gaze. "Really. Seriously."

"Just be careful."

I was getting a little tired of that admonition. "I promise I'm not going to do anything to hurt my arm."

He surprised me by saying, "I'm not talking about your arm. All your others parts are still working well, I presume?"

"Dad…" That caught me off-guard, especially his tone. As if I were still a kid.

"I haven't forgotten how it feels to be young and in love, Dylan." His own cheeks colored slightly. "I wanted your mother so much you could've been a very premature baby if I hadn't kept a tight rein on my own emotions."

Before I could think how to answer that, Letty called us to supper.

****

Excerpt from Dylan Roth's journal, September 30, 1925:

The house has been finished and Jules gave a party to celebrate, a housewarming, he calls it. I wore my best suit and Annie looked beautiful in the dress she sewed for the occasion. It was made of a fabric she called silk voile, soft translucent stuff with large roses on a pink background. She looked beautiful and I was certain she'd outshine every woman there. That made her laugh but I think she was pleased. We arrived in style, in my Model T truck. The party was in full swing when we got there. All who worked on the construction were invited, as well as some local bigwigs, including Annie's cousin, the sheriff. He looked odd without that ax handle he usually carries. I also saw the pastor from Gilead Harmony Church where Annie and I worship, and Jules does, also.

It was odd to see Jules also dressed up and not in his usual dungarees and work shirt. He was wearing a tuxedo with peaked lapels. Annie whispered she thought I'd look 'elegant' in one. I replied I'd feel awkward. His wife wore some kind of gauzy concoction that looked to cost more than all the other dresses in the room combined, but she couldn't rival my Annie and I said so, making my sweet wife blush.

Jules had a string quartet set in a corner of the ballroom, and we had a dance or two—waltzes, no Charleston—then were enjoying a cup of punch when Mrs. Mercier approached.

'Jules is going to have the garden landscaped and I'd like your opinion on what type furniture I should have.'

I excused myself from Annie and she led me through

the kitchen to the backdoor and onto the porch. There were no outdoor torches and the garden was in shadow.

'It's too dark to see anything,' I said. 'I'll come back in the daytime...'

I got no further. She threw herself at me, wrapping her arms around my neck and pressing her mouth to mine. I was so startled, I'm afraid I was a little rough as I pushed her away and disentangled her arms.

'Mrs. Mercier...what's the meaning of this?' I was outraged as well as confused.

She said the most astonishing thing: 'Don't pretend, Dylan. I know how you feel about me. I love you, too. I'm ready to go away with you. Tonight.'

'What are you saying?' I must have sounded unbelievably stupid, but I was shocked.

'I don't love Jules,' she declared. 'I love you. Darling, admit you feel the same...' She didn't finish but again tried to embrace me.

I backed away and fumbled for the door, escaping back into the house. She followed, in tears, making even more outlandish avowals of love. I was thankful no one was in the kitchen to hear. As I came into the ballroom, I saw Jules standing nearby, talking to a group of men. He noticed my distress and came over.

'Dylan? What's the matter? You look...'

'Jules...Your wife...' I stammered. I couldn't go on. Not with all these people around. I finished lamely, 'I have to go.'

I pushed past him, finding Annie. She took one look at my face and asked, 'What's happened?'

'We're leaving.' I took her arm and nearly dragged her to the door.

'But...I wanted to dance some more,' she protested.

'Why must we go?'

'Don't argue. We're leaving, Annie. Now.' I'm afraid I raised my voice. She didn't argue, just followed meekly behind me as I went into the foyer.

As I glanced back, I saw Marianne Mercier standing at the door, an expression I couldn't interpret on her face. Annie looked around, saw her, and looked back at me but didn't speak.

I helped Annie into the truck and we drove home in silence. Once there, I took home Annie's cousin Charlotte, Ezra's daughter, who'd agreed to stay with the children. When I returned, Annie was waiting for me.

'Dylan, won't you tell me what's wrong?'

I couldn't repeat what had happened. I don't want Annie to know about this. Besides, Jules Mercier is my friend and I value him. I simply can't understand how such a good man could have such bad judgment in his choice of a wife.

At worst, Marianne Mercier is mad. At best, she is seriously deluded. Either way, I will never set foot on the Mercier property again, and my friendship with Jules is now in jeopardy as well.

I have to talk to Jules.

Chapter 22

The next day, we were back at the newspaper office. Letty didn't protest or say anything, except, "Well, are you ready to leave?" as soon as Mom and Dad drove away.

We found Mrs. Ellis again. She greeted me as warmly as before and I got right to the point.

"I know this is probably a useless question, but is there any chance the reporter who wrote that June 1927 story is still around? His name was…"

"…Robert Bascom," she finished for me. "Oh yes, Bobby B—that's what we call him—is very much around." She smiled.

"You mean, he's still alive?" Letty was so surprised she joined in the conversation.

"Alive and kicking…well, perhaps not kicking, since he's in a wheelchair now, but still pretty active. He pops in from time to time, though he has to have someone drive him." She laughed. "I'm amazed how that man gets around, for someone his age."

"Exactly how old is he?" Letty asked.

"I think he's around a hundred and twelve."

"You're kidding." Letty looked shocked.

Mrs. Ellis shook her head, smiling, as if she enjoyed Letty's surprise.

"Could you give me his address?" I asked. "I'd like to talk to him. If it's okay, I mean?"

"I don't think he'd mind seeing some new faces." She scribbled something on a memo slip and handed it to me. "He's always complaining about not being as mobile as he'd like. Some of us from the paper occasionally go and visit him."

I glanced at the paper. It read, *Cedar Hills Assisted Living*, and an address in Amesville.

"Thank you, Mrs. Ellis." I caught Letty's arm. "Let's go."

"Tell him 'Hi' for me," Mrs. Ellis said, "and that the new mystery novel he requested is in. He loves mysteries."

That was good to hear. I was counting on his helping solve this one.

Cedar Hills Assisted Living was a single level, sprawling building set in the middle of an acre of land decorated with trees and flowers.

"Where do they get the names for these places?" I complained. "There's not a cedar tree or a hill in sight."

Letty didn't answer. Instead, she clasped my arm and propelled me toward the door. Apparently, she was as eager to meet a man past the one hundred year mark as I was.

"Now, remember," she warned, apparently still having some reservations. "If he's deaf or nearly blind or senile and can't remember his own name, don't be disappointed."

"From Mrs. Ellis' description, I kind of doubt he's any of those," I reminded her.

Inside, it was a neat, very clean place, the lobby looking as if it should belong to a small but respectable hotel instead of a nursing home. I took a deep breath. There wasn't any of that antiseptic smell I'd always associated with nursing homes since the one time I'd visited Grandpa when he had to stay in one for a while after he fell and broke a hip. Once he was home, he'd told me he thought he'd never get the scent out of his nose.

The receptionist was polite and a little surprised when I asked to see Robert Bascom.

"Are you family?"

"No, just friends." That was stretching a point, but so what?

"I ask because I've never seen you here before."

"Mr. Bascom *is* allowed visitors, isn't he?" Letty wondered.

"If you're asking is he competent…oh my goodness, yes." The girl laughed. "Bobby B is as well put-together in the head as they come. He's always entertaining us whippersnappers—that's what he calls anyone under the age of thirty—with stories from when he was a reporter for the *Daily Courier*."

"That's good to know," I said. "Because I want to talk to him about one of his stories."

"I imagine he'll be glad to see you. Just the other day, he was complaining that he was bored." She pushed a large book looking like an accounting ledger toward me. "If you'll just sign in…name…person visiting…and the date, I'll have someone take you to him."

She picked up her phone, speaking into it while Letty signed for us. In a few moments, a tall black man in white shirt and trousers appeared. He was about my age and looked as if he could've been a quarterback in college. I wondered if being muscle-bound was a requirement for working in a place like this.

"Jax," the receptionist said, "these folks are here to

see Bobby B. He's in the garden."

He nodded and stepped back, gesturing. "This way, please."

We walked down a corridor intersecting another. I glanced down it, seeing a sign saying *To Dining Room* and another, *Hair Dresser/Barber Shop*. Jax led us out a side door into a patio and from there to a garden overhung with weeping willows and brightened by pink Japanese magnolias. The flowerbeds were crimson with geraniums and salvia. We walked down a path, its cement roughened to provide better traction for wheelchairs.

As the path curved around a rock and caladium arrangement with some of those silly gnomish garden figures peeking from the foliage, a voice floated to us...

"...don't ever underestimate me just because I'm older than you..."

The path straightened and the speaker came into sight, a man sitting in a wheelchair. He was parked to the side of a cement table with bench seats attached. On the top of the table was an inlaid checkerboard, black and red game pieces stacked neatly on each side.

So this was Bobby B...Robert Bascom, reporter who asked the wrong questions.

He hadn't seen us yet, and I studied him while he was unaware. He wasn't too tall and was thin, his body having that collapsed look the very elderly often get. He didn't look ill or sickly in any way, however, though his face was a mass of wrinkles and his skin very pale with a waxen color as if he didn't get much sunshine. His hair was steel-gray and there was a surprising amount of it. To my surprise, he wasn't wearing glasses or a hearing aid, and his movements as he leaned forward and gathered up the checkers and replaced them in the little stone holder were very brisk.

"How many does that make?" he asked and laughed. "Don't tell me…I'm still one hundred percent ahead, aren't I?"

"Rub it in, Bobby." His opponent slid off the bench and reached for his walker. He was a chubby little Santa Claus of a man, with white beard and snowy hair. He gave Robert Bascom a disgruntled look. "I'm going to invest in a book on how to cheat at checkers."

"Come back for a rematch after you read it." Bobby laughed again and turned his attention to us as his friend wobbled away. "Excuse me for ignoring you, Jax. Just had to lord it over Rudy a bit. That's the fifteenth game he's lost to me this week." He peered around the orderly. "Who do we have here?"

His eyes were a bright blue, and twinkling with the triumph of his latest checker win, no doubt.

"These folks wanted to talk to you, Bobby." Jax gestured at us.

He looked at me. "It's nice to see young folks. Thanks, Jax."

The orderly nodded and left us.

We watched him walk away, then looked back at the reason for our being there.

"Sit down, don't stand on ceremony. He might not like it." He laughed at that little joke.

I went around him and slid onto one of the stone benches. Letty took the other. He spun the wheelchair so it faced the table squarely…and the silence fell.

"Well? Talk away." Those blue eyes shifted from me to Letty, lingering there.

Bobby B, I decided, must've been a ladies' man in

his youth and hadn't forgotten it.

"Mr. Bascom…"

"'Bobby,' please. Mr. Bascom was my father, bless his soul…and also my son. No one calls me anything but *Bobby.*"

"Bobby…" I hesitated. How to get started? "My name's Dylan Roth, and this is Letty Mercier…"

"Roth?" He frowned. "Hm. That sounds familiar." He rubbed his chin.

I stopped. Could he possibly remember so quickly, after so long?

"Roth…Dylan…" He shook a finger. "Wait a minute…don't tell me…yeah…I've got it…A tornado, 1926, or was it 1927?"

"1926," I confirmed. Was it going to be this easy?

"You couldn't have been involved in that." He shook his head. "You're definitely too young, unless you've discovered the Fountain of Youth, and if you did, tell me where it is. *Please.*" He laughed. "The Dylan Roth I wrote about would be about a hundred and twenty now." He peered at me. "You don't look a day over thirty."

"You're pretty astute," I let my astonishment show. "He was my great-grandfather." I explained, reaching across the stone tabletop and squeezing Letty's hand as if to draw her attention to his reply. She squeezed back. "You really remember that? After all this time?"

"Young man, I remember *everything*," he stated emphatically. "Born with an eidetic memory, what they call a photographic memory. I never forget anything. Sometimes unfortunately." He sighed.

"Then what can you tell me about your story on the disappearance of my great-grandfather and Letty's, back in 1926?"

"Anything you want to know," he answered promptly. He leaned back into the chair. "You need information on a specific part of what I wrote?"

"I was interested in the one you wrote in 1927, and also wondered why there wasn't one directly after the storm in 1926."

"Would've been that damned sheriff," he said and grimaced. "Ezra Benson. We were putting out a special post-storm edition. The paper had already been put to bed and was being printed when he stormed in, went straight into Carl Everett's office—he was the editor—and slammed the door. In a few minutes, they dragged Steve Naismith in. He was the one wrote the story. Don't know what Benson had on Carl but Steve's story was removed and rewritten, and the few papers that had already been printed were taken out back and burned. The entire edition was delayed a full day."

"What can you tell me about the original story?"

"Not much. Didn't get a chance to read it before it was gone, but I talked to Steve. He said it was a fairly standard story. How the storm developed, the direction it came from, how it bypassed Amesville completely and swept kind of south central, swooping down just outside Estonko before going on into Florida. It mentioned two people from Estonko were missing, told a little about who they were, and how one was from Savannah, and had moved around a bit...I think Brunswick was mentioned...before he settled in Estonko. Didn't see anything there to warrant rewriting the story."

"What about in the follow-up?"

"Got all the info straight from the horse's mouth...the sheriff's, I mean," he retorted. "That's why

I remember your name. He practically told me what I was to write about those two…Dylan Roth…" He pointed at me. "And the other, Jules Mercier…" He glanced at Letty. "You said that's your great-granddaddy?"

She nodded.

"They were reported missing by their wives. It was thought they'd got caught in the storm. Neighbors and very close friends, the story said. The sheriff expressed the opinion—a little forcefully, I thought—they were probably plunked into Black Creek and drowned. He thought they were at the bottom of a river somewhere and would never surface. They dragged the creek for a mile in either direction and didn't find anything, so it seemed he might be right."

"Did you agree?"

"Hell, no. I'd managed to talk to a couple of the searchers before the sheriff got wind of what I was doing. One said there was a hint of something fishy in the story. He said the story was the two had been more than neighbors and close friends, a little *too* close…" He glanced at Letty. "…if you know what I mean."

"If you're hinting they were gay, don't waltz around it on my account, Bobby, though I appreciate your delicacy," Letty said.

"Well, you're a plainspoken little lady. I like that." He flashed her a smile, and if those pearly whites were dentures, they were the best I'd ever seen. "Okay. He said there was a rumor the two were lovers—only he didn't use that word—and had used the storm to run away and the search was merely a cover-up started by the sheriff because Mrs. Roth was his cousin."

"Did he say where he heard the rumor or who started

it?" I asked. "How reliable was your source?"

"Pretty reliable. He was one of Benson's deputies. Said he was there when Mrs. Mercier told the sheriff and he'd immediately been sworn to silence. He was pretty nervous that Benson might find out, but I assured him he'd never hear it from me. I'd seen the sheriff in action. He carried an ax handle and knew how to use it, and I didn't want to be on the receiving end of that thing."

"So you printed the story as Benson told it?"

"Decided to exercise caution in this instance." He winked. "It was only a year later when I suggested doing another follow-up that I got into trouble."

"When you interviewed Marianne Mercier and Anna Belle Roth?"

"That's right. Nearly got myself shot by Marianne Mercier. My reporting career could've ended right there if I'd been a little slower."

"Why did she get so upset?"

"Damned if I know. I never came out and asked her point-blank if her husband and Roth were canoodling…"

Letty stifled a smile at that.

"…though I tiptoed around it. I did ask her exactly what kind of relationship the two had…how long they'd known each other…not if either had ever done anything in word or gesture hinting they were sweetie-pies or something. If I had, the editor probably would've killed it without Benson's help. As it was, the paper was forced to write that damned retraction. And I got demoted to the society page, covering garden parties and dog shows for the next year."

Even now, he looked chagrined.

"After that, I was told it might be best for my future employment history if I didn't do any more stories about either Roth or Mercier." He looked up at me, still angry after all this time. "I really liked Anna Belle Roth. She seemed a levelheaded lady. Strong, holding up well under whatever was going on and really in love with her husband. She showed me his picture. As I remember, you look a lot like him."

"Yes, I know." I wondered if it was the same picture now stuck on my corkboard.

"That Marianne Mercier, though…she reminded me of a stick of dynamite with a short fuse." He glanced at Letty. "Sorry about that, Miss Mercier, being as how she was your great-grandma, but…"

Letty shook her head in an *It doesn't matter* manner.

"The whole time I was talking to her, she was looking around, kind of twitchy-like, jumped at every bird tweet and branch snap, as if expecting someone to come rushing out of the pecan grove to the side of the house and attack."

Into my mind flashed that white thing fluttering from one tree to another the night I drove back to the house. It took a great effort not to shudder.

"It was definitely scary, and I didn't consider myself one to be scared easily." He looked at Letty. "You kind of remind me of her…not that you're scary, but you've got that same red hair. You're prettier, though."

"Thank you." Letty managed a slight blush.

We talked a little longer, but then I decided I had all the information Bobby B could give.

"I want to thank you, Bobby, for talking to us." I got up, making preparations to leave.

Letty stood also.

"Think nothing of it." He waved away any gratitude. "I'm glad to have a visitor. Don't get out much now that

I can't drive. Have to rely on one of my great-grandsons, and the younger generation seems to think us oldsters want to stay in one place all the time."

"May I say you're remarkably spry for someone a hundred and twelve?" I thought that would be a good way to end the conversation.

He laughed. "That's because I'm *not* a hundred and twelve."

"No?" I didn't pretend surprise. I was. "How old are you?"

"I'm only a hundred and eight. The paper wouldn't hire anyone under the age of twenty-one. I was eighteen, so I lied about my age. It's no secret now, for anyone who asks. Had to give my actual birthday when I started collecting Social Security, but back then no one knew."

"Well, thank you, whatever age you are." I held out my hand.

"You're welcome, Mr. Dylan Roth." He shook it firmly, then released it.

I took Letty's arm and turned away.

"Say…"

I looked back.

"Why are you asking all these questions? Are you planning on writing another novel?"

I must've looked surprised because he went on, "Yes, I know who you are. Read your book, too. Good writing, almost as good as your exposés."

"Thank you." I remembered Mrs. Ellis' message. "Oh, by the way, Mrs. Ellis said to tell you that book you wanted has come in."

"Great. I'm looking forward to reading it. Always did like a good mystery. Let me know how *your* mystery ends, will you? I want an autographed copy when it's released."

I promised he'd have it. Like I was going to dare write another novel.

As we walked back to the car, Letty said, "Why do you suppose the sheriff had them pull that story? From what Bobby said, there was nothing in it that sounded incriminating."

"I agree, unless it's the fact that he mentioned the many places Jules had lived. Maybe Benson thought someone might get curious and start checking those places and discover something he shouldn't."

"You mean, like Jules left a string of broken male hearts as he went from town to town?"

"Something like that. I think we can accept what Bobby said as accurate." I shook my head. "Damn, a hundred and eight, and he sounded so…lucid."

Letty searched through her purse for the keys. "I think it's great that not everyone fades away as they get older."

"I hope I'm like that. Still able to get around, talk coherently."

I'd never thought about getting old before. Now, it fell over me like a pall. Grandma and Grandpa were getting up there. Mom and Dad were now in their fifties, and Letty and I would soon edge into their places. That brought on another shiver I couldn't stifle.

"So do I," she smiled, and aimed a gentle fist against my left shoulder. "Otherwise when you get to be ninety, I'm going to trade you in for a more lively seventy-year-old."

"Not if I can find a sprightly fifty-year-old to take *your* place," I retorted as we got into the car.

She ignored that, asking instead as we pulled back

onto the highway, "Do you still want to go to that hospital?"

"Yep."

"If you're looking for medical records, you may run into a roadblock. Those are confidential, you know. Only family members allowed access."

"Confidential only if the patient's still alive, I think. If not, I have a family member right here, don't I?"

She looked thoughtful. "You're paying for the gas."

"Done."

"But not today. By the time we get home, your folks should be there."

"Damn."

"Watch your language." She gave me a prim grimace, making me laugh. "You should take a lesson from Bobby B."

****

From the diary of Marianne Mercier, September 30, 1925:

Tonight I made a terrible mistake. My only excuse is that the love Dylan has for me made me indiscreet.

It was the grand house party I wished for, so I could lord it over these country bumpkins. I had a big surprise for Jules planned also, for tonight Dylan and I were going to run away together. I couldn't wait for him to arrive, though he had that mousy wife of his with him. It was so easy to lure him away from her with a few questions about furniture for the garden. Once we were alone on the back porch, I lost all caution. I threw myself at him and kissed him. He backed away, practically slinging me from him. When I told him I was ready to leave, he acted astounded by my remarks.

I understood. He was surprised and unprepared

though we'd exchanged smiles and knew what was in each other's minds. It was wrong of me to be so blatant since until now we'd been circumspect. Before I could apologize and explain, he returned to the ballroom, where he said something to Jules, then swept up his wife and they left.

Jules didn't say anything to me, though by the look on his face, I knew he was aware what had happened. It was only after everyone left that he confronted me.

"Is it happening again, Marianne? Are you making my best friend the object of your lustful fantasies this time?"

I should've denied it, but I don't care if he knows. After all, he found out before and foiled my plans...but not this time.

"What if he is?" I flung at him. "It's no fantasy, Jules. Dylan loves me and he wants me to go away with him. We would've left tonight if he'd been prepared."

We argued, as we've done before when I've found someone to love and he's interfered. Then I struck him. We were standing on the upstairs landing. Eddie had awakened and come to his door. He saw and began to cry. I had to calm him and put him back to bed. Little brat. He's such a crybaby. Why do I have to tend them? All I want is to be free to love Dylan. When I returned, Jules had gone to sleep, his back turned to me. How I wish he would die. If I thought I could get away with it, I'd plunge a knife into his back while he sleeps. Then Dylan and I could leave.

Someday I may do it.

Chapter 23

The following morning, Letty nixed our little road trip, reminding me I had an appointment with the physical therapy department at Janssen Memorial.

"Also, I looked up a few things on the Internet last night. About patient confidentiality and such…and if I interpreted what I read correctly…"

I bit my lip and waited for the punchline.

"…aside from some general rules relating to specific health laws and general catastrophes, the only time a doctor can revoke patient confidentiality is if non-disclosure would result in harm to the life or health of a family member. I don't think your excuse that 'something doesn't sound right' is acceptable."

She picked up the keys.

"Therefore, trip is cancelled because of inaccessability."

I went reluctantly to my appointment, rationalizing it was necessary to keep muscles from atrophying while my arm was immobile but not liking that Letty's legal tidbit was going to cut into my investigation.

Afterward, as I made preparations to leave, I decided to see what my options were, saying to the therapist, "Is it necessary that I come in twice a week? I mean, that's a lot of miles and a lot of gas. Could I do the exercises at home?"

"You could," he answered, "if you will. However,

I've found that most patients who promise faithfully to follow whatever regimen I set up, leave here, toss the instructions into the trash, and end up complaining how physical therapy didn't help."

"I'll make sure he does whatever you tell him." Letty spoke up, giving me a stern look. "If I have to stand over him with a whip."

"I'll bet you would, too." He laughed. "You're got yourself a slave driver here, Dylan."

"Wouldn't have her any other way." I decided to get really bold and give her a hug then and there.

She laughed and didn't pull away, instead, entwining her fingers in mine.

"Okay," he said. "I'll give you the benefit of a doubt...written exercises, and see you back in two weeks. If it looks like you've followed orders...good enough. If not..."

He gave me what he thought was a threatening grimace. It made him look as if he'd tasted a lemon, and I laughed.

"I promise." I held up my right hand, releasing Letty's long enough to touch the other to my heart.

We left with three pages of printed instructions, fully illustrated, and safely entrusted into Letty's care. They consisted of exercises I was to do twice a day for the next fourteen days. I was also given a long strip of yellow stretchy material, told to tie it to a doorknob and pull it in various directions as the set of instructions on the last sheet said.

Sounded like fun.

"Now then..." Letty pointedly aimed the truck for home while asking, "Where to?"

"Nowhere, since you've destroyed my hopes of

going to the state hospital," I answered.

"Your notions may yet drive me there as a patient," she retorted.

I glared.

She gave me a sassy smile. "Let's go somewhere else."

"Where?"

"Wait and see."

The truck sped down the highway. Seemed we were going back home, as far as I could tell. We turned into town, speeding past a drug store. Something nagged in my memory, telling me we should stop there, but I couldn't figure out why.

It was only as we followed the route I usually took to get to the construction site that I realized our destination.

"To the farmhouse? Why are we going there?" I asked.

"Don't you want to see how work's progressing?" She didn't look at me.

"I guess."

"Don't sound so enthusiastic."

I didn't want to admit I hadn't thought about the house itself since the moment I accepted the fact that by the time I was able to work again, work would be finished. Frankly, I was in no hurry to get up on a scaffold if my 'dream woman'—I used that term in a completely unromantic way—might again attempt to push me off.

Letty glanced at me. "What's the matter?"

I guess I was letting my thoughts show.

"Nothing," I denied and attempted to look interested. "Have they finished the first floor yet?"

Didn't I say I'm not an actor? Letty saw right through me, though she obviously couldn't figure out why I wouldn't want to go back there. She didn't push the subject, however.

When we got to the turn-off and rolled down the road, I saw immediately more groundwork had been done. Now, the track looked like a driveway. The strip of land between the pecan grove and the road had been mowed neatly, as had a twenty-foot swath of the meadow. Letty's little car could safely travel now. I was surprised she hadn't asserted her independence and started driving the little sportster again instead of riding with Dad.

We came around the curve and Letty pulled the truck to the right, parking it alongside the other vehicles crowded together in the closely-trimmed meadow. I got out and stared.

The ramshackle ruin was no more. It had been transformed.

The porch, steps, and first floor were fully completed. The hedge, cut to a height of eight inches on either side of the steps, was already showing green-leafed new growth. When it grew out, it was going to look great, as well as being a cover hiding the underside of the house.

The roof over the porch hadn't been shingled yet, but it looked solid and sturdy. I could see that work had begun on the balcony. Sun reflected off windows on the first level.

"Wait right there." Letty left me and ran to the front steps.

"Hey, wait…" I called after her, then saw Bill coming around the corner of the house.

"Hi, Dyl." He raised the hand not holding the camera.

Behind him, Biff waved the boom in greeting.

"Hey." I concentrated on Letty. She was standing on the third step up, watching me as Bill raised the camera and aimed it.

"Walk toward Letty," he ordered.

It took me a moment longer to realize what was going on. They were filming *Dylan Roth's first glimpse of the Mercier home since his accident.*

Okay.

I stepped away from the car and aimed myself for Letty, walking with a no-nonsense stride.

"Dylan, hi," she called and held out her hand. "Welcome back."

"Thanks, Letty."

I caught her hand with my left one, giving it a friendly but noncommittal squeeze.

Wonder what would happen if I took her in my arms and kissed her? Bet that'd give the viewers a thrill.

I decided to improvise. "Thought I'd stop by and see how things are going."

She relaxed. I hadn't realized, until that moment, she'd been tense. Expecting me to react negatively to being here?

"Well, what do you think?" She waved a hand at the house.

"From where I'm standing, it looks good," I announced.

I mounted the steps so we were standing side by side. Behind me Bill adjusted the lens to get us both in the shot.

I looked down. "Won't have to worry about falling

through *these* steps. Can we go in?"

"Sure." She turned and went up the steps to the porch.

I followed. "I'm anxious to see how it looks," I confided.

That was the truth.

We went through the doorway. It still didn't have a door. Letty saw me glance at that.

"Your dad said they won't put up the door until they begin painting."

Inside, it was difficult to believe it was the same place I'd been in before. All the broken glass was gone, leaves, branches, and everything else left by wind, weather, and vandalism had been cleaned away. The floors were strong and smelled of fresh-cut hardwood.

The stairs going up to the second floor had been repaired and the banister replaced. I stopped, studying it. It was plain, none of the fancy woodcarving I imagined had been on the original.

I touched the finial.

"Too bad my great-grandfather isn't here to put the finishing touches on this for you."

She froze, eyes meeting mine, silently asking, *What are you doing?* I didn't move, looking from her to the post.

"Oh…that's…right." She sounded like someone who'd forgotten her lines and was struggling to remember. Then, she said, "Your great-grandfather worked on the original construction, didn't he?"

I nodded, saying, "He was a carpenter," and went into the parlor.

She followed.

"He did the scrollwork on all the fireplaces." I

indicated the one before us, stepping aside so Bill could get a good close-up of the sidepieces and the mantel. "I'm glad you decided to keep the original fireplace frames."

By now, Letty had relaxed. "He was certainly talented."

"Were the plumbers able to get the pump working?" I went through the dining room to the kitchen.

Letty demonstrated they had. She worked the handle a little too vigorously, splashing water into the sink. I jumped back as she cautioned, "Careful, don't get your cast wet."

The work island cabinet was being restored, she added as we went into the ballroom. With the doors slid back, it seemed vast. Once again, I imagined the housewarming party, only to have it marred by memory of Dylan's argument with Marianne.

"They'll sand and varnish the floors, then hang the chandelier." She pointed to the ceiling where wires hung in a red, blue, and yellow plastic-encased tangle, "and the other light fixtures."

I spun in a circle, not having to pretend to be impressed. "This place is going to be a showcase."

Outside once again, she asked the question I imagined the audience would be wondering about. "How are you, Dylan?"

"Doing pretty good." I gave her a smile saying, *As if you didn't know*.

"Was your injury very serious?" She pressed a hand against her heart, looking concerned. "I can't tell you how worried I was."

You don't have to. I know. I thought of all the things I could say to throw this conversation into chaos and ruin the take, but why would I?

"Thank, Letty. I appreciate that." I raised my casted arm. "I broke both bones in my forearm, but it's healing fine. I do have some hardware, however." I laughed. "From now on, when I fly, I'll set off metal detectors."

"I don't suppose you'll be coming back to work any time soon?"

"I'm afraid the cast won't come off before the house is finished." I looked regretful while thinking, *It damn well better*. Then I smiled. "However, it looks as if you've been getting along pretty well without me."

At this, there was a long pause.

"Dylan, believe me, it hasn't been the same since you got hurt."

Letty looked up at me and there was something in her expression that made me forget where we were, that Bill's lens was taking it all in. I almost bent and kissed her. Just in time, I managed to stop my step toward her.

"Thanks, Letty. I appreciate that." I hoped I covered the movement well enough.

"…and *Cut!*" Bill lowered the camera. He came toward us. "Dylan, about that film you wanted checked…"

"Yeah, I was wondering if you'd forgotten."

"I finally managed to do some work on it this past weekend. I'll bring it by after work tonight and we'll take a look at it."

"Great. Did you find anything?"

He gave me an odd look, almost secretive. "Let's talk about that tonight."

"Okay."

He called to Biff, and they went down the steps and around the house. Letty and I followed, going to the right where another scaffold like the one from which I'd fallen had been set up around the other chimney.

"Hey, bro!" From its top, Ben walked to the edge, shouting a welcome.

I was surprised to see him up so high. "What are you doing up there?"

"Decided it was time I put on my Big Boy jeans and got over my height-fright. What are *you* doing here?"

"Just a little follow-up film work," Letty explained.

"Did Mom tell you Liz and I are coming by for supper tonight?"

"Nope. What's the occasion?"

"Got something to tell you." He grinned.

"Oh? What?"

"Tell you then." He winked and did that little victory fist-shake. "Got to get back to work." With a wave, he turned away from the edge and out of sight.

"Guess I'd better get you home." Letty went to the truck.

"You could've told me where we were going," I said as she opened the door for me. "Did you think I'd kick up a fuss if I found out we were coming here?"

"I wasn't certain how you'd react, considering all we now know. You really shook me when you mentioned Dylan."

"*You* didn't warn me, *I* didn't warn you, but you needn't have worried that I was going to let loose any of *those* worms." I climbed in and she slammed the door. I waited until she'd gone around and gotten behind the wheel before I continued, "I'd never do that. Not on camera."

This time, she let me struggle with the shoulder harness and didn't help me. Paying me back, I guess.

"I'm sorry. I know I should've trusted you not to spoil everything, but…"

"Hey…" I pulled her toward me. "It's okay. We've still got a lot to learn about each other. Just have a little faith, Letty." I kissed her, then leaned back. "Home, James."

"That's Miz Scarlett," she snapped.

When we reached the highway, however, I said, "Wait a minute."

She braked, waiting.

"Go right."

"But home is…"

"I know, but there's somewhere else I want to see first."

"What?"

I didn't answer.

"Is this payback?" Nevertheless, she didn't argue. "Okay."

We had driven about fifteen minutes when another turn-off appeared.

"Turn here."

It was fenced in with barbed wire, just as the Mercier property was, but the wire and posts were in better condition. There was also a *Posted* sign. Other than being a little weathered, it was unmarked by buckshot or vandals.

The track was barely visible, but the pickup crashed over it like a stampeding rhino, flattening every weed in its path. Some were pretty high and the tops of a few actually flew off, made a curve, and slapped against the windshield before rebounding onto the hood and sliding to the ground.

"Dylan, where are we going?" Letty asked.

"I'm not sure," I replied.

"That's encouraging." The road curved and she slowed the truck, then stopped. "I think this is the end of the line."

Before us lay the remains of what had once been a house. Nothing much was left…the foundation, part of the porch…it was in worse condition than the Mercier place had been. Way worse.

I struggled to get the door open and slid out of the truck. Letty did the same and we clambered through the surrounding weeds, meeting in front.

"What is this place?"

"This, my dear Letty, is the Roth Old Home Place."

"The…your family owns this? This is Dylan Roth's home? Why haven't you said something before?"

"I wasn't even aware we owned this property until a couple of weeks ago. I thought it was part of the Mercier homestead."

"Why are we here, Dylan?"

"Because I wanted to see my great-grandfather's home—or what's left of it—and I thought you might like to see…"

"…how the other half of the story lived? Well, let's take a look."

She pushed her way through the weeds. I followed. We circled the house, sticking close to the foundation where vegetation hadn't yet encroached.

Compared to the Mercier place, it was small, five rooms in all, originally a one-story shotgun house, three rooms built one behind the other. The two rooms at the front abutting the porch were probably added later, with the kitchen in the back making the shape into an L. Nothing remained now but the brick supports of the foundation showing where the rooms had been, rising out of the weeds, with a few termite-riddled boards over what was probably a root cellar. Behind the house was a well, and a stack of planks a little farther back that must have been the barn.

It didn't take us long to go completely around the house, and when we were back at the truck again, Letty shivered.

"What is it?"

"I don't know. It just feels…eerie. Don't you think?"

"Not really. Though I'll admit I got a kind of creepy feeling the first time I saw *your* old home place."

"Guess that makes us even, because your ancestral digs are spooking me out." She caught my hand, looking toward the truck. "Let's go."

"Not yet." I pulled away. "There's something else I want to do first."

"Dylan, this place is in worse shape than my house ever was. What could you possibly…"

I held up a hand.

She stopped.

Leaving her standing there, I went around to the truck bed. I'd taken the lantern out but never removed the mat and sleeping bag. Instead, I'd simply stuffed them into the toolbox.

Letty followed me, watching as I unlatched the tailgate and clambered inside, hauling myself up by gripping the top of a side panel. I flipped open the toolbox lid and pulled out the foam pad, unrolling it and placing it on the floor of the truck. That took a bit of maneuvering because I had only one hand to use.

"What are you doing?"

I didn't answer, just made certain the mat was as flat as possible, then offered her my hand. Hesitantly, she placed her own in it. I braced, and lifted her up and inside. Then, I put my arms around her.

"Letty...I love you and I want to make love to you..."

"I love you, too, Dyl, and I want the same thing, but as long as your arm's..."

"Forget my arm. That's becoming less and less of an excuse every day. Sometimes we have to seize opportunities, and I've decided today is one of them." I gestured at the mat.

She looked at it and back at me in disbelief. "You mean...here? Now?"

I nodded. "Here. Now."

She looked around, giving a self-conscious laugh that trickled away into a sickly giggle. "I've never had sex in the open before."

"I should hope not." I punctuated my reply with a kiss to her forehead. "...and I hope you never do again unless it's with me, but this isn't going to be sex," I added.

"It isn't?"

I shook my head. "This is going to be making love."

****

It didn't happen.

As a seducer, I'm a complete failure. Casanova would've laughed me out of Italy, then turned his back with a sneer. In spite of my assurances, kisses, and caresses, Letty was uncomfortable being exposed to the wind and sky, unshielded by four walls. She started at every sound coming from the pines surrounding us. Once my phone buzzed and she pulled away from my kiss.

"Aren't you going to answer that?"

"I hope you're kidding." I took the phone from my back pocket, tapped an icon turning it off, and dropped it behind me, returning to kissing her.

I tried my best, I swear, and then, just as I'd managed to get her shirt unbuttoned, and recovered from the disappointment of discovering today she was wearing a bra, in the midst of what I felt was a soul-searing kiss, *Responsibility* stamped into my brain.

"Letty…sweetheart…there's a storm coming in and I didn't bring a raincoat." I pulled away from her. "Are you on a pill, patch, or any kind of contraceptive like that, I hope?"

Her gaze met mine. Clear, unglazed by passion. "Until now, I've had no reason to be."

Well, damn. I knew now why I'd felt we should stop at the pharmacy. I sat up, willing my erection to wilt. *Down, boy.*

"Sweetheart, I've suddenly understood something Dad said to me yesterday. I've also been reminded I'm not a randy teenager who has sex first and then is shocked when the baby arrives."

Curses, foiled again.

"In that case, I guess there won't be any downpour today, will there?" Damned if she didn't look disappointed.

"I'm sorry, Letty." I was sincerely apologetic. "This was a bad idea, but I…" I decided to get serious. "Damn it, I want you, and I thought…but I see now I was forcing you to do something you didn't want, and I'd never do that."

I sighed and the sensation seemed to come from the very bottom of my soul.

"We can't have any privacy at home unless you want to sneak downstairs while the folks are asleep?" I suggested, half-hopefully. "If you do, be careful, because the third step from the bottom squeaks."

She bit her lip. I couldn't tell if she was stifling a smile or seriously considering my suggestion. She shook her head.

"In that case, I guess…" Something inside slipped, a feeling of surrender. "Guess this means we won't have sex until we're married. Damn it."

Married? That may have slipped out, but it didn't startle me because it seemed a natural thing to say. I wanted Letty around forever. Hadn't I been thinking that all along?

Her sharp little ears didn't miss it, either. "Is that a proposal? Because if it is, I'd say you can really pick the moments."

"I've always been aware there's a time and a place for everything." A pine twig lay in one of the recessed grooves is the bed. I plucked it out, twirling it between my fingers. "Why shouldn't it be when I've just realized I'm never going to be alone with you long enough to do the deed unless it's legal?"

Pulling loose a couple of pine needles, I looped them into a slightly misshapen ring and took Letty's hand.

"Miz Scarlett, will you marry me?" I slid the twisted pine needles onto her finger.

She looked at it and then at me. "Why, Mr. Roth, I do believe I will."

I hugged her. "In that case, let's get out of here and go home."

I helped her rebutton her shirt. She assisted me in rolling the mat and replacing it in the toolbox. Then we slid out of the truck bed and got back into the cab.

For some reason, I didn't consider the afternoon a failure at all. All I could think was, *Ben's definitely going to be happy.*

When we got home, it was after six. I was expecting to see Dad's pickup in the yard, but it wasn't there. No one was in the house, either.

"I wonder where they are?" Neither had said anything about going anywhere before coming home.

"Maybe your Mom stopped to get more groceries," Letty suggested. She smiled. "After all, she's feeding an extra mouth these days."

She went upstairs to change her shirt. There had been some dirt and pine needles in the truck bed and somehow she'd managed to get smudges and green stains on its back. Guess she wanted to make certain neither parent saw them.

"I also want to put my 'engagement ring' in a safe place." She slid the pine needles off her finger. They were already coming apart.

I hurried downstairs to my bedroom, making a beeline for the bedside table. Pulling out the drawer, I thrust my hand inside, raking out its contents...pocket-sized packet of tissues, a deck of cards, a box of toothpicks—why weren't those in the kitchen?—my reading glasses, which I never used, and, in the very back, an unopened box of condoms.

Yes!

I'd bought them shortly after arriving home, determined to show my loss of Jilly didn't matter, but never found an opportunity when I'd wanted to use them. I glanced at the expiration date. Still viable, thank God. I tore open the box, ripping off one of the foil packs and stuffing it into my wallet. Next time…no matter where or when, I'd be ready. Surely I could manage at least one more attempt before the wedding, whenever that was.

I went back upstairs.

It was now nearly six-thirty and still no parents.

"Do you suppose something happened?" Letty asked, reflecting the worry I was trying to conceal. "Perhaps you should call."

"Right." I reached into my hip pocket. No phone. "My phone's gone." I slapped all my pockets. "Where…?"

"You turned if off when we were…" Letty reminded. "Remember?"

"Oh, yeah. Damn, hope it didn't bounce out of the truck." I hurried outside.

The phone was where I'd tossed it, lying in one of the bed's grooves. I scooped it up, turned it on, and was immediately informed I had four voice mails.

The first one was from Mom, "*Dylan, call me.*" As was the second, a little sharper, "*Dylan, call me now,*" and the third, anxious and distressed, "*Dylan, where are you? Call me!*" I didn't listen to the fourth because just then the phone rang.

Guess who?

"Dylan, where have you been?" Mom's voice screeched through the speaker, a hint of tears behind it. "Why didn't you call me?"

"Mom, what's happened? Where are you?"

"I'm at the hospital. Ben's hurt."

Chapter 24

Both the chimney and the scaffolding around it had collapsed while Ben and two others were on it.

The other men, Chris Thompson and Jeff Holsom, childhood friends and classmates, weren't badly injured. Somehow, they managed to ride the platform to the ground and leap off at the last minute. They only got a few bruises and scratches from landing in the weeds. They now sat in the waiting room with the others.

Ben, however, had been directly next to the chimney. A chunk of bricks literally fell into his lap, causing him to land on his back and fall though that part of the scaffolding as it shattered under him. He'd broken a leg and several ribs and had a concussion. It was the head injury that worried everyone because he was still unconscious.

We went to Janssen Memorial in the sportscar, Letty wanting to get there as fast as possible, though it was difficult for me to get in and out of the sportster. Desperation made me manage, if clumsily.

The receptionist directed us to where they were. Mom met me with tears. Though I never replied to her question as to why I hadn't answered my phone before, she didn't persist in demanding to know the reason. Dad was as worried as Mom, though he was struggling to stay calm and attempting to soothe her.

"There's no use for you to stay," Mom told me after

a hug each to both me and Letty. "Ben's in ICU. He isn't going to be allowed visitors until he's fully conscious. Liz is with him now. I'm going to sit with him tonight so she can get some rest. She doesn't need to be upset in her condition."

"What does that mean?"

She grimaced. "I know this isn't the way Ben was planning on telling you you're going to be an uncle. They were coming to supper tonight to make an official announcement."

I remembered what Ben had said. That made what happened even worse. He'd looked so excited when he spoke to me. Had my being there made him careless? Was it because he was attempting to overcome his fear of heights? No, wait...the chimney *collapsed*. Carelessness wouldn't have caused that.

"Dad...what the hell happened? We checked both chimneys. They were in good shape."

"Dylan, don't," he snapped, putting an arm around Mom as her eyes again filled. "We don't need any conspiracy theories just now."

Conspiracy theories? That hurt.

He kissed Mom on the cheek. "I'm going home, Ella." He sighed heavily and sadly. "Got to keep things going, don't we? Call me if anything changes. I don't care what time it is." He glanced at me. "You two may as well leave, too."

Letty hadn't said a word the entire time. In fact, except for hugging Mom, she simply hovered in the background. Now, she nodded, gave Mom another hug and whispered, "Call me if you need anything," and seized my arm, dragging me out of the room.

I managed a nod and a quick word to Chris and Jeff

as we passed. One had his wrist wrapped, the other wore a couple of butterfly bandages on his forehead and cheek. I saw Mom go over to them, probably saying the same thing she'd said to me.

Once home, Letty made a listless supper. I don't remember what it was or how it tasted. We simply ate, automatically. Afterward, she cleared the table, equally quietly. Dad went to bed, and we sort of stood there, looking at each other, not knowing what to say. The sound of a car interrupted our silence. Someone knocked at the back door.

"I'll get it." Letty looked relieved to have something to do.

It was Bill. I'd forgotten he was coming over.

"Starting to sprinkle," he said, as he stamped his feet on the doormat before coming in. His shoulders were damp and water beaded in his hair. "Weather forecast says we may have rain from that tropical storm."

"Please, don't tell me you filmed Ben's fall," was the first thing I said in greeting. I didn't think I could bear watching my brother and the others encore my downward spiral.

"I was on the other side of the house," he answered, and frowned when I relaxed, saying defensively, "Even if I *had* filmed it, I wouldn't send it in. Catching your tumble on film is one thing, shooting a repeat performance would be completely unfeeling, as well as in bad taste. I'm not a ghoul."

"Inappropriate metaphor," I mumbled. "Ghouls eat corpses." I gestured at the case containing his laptop. "I don't feel like looking at that, tonight."

"In view of what's happened, I think you should."

"What does that mean?"

He didn't answer, but I've never seen anyone look so serious.

"Okay." I didn't argue.

He swung the case off his shoulder and onto the kitchen table. "I'll set it up here."

It took a few minutes for him to get the laptop out of the case, fire it up, and plug a thumb drive into a USB port. He punched keys, typed in a couple of commands, and clicked *Open File.* A screen holding a series of images resembling film clips with the video player icon appeared. He selected one, and another screen opened, with a grid at the bottom showing video-length, a sound on/off switch, and the *play/stop* icon.

"The reason I didn't get this to you sooner is because I had to do a lot to it. Adding filters…gamma correction…sharpen the luminance, define radial and linear gradients…use a grayscale…"

"Bill," I snapped impatiently. "If you want me to say I appreciate the effort, I do. Just get on with it."

"Okay." He looked disappointed that I wasn't properly awed by his expertise. "First, here's the original."

"We've seen that."

"You need to see it again for comparison," he said, and clicked the cursor over the *Play* arrow.

Once again, I watched my onscreen self turn around and speak, saw the flutter of white blur the screen. Then I was subjected to the sight of my body disappearing over the rim of the platform. There was a jumble of images as Bill lowered the camera and ran to the edge where he involuntarily recorded the sight of me crumpled on the ground with Letty, Dad, and the others around me.

Letty gave a choked sob, putting a hand to her

mouth. I reached behind Bill, groping for her hand.

"Sorry, Letty." Bill muttered. As if in afterthought, he gave me a sympathetic look.

He rewound the scene, typing in something else. The picture faded, turning as near-neutral as possible without actually becoming black-and-white. The sky became a pale taupe, my shirt and jeans dark brown, the platform a washed-out yellow. Bill replayed it.

This time, the action was slower, too, not exactly slow motion but a more sluggish tempo than natural movement. On the screen, my color-muted image turned, my voice coming through like a battery-run item using its last bit of juice, "Loooksss Goooddd…"

…and there it was…

A blink and a flutter and a figure appeared between me and the camera. Bill had been standing to the side so he caught her in profile. Her hair was pulled back from her face, little wisps floating about her ears and forehead, the rest knotted at the nape of her neck. She was wearing a sleeveless, long-waisted dress seeming to fade into misty wisps past her knees. Her hands were outstretched.

She lunged forward, striking me in the chest. I staggered backward into space.

Her face contorted in a grimace that might've been a scream or a laugh, and…she disappeared.

Again, there was the bouncing, shaking camera as Bill ran forward, directly through the space where she'd been standing.

"My God." Letty gasped. "What was that?"

"That, folks, was a free-form, unattached, fully ectoplasmic entity," Bill intoned.

"This is no time for levity," I snapped, more unnerved than I had been when only *I* had seen her.

Being proven right didn't help. "Or for quoting movies."

"I'm not being funny," Bill answered. "Dylan, I apologize for what I was thinking. You've got yourself a real ghost."

I didn't say anything, though I swallowed so loudly it echoed through the kitchen.

"Who are we going to call?" Letty spoke up, giving me a guilty and apologetic stare.

"Don't," I groaned. "Please."

"You didn't send that to the home office, did you?" she went on.

"What would they do if they saw it?" I asked.

Bill laughed. "Probably call in some real ghosthunters. *DHU* remodeling a genuine haunted house? The boss would love that. Think of the ratings."

Neither Letty nor I reacted. I think we were both too stunned.

"Care to take a wild guess at our ghost's identity? Got any ideas?"

"It's Marianne, of course." I didn't have to guess.

Ben's accident had happened shortly after Letty and I left, around the time I was attempting my abortive open-air seduction. I had angered Marianne and she hurt my brother in retaliation.

"Who else could it be?"

"What's her spirit doing *here*?" Letty didn't challenge what I'd said. "She died in the state hospital, and is buried in Savannah."

"I've no idea. Ghost and ghoulies are beyond my expertise. Maybe she's drawn back to whatever happened that night and she's been haunting the place all these years, waiting…"

"For what?"

"How would I know?" I snapped. "One thing for sure, when you and I showed up with a construction crew, we became a catalyst."

"There's something else…" Bill continued, closing the file and opening another. He went through the same routine as before. "This is from the first day of shooting. In the nursery."

"You got something then, too?" I remembered that voice. "Why didn't you mention it before?"

"Because I convinced myself it was a sound glitch in the equipment, an audio syndrome or something. I deleted it and sent it on, but after seeing *that*…" He nodded at the screen. "I gave the original some tweaking and came up with this…"

He played the piece, not starting at the beginning but where Letty and I entered, talking about the fact that the door looked as if someone had taken an ax to it.

I leaned over the crib, saying, "This is…"

Let me go!

My flinch was very obvious.

For effect, Bill reran that part and replayed it, with the volume increased.

I stared at the screen, thinking furiously…*trying* to think, actually. All that happened was that my thoughts kept bumping into each other. *There's really a ghost. We've got a voice and an image. What the hell are we going to do with it? What* can *we do?*

As if she heard me, Letty put my thoughts into words. "Dylan, what are we going to do?"

"I haven't a clue." I'm so damned eloquent. What happened to all that verbal gility I employed as a reporter?

Bill ejected the thumb drive, unplugging it.

"Is it okay if I keep that?" I reached for it. He released it into my hand.

"It's a copy." He nodded at the laptop. "The original's saved to my hard drive."

"Thanks, Bill." I pocketed the drive.

"Dylan." For the first time, he looked worried. "We aren't in any danger, are we?"

"Bill…" I didn't have to think about it. "So far, four people have been hurt in accidents that shouldn't have happened. I don't think I'd be out of line if I said, *Damn right we're in danger*."

"Guess it's a good thing Mr. Roth closed down the site…*again*…isn't it? What are we going to do?"

I noticed he didn't say, "What are *you* going to do?" Bill apparently considered himself part of the solution, whatever it was. I was glad he let me know I could count on him, no matter the plan.

"Yeah, good thing," I agreed. "I'm going to have to think about it. At the moment, I don't know what to do. I've never been in a situation like this before."

He nodded and repacked the laptop. "If you need me, I'll be at the motel with Biff. I haven't let the home office know what's happened."

"Have you shown this to Biff?" Letty asked.

He shook his head. "I wasn't sure how many people you wanted to know about it."

"Show him," I said. "It might be good for him to be forewarned, too."

After Bill left, Letty gave a shudder so heavy it looked exaggerated. "That voice I thought I heard when we were downstairs…it was her, wasn't it? Dylan, I'm afraid."

"I'd be lying if I said I wasn't, too." I put my arms

around her. "If this were a novel, the hero would know exactly what to do, but I'm no hero, and I haven't a clue."

She didn't answer, just burrowed her cheek against my chest.

"I'm sorry, sweetheart. All I can think of right now is Ben. That's all that seems real."

I needed her so badly then, wanted her to hold me and tell me Ben would be okay, that he wasn't going to die and leave my unborn niece or nephew half-orphaned. As selfish as it sounded, I wanted to reaffirm Life by making love to Letty, while at the same time sobbing my fear that I wasn't about to be my parents' only surviving child…and I didn't consider those kinds of tears unmanly.

"Maybe tomorrow, I'll know what to do. By then, perhaps an answer will present itself." I forced myself to smile. "After all, Miz Scarlett, tomorrow is another…"

"Don't say it," she snapped. "I can't take any levity right now, Dyl."

This from the woman who'd thrown that other movie tagline at me.

"You're right. Sorry." I placed a half-hearted kiss on her cheek and pushed her toward the stairs. "Good night."

She turned and ran up them, not looking back.

I went to bed, struggled out of my clothes and into my pajama bottoms, shocking myself by muttering a prayer, "Please, God, let Ben be all right." Then I settled down to think.

Best place to start was by finding out more about Marianne Mercier, but how?

Instead of arriving at a solution, I fell asleep.

****

I don't know what woke me. Some slight sound, a beam popping. I opened my eyes, looking toward the stairs.

I'd left the door to the bathroom open. Outside light from the two half-windows filtered through, illuminating the bedroom enough for me to see a blur of white hovering on the stairs.

No, damn it! After all I'd been through today, her appearance made me furious. *Not tonight, babe.*

I sat up, raising my right arm so the fingers of both hands touched, forming a cross. "Go away. I'm not going through that again."

"Dylan?"

"In the Name of the Father, the Son, and the Holy Spirit, leave this place. I don't want you!" I closed my eyes, rolling onto my left side. That immediately caused a stab of pain through my right arm as it fell against my body. I gritted my teeth and didn't move.

"You don't want me?"

That wasn't right. The voice wasn't inside my head but coming from the stairs. She sounded so hurt and forlorn I opened my eyes and looked back.

Letty stood on the next to the bottom step.

"Letty?"

"Why did you say that?" Her voice was stricken.

"I had a nightmare," I lied. "What are you doing here?"

"What do you think?" With that, she was off the steps, running to the bed.

She stopped beside it. Before I could speak again, she pulled her arms out of the nightgown, slid it to her waist and let it fall to the floor.

Even in the dim light from the bathroom windows,

she was beautiful. I wanted to tell her but suddenly couldn't speak. *Lord, please don't let this be a dream, too.* Instead, I took her hand and pulled her into the bed. She put her arms around my neck and kissed me.

"Are you sure?" I whispered.

She nodded.

It was awkward at first. I had to maneuver my cast so my arm wasn't twisted, to say nothing of wriggling out of my pajama bottoms.

Letty was patient. Once we were in a comfortable position, I reveled in the smooth sensation of her flesh where our bodies touched. There were moments of tentative foreplay, then more abrupt and heated caresses, becoming frenzied as I buried myself in her passion. I think once I cried out when the pleasure of it all became almost too much to bear.

At some point, I paused long enough to reach into the drawer and extract a condom, then endured the embarrassment of Letty helping me put it on. At my peak, I poured myself into it, but it didn't matter because even with the barrier of latex between us, I'd filled Letty with my heart and my soul and she'd done the same to me. We were joined now, in body and spirit, bound with a bond of loving trust, making a nonverbal commitment we'd spend the rest of our lives upholding.

Afterward, I hurried to the bathroom to get rid of the evidence, then ran back to the bed. My sigh as I lay beside her said it all: I had everything I wanted. I was happy, complete...and no damned ghost had better disrupt it.

I put my arm around Letty, cuddling her. She snuggled closer, skin hot against mine, branding me as hers. With a sigh, she rested her cheek against my shoulder.

"Hey, don't go to sleep," I warned, giving her a gentle shake. "You have to go back upstairs in a bit."

"Why?" Her question was drowsy.

"Because if *you* go to sleep, *I'll* go to sleep, and Dad'll find us here in the morning."

"…and it's none of his business, is it?"

How could she guess so accurately?

"Not this part." I caught her cheeks in my hands, turning her face toward me. "I love you, Letty, and I don't want anything spoiling it. I've enough on my hands worrying about ghosts without having problems from the real world, too."

Like a good diplomat, she changed the subject, but not for a better one. Reaching into the still-open drawer, she brought out the condom box, shaking it. The lone occupant rattled around.

"Only one left. It says, *Contains three*. Where's the other one?"

"In my wallet. Put there this afternoon. Jealous, Miz Scarlett?" I kissed her. "No need to be."

Instead of agreeing as I expected, she asked, "Why did you say you didn't want me? Don't tell me you were talking in your sleep. You were wide awake."

What kind of pillow talk is this? It took me three seconds to decide to tell the truth when what I really wanted was to snuggle sleepily.

"Would you believe me if I said I'm the one being haunted and not the house?"

There was a silence. She shifted position, turning so her back was to me.

"Yesterday I would've said you were crazy. After seeing that video? I believe you. Tell me."

I released her, sliding my hands to hers. Twining our fingers, I wrapped her in a tighter embrace as I spooned against her.

"I wasn't saying that to *you*, Letty. It was to *her*."

"Her? You mean…Marianne?"

"She's come to me twice. The first time was the night I spent at the house." I decided not to hold back but to tell her the complete truth and hope she'd accept it. "I wanted you even then, Letty, and she took advantage of that. She fooled me into thinking she was you. I believed I made love to you, and then…when you woke me…"

"So that's why you nearly made a hole in the wall trying to get away from me." She didn't laugh as I expected. "You said, *twice*."

"After I came home from the hospital. Mom heard me through the baby monitor and woke me." I nodded at the bedside table. I'd since switched off the little eavesdropper.

"So, tonight you thought…"

"I thought she was back, and I wasn't about to get drawn into her spell again."

"That's unnerving, knowing my great-grandmother is my rival." Letty moved uneasily. Her fingers tightened around mine. "You don't know how close I came to going back upstairs."

She wriggled around to face me again.

"I don't understand. If Marianne hated Dylan so, why these attempts at seduction? That's quite a switch from pushing you off a platform."

"Because we share the same name? Because I look like him. I'm the same age he was when… Hell, I don't know!"

"If she's singling out you, why attack Ben and the

278

others?" she persisted. "I'm going to quote you...'That doesn't add up.'"

"I think I angered her when I tried to seduce you." Let's not talk about it." I was sick of all these questions with no answers. "For tonight, let the dead rest in peace." I kissed her. "Let's concentrate on *us*."

By the time Letty tiptoed back to her own room, the condom box was empty. I, on the other hand, was filled with a happiness no one was going to destroy, and a future I saw as brighter than gold.

Chapter 25

The next morning, I was dragged from a dreamless sleep by Dad calling to me.

"Hey, you okay?"

"Um…yeah…" I struggled upright, pushing my hair out of my face. *Memo to self: Haircut or not?* "What time is it?"

"Eight o'clock. Letty was worried because you hadn't gotten up." He came down the stairs, stopping at the foot of the bed. "I told her I'd check on you. Plan on taking a shower this morning?"

At my nod, he went into the kitchen. As I threw back the covers and slid my legs over the edge of the bed, I could hear him opening a cabinet and taking out the plastic wrap. It was only as he came back around the wall and stopped, staring at me, that I realized I'd never put back on my pajama bottoms.

"Sleeping nude, Dylan?" One brow went up.

"It got hot last night."

Was it ever.

That excuse sounded feeble, however, and even more so when he asked, "Why didn't you turn on your air conditioner? That's what it's for."

I shook my head, saying, with a bit of a whine, "Sorry, Dad, I didn't think about it. I was too worried about Ben."

He accepted that. Nodding, he pulled a length of

plastic wrap out of the box and started entwining it around my cast.

"Go ahead and shower. Call me when you're ready to get dressed."

****

This time wearing a pair of jeans and a dark blue tee because I'd run out of muscle shirts, I made my appearance in the kitchen where Letty was bustling around as if she'd cooked breakfast for us all her life.

Breakfast was fairly quiet except for a few compliments from Dad about Letty's cooking. I decided I'd better toss in a couple, also, before I got the Evil Eye from my future wife. She accepted those with a smile that said, *It's about time.*

"I'm off to the hospital," Dad said as he finished, continuing before I could get out the question, "Your mother called me earlier. No change. She's going over to Ben's and check on Liz, maybe stay there and rest instead of coming home."

He opened the door as he spoke.

"You two going to be okay? Got anything planned?"

"Nothing," I answered. "I'm sticking close to home. Call me if anything changes."

He nodded and went out. I waited until I heard the truck drive away before I spoke.

"Well! What shall we do today?" I put my arms around her, waggling my eyebrows. "Want to go back downstairs and pick up where we left off last night?"

"How many condoms do you have left?" Letty gave me a stare I thought a little assessing.

"One." I hoped I wasn't being weighed and found lacking. She certainly hadn't acted as if I were last night.

"None," she corrected. "I can count, you know, so I

guess we'd better not." She kissed my chin. "Ouch…didn't shave this morning, did you?"

"It's a little difficult to open a can of shave cream with one hand," I excused myself. I ran a hand over my cheek. It felt a little sandpaperish, but it usually was that way in the mornings. "Is it that bad?"

"Let's just say I guess you haven't looked in the mirror lately." She patted the same cheek. "You're beginning to look like Blackbeard. How long's it been since you put a razor to that handsome face?"

At least she called me handsome.

"What's today?"

"June 28."

"Only three days."

I wasn't about to admit I'd enjoyed freedom from razor-burn all that time. If it'd been left to me, I'd have a Santa Claus adornment by now, but Jillian had never cared for male facial hair, not even a five o'clock shadow. With my coloring, I generally sported one by noon, so for the length of my married life, I'd resigned myself to shaving in the morning and as soon as I got home from work.

"No matter." Letty's response was a surprise. "It looks good. In fact, I wouldn't mind if you grew a beard. Like Robin Hood's, maybe."

Well. If Letty didn't mind it. Maybe I'd do that.

"I think I'll read the paper and see how the rest of the world's faring." She dismissed the subject.

She went into the den where the morning paper lay folded by Dad's chair. Dropping into it, she began to leaf through the pages. Amazing how that woman was fitting herself into this household. No one sat in Dad's chair. That was his private domain and sacrosanct, but I had a feeling he wouldn't have said a thing if he'd walked in just then and seen Letty sitting there.

In spite of what I'd said to Dad, I wasn't happy about staying home. I wanted to be out, doing something, trying to find out more about Marianne Mercier, and also keep my worry about Ben at bay.

I accepted an offer of the sports section, speed-read through it, and set it aside. Wandering back into the kitchen, I poured myself another cup of coffee and heated it in the microwave. After two sips, however, I left it on the counter. Going back into the living room, I found myself before the bookcase, pretending to look over the titles.

Nothing there I wanted to read but I already knew that. At this point, my attention span was probably less than that of a two-year-old's, if the subject didn't have to do with Marianne Mercier.

Sighing, I went downstairs, ending up in the kitchen staring at the storyboard. I studied Dylan's picture, leaned in for a closer look at Anna Belle's features, wished again I had one of Jules and Marianne, then proceeded to re-read every news article one word at a time.

That gave me no insights, though it did waste a good fifteen minutes. Afterwards, I went back upstairs and reclaimed my coffee. Two more sips of now room temperature liquid and I repeated the entire circuit.

By now, I was impatient and also jittery with a sense of approaching disaster, and I didn't know why. Did I sense something had happened to Ben? I could call the hospital and ask, but I probably wouldn't be told anything, except perhaps 'he's holding his own,' which meant absolutely nothing. Surely Dad would let us know if his condition changed.

Whatever the reason, I was now so edgy I couldn't sit still.

Letty had studiously ignored my comings and goings. As I came up the stairs again, however, she dropped the paper to her lap.

"For goodness' sakes, Dylan. Will you please sit down and quit this roaming around? You're about to drive me up the wall!"

"Sorry." I dropped into the chair and immediately popped up again. "I thought maybe Dad would call and give us an update." I looked around. "I need something to do." I held out a hand. "Let's go somewhere."

She looked at the hand and then at me. "I don't think that's a good idea, if a storm's coming in." She shook the paper. "Newspaper forecast says there's a ninety-five percent chance it's going to become a hurricane."

I glanced out the window. Clouds were gathering, heavy gray ones. It had started sprinkling again, the windshields of my truck and Letty's Beamer dotted with raindrops. As if to emphasize what she'd said, there was a distant rumble that could only be thunder.

"Yeah, guess you're right." I began to pace.

Letty watched me a moment, then set aside the newspaper and stalked into the kitchen. Very quickly, she was back.

"Here." She thrust a handful of paper at me. "Do your exercises. You've neglected them."

"I don't want to—"

"I promised you would. Don't make me a liar." She shook the papers impatiently.

I accepted them, looked them over, handed them back, and got to work. With Letty reading the instructions, I went through all three pages, performing such idiotic maneuvers as finger-walking up the wall to a height an arm'slength above my head, and rotating my shoulders forward five times, then backwards the same number. I ended by tying the strip of yellow rubber around the kitchen doorknob and hauling on it ten times as if pulling on the reins of a runaway horse. On that one, I actually got into the swing of things and shouted a hearty, "Giddup, horsie!" as I finished up.

"Okay, cowboy, leave it tied to the door," Letty ordered, rolling her eyes at my clowning. "That way it'll be there for your next session."

"I don't see how this is going to help my arm," I huffed. For some reason, that minor bit of isometrics winded me.

"Trust me, it will," was all she said.

"Okay…that's done, now what?" I gave her a woebegone look, lower lip thrust out. "Mommy, I'm bored." I put my arms around her, resting my forehead against her shoulder, and managed a theatrical whimper.

"There…there…" She patted my arm, sarcastically. "I'm sorry, Dylan. I don't have a solution as to what to do. Don't act like such a baby." She looked thoughtful. "Actually, it'd be easier to keep you entertained if you *were* a baby."

"I can think of one way, but you've already nixed it." My sigh was a lot gustier than hers. "To tell the truth, I doubt I could be very amorous right now anyway. Too much going on in my mind."

"Okay." With a sigh of defeat, she sat on the couch, patting it. "Let's stop ignoring the great-grandmother's ghost in the room."

That was all the encouragement I needed.

"I need to know more about Marianne." I didn't wait to sit down but spoke before I got to the couch. "If only we had access to her medical records from the hospital." I gave a sharp laugh. "Do you suppose a ghost would be considered a threat to the health of a family member?"

"Even if it did, Marianne's files have been ash for over half a century."

As I stared at her, she continued, "I forgot to tell you... Georgia hospitals are only required to keep records for ten years."

My beloved was definitely becoming a spoil-sport.

"Damn. I'm sure they would've given me all the answers I need...in her own words, too." I thought about that. "Does your family happen to have any of her belongings? Maybe she kept a diary."

"No one's mentioned it."

I got to my feet. A sudden idea wormed its way into my thoughts. "I wonder...maybe there's something as good." I held out my hand. "Come on."

"Where are we going?" She took it, however.

I led her up the stairs, stopping in front of Ben's old room. A chain hung from a large wooden panel in the ceiling.

"Attic." I gave it a tug. It slid downward, revealing a set of stairs doubled-over against themselves.

I unfolded the stairs and started up, Letty following. At the top hung a second chain, this one switching on a bare light bulb in the ceiling. That, and the gray sunlight coming through small windows at each end under the eaves, revealed stacks of boxes, a couple of kitchen chairs, various odds and ends, and a large trunk.

Letty went around me, making a beeline for something in a corner, a highchair, complete with tray, its metal slightly battered. "Was this yours?"

"Mine, then Ben's," I admitted. "We were rough eaters," I added as she touched a dent in the tray.

There was also a rocking horse, one of those bouncing ones, with coiled springs. She stared at it. Remembering the wooden relic abandoned in the nursery?

"What are we looking for?"

"Anna Belle's diary, if she kept one. It'd be from her point-of-view, but it should offer some insights." I gestured to the trunk. "If there's anything here, it'll be in that."

There were boxes on top of it. She helped me remove them, very carefully so we wouldn't upset the dust of ages covering them. It wasn't easy. We were both sneezing and brushing a gray film off our hands before we got everything set aside.

The trunk was bound in leather secured by brass brads. Probably the lid had been held in place by thick metal buckles, but those were now missing. It opened easily when I lifted the lid, letting it fall against the wall.

A faint sour scent floated out, the fragrance of old things long locked away. I poked through the topmost contents…cardboard boxes, letters bound together with faded ribbon, loose greeting cards, neatly folded bits of…something…

Gently, I lifted out a box about a foot square. The edges of the lid were split. One end had been repaired with cellophane tape that long ago lost its adhesive and hung in stiff yellow shreds.

"Here, see what this is."

Letty took it, pulled up one of the chairs, and after determining it would hold her weight, sat in it. With the box balanced on her knees, she lifted off the top.

"It's a photo album." Very carefully, she turned the pages. "Is this you?" She tapped a photo.

I leaned over, peering at the picture of a little boy playing in a sandbox. "Yep...and that one's Ben." I nodded to the next picture.

She turned a page, and another.

"If you want to look at childhood pictures of me, we can do it another day. First things first," I reminded. I took out another box, even older and in worse condition. "Here."

I held it out.

Reluctantly, she closed the box and set it in the other chair, taking the second one. The top had completely split on the sides and came apart as she removed it. Carefully, Letty laid the lid in the chair atop the first album.

Inside was another album. On this one, the ribbon holding the cover and the pages together had completely disintegrated. She turned a few pages, then looked at the black flakes adhering to her palm. Gently, she brushed her hands together, watching the pieces float to the attic floor like bits of dark snow.

"Dylan."

"What?" I pushed aside a stack of fabric, delicate squares of yellowed muslin with embroidery and laced edges. Handkerchiefs?

"Look."

Straightening, I swung around. She held up a page from the album, so worn it looked as if it might fall to pieces if breathed on. Unconsciously I held my breath. Most of the photos on the page had fallen off, the glue on the little corner stickers having long ago lost their bonding power. They lay in a corner of the box amid a mound of black shreds.

Only one picture still adhered to the page. It had been folded in half.

Letty pulled the photo out and unfolded it, vainly attempting to smooth the ragged cracks in the paper. She studied it briefly, then held it out to me.

I took it, examining it silently.

Two men and two women...clothes circa 1920s...the men were in dungarees and work shirts, the women in waistless dresses with hemlines just above their knees, white stockings and clunky Mary Jane-type shoes.

It took only a second to recognize Dylan and Anna Belle. Her hair was cut in a boyish bob, uncomfortably similar to some I'd seen on girls recently. It was light, probably blonde. Dylan had his arm around her waist. He was looking down at her, meeting her smile with one of his own.

The other couple... The man had to be Jules Mercier. He was stern but I imagined would've been fairly good-looking if he'd smiled. His hair was dark, and slicked back in that patent-leather style a good many men favored back then. Even in work clothes, he appeared very tidy. Beside him, Dylan looked rough and a little unkempt.

I shifted my gaze to the woman beside him, and got my first look at Marianne Mercier.

She was short and small. She barely came up to her husband's shoulder. Her eyes were light, her hair that grayish color red hair becomes on black and white film.

Bobby B had told the truth. She looked a little like Letty, but Letty *was* prettier. Jules wasn't looking at her, however. He was staring straight ahead with what appeared to be fierce determination to ignore the woman standing next to him. Likewise, *she* wasn't looking at *him*.

Oh God. I must've gasped.

She was looking at Dylan, and her expression…

"You see it, too, don't you?" Letty said quietly.

"That isn't the look a woman gives a man she hates," I whispered. For some reason, I couldn't speak any louder. "If both she and Jules… God, Letty, this just became more than complicated."

"I'm surprised Anna Belle kept this." Letty touched Dylan's image with her forefinger. "Guess we know why it's folded."

I swallowed and made my voice decisive. "This doesn't help. If anything, it only adds to the confusion." I looked back into the trunk. "We can put that photo on the board, but it looks like this was a wasted ef— Wait a minute."

My gaze caught something in the bottom of the trunk, wrapped in tissue paper. I pushed aside what looked like a folded crocheted tablecloth and a handful of doilies to get a better view.

The paper was so yellow it looked as if it had been gilded. Pulling it apart, I lifted out two slender books. The top one was bound in dark red, its edges faded and splotched with mildew and spatters, as if water had been poured over it.

I didn't have to look at the inscription on the front, *Personal Diary*, to know I'd found what I was looking for.

"Eureka." I turned to Letty. "Take that photo. Let's put everything back and get downstairs."

We settled in the den after Letty had very gently wiped the red book with a clean dishtowel.

It took me several moments to open it. I was abruptly seized with a fear that what it might hold would make some drastic change not only in what I'd been told but perhaps in our lives.

Letty didn't say anything. She simply sat, clutching the towel, waiting for me to do something. At least, she didn't prod me with some impatient remark.

I studied the diary.

It was only about four by five inches and maybe an inch thick. Could something that small actually hold five years of one's life?

There was a little lock on the front, a strip of cloth with a metal flange extending from the back cover sliding into it.

If it's locked, if I force it and it tears... I fumbled with it, pressing a tiny button set into the center. It fell open.

This is my Personal Diary, Anna Belle Rowen, was written on the inside of the front board. The last name had been scratched out and "Roth" written beside it.

I wondered if Anna Belle reread her diary often, attempting to bring Dylan to life again in her mind. Had she thought of what happened and perhaps shed a tear at the irony of that little inscription?

The other book...

I admit my hand shook as I opened it.

Dylan Roth.

It was that same bold handwriting as on the back of the picture on the storyboard.

My Journal.

It didn't really look like a journal but more like a

miniature account book with blue horizontal lines and vertical red ones dividing them. Perhaps Dylan hadn't been able to afford a true journal so he bought whatever was available.

There was one sentence written on the front page. Breath tightening, I let my gaze skim over it.

...This will be written in English because that is the language of my new home and I am now a new man...

I looked up, holding out the red book to Letty.

"You read Anna Belle's, I'll read Dylan's."

We decided we would skim the entries and read aloud relevant passages. If one found a pertinent paragraph, the other would try to find one on the same or a near date and we'd compare them. That way, we'd possibly get two views of the same event.

Anna Belle's diary was more detailed than Dylan's. The first entries were of her receiving the book as a birthday gift, then of meetings with friends, picnics, and such. Dylan's was more sporadic...a notation here, a word or two there, telling of his arrival in Amesville, then the move to Estonko, and his being accepted by the townspeople because of his friendship with the young man from Amesville whom he called 'my friend Benson.'

Could his sponsor have been the sheriff's relative? Maybe the sheriff himself? That would be more than ironic and would definitely explain why Sheriff Benson had done his best to hide the truth.

Two years were covered very quickly in both diaries, with Dylan's one to ten word notations mentioning his work as a carpenter going so well he managed to buy a house and that acreage we still owned. It was all so brief and mundane I was beginning to despair finding anything cogent, when Letty said, "Listen to this…"

I stopped reading to look over at her.

"*Today I met someone and I think he's going to be important in my life. His name's Dylan Roth and he's from Rumania or Romania—oh, I don't know how to spell it!—of all places. He's a carpenter and he's so cute. He has the most beautiful curly black hair and blue eyes.*"

After hearing that, it took a great effort not to self-consciously run a hand through my own hair.

"What's the date?" I asked.

"April 25, 1921."

I flipped forward in Dylan's journal. That date wasn't many pages over from the beginning. He'd really attempted to conserve as much paper as possible.

"Here it is, but it's not much. He went to the hardware store to buy some nails and saw Anna Belle, introduced himself but worried she might think him an 'insolent foreigner.'"

Letty was already reading further. As I stopped, she picked up the story. "*May 1. Dylan came to call, politely asking Daddy if he might escort me to the church's May Day Festival. A group of us were going so we weren't alone. He fit right in. He is so polite and sweet.*"

Dylan's entry was a single line: *Annie's father allowed me to go with her to a church celebration.* I looked at the next line, dated two weeks later. "He decided to ask Anna Belle to marry him. Talk about a fast worker! *Mr. Rowen asked me what religion I am. When I told him I am Greek Orthodox, he said he wasn't certain he could let someone who followed a religion he'd never heard of marry his daughter. I told him I*

*would accept whatever faith he wanted. God has allowed
me to find the woman of my dreams. Surely He won't
care in what form I worship Him."*

Well, that answered my question of whether he'd
converted or not.

"They married a year later, in June," I said. "A
definitely long engagement to offset the whirlwind
courtship."

"Here's the engagement announcement." Letty held
up a folded bit of newsprint that had been tucked
between the pages. She handed it to me. It showed Dylan
smiling sheepishly at Anna Belle. I gave it back to her
and she replaced it in the diary. Anna Belle had several
entries after that, of wedding parties, and showers given
by friends.

Dylan's had no entry between the announcement of
the engagement and the wedding. *June 10, 1922: This is
the happiest day of my life.* It was the same thing he'd
written on the back of that photograph. *Today I marry
my Annie and must mark this momentous day.*

"Damn, Letty, Great-Grandpa was nothing if not
succinct." I turned the page. "Wait a minute…there's
something else on the next page…*While my bride sleeps,
I rise from my marital bed to write this because it is
something I can say to no one, but I must put to paper
what is in my heart. My heart…over which Annie's gift
to me, a cross inscribed with our initials, now rests. I
have known only two women, but after tonight I never
wish to know another. Annie is everything I could wish
for."*

A sound from Letty, not quite a gasp, more like a
sob, made me look up.

"That is so beautiful." She blinked. "I'm afraid

Annie didn't put down any post-wedding night thoughts, but she did say this on their wedding day: *I'll be leaving for the church in a few minutes but have to write this down. I am so happy and am impatient for tonight. Perhaps that makes me wicked somehow, but I want to be in bed with Dylan and learning what it is to be a wife. I'm also a little afraid, as it always is with the unknown, but I look forward to being loved by my husband."*

I didn't reply to that, couldn't without sounding like a sentimental sap, so I found the next entry, dated the following year. "*Annie Belle tells me I will be a father soon. I am now a man blessed in all things.*" After that was the notation, dated seven months later, "*Today is the second happiest day of my life. My son Theodore born at two o'clock this morning.*"

After that, there was another entry a year later announcing the birth of Ila Mae, and then…

"Letty, listen to this. I think this is when Dylan and Jules met." I sat up from where I'd slouched in my chair. "Jules advertised for workers to build his new house and Dylan applied. *I can always use more income, with two little ones now.*"

"Anna Belle mentions that, too," Letty said. "Just a note that Dylan applied to help build their neighbor's new home and was accepted."

I read a little further before saying, "Here's where the plot begins to thicken."

"How?"

"Seems Marianne was trying to get friendly with Dylan and he didn't want it. He says she watches him and it makes him uncomfortable. *I wish I had the courage to tell Jules' wife that, but it may be I am mistaken in what I sense, and if I were to say it aloud, it would destroy the friendship I have with him.* What do you think of that?" I looked over at Letty.

"It certainly sounds like there was something going on," she agreed. "If one-sided."

"And definitely off-course, since he's talking about Marianne and not Jules. It sounds like Dylan and Jules were just friends."

"At that point, anyway," she said ominously. "He didn't mention it to Anna Belle, either. The only thing she's said about the house is that *Dylan is happy in his work for Jules Mercier.* Did you notice he calls her 'Annie?'"

I went back to reading, skimming the next passages. In a few minutes, I sat bolt upright.

"Holy…"

"What is it?" Letty looked at me in alarm.

"I think I've found part of the answer." I cleared my throat. "*Jules Mercier is my friend and I value him but I can't understand how such a good man could have such bad judgment in his choice of a wife.*"

"Wow, that's harsh."

I continued reading. "*At worse, Marianne Mercier is mad. At best, she is seriously deluded.*"

"For crying out loud, Dylan. Don't stop now. Does he say what happened?"

"Give me a minute." I backtracked, reading over the entire passage I'd carelessly skipped.

"Oh, shit, Letty. At the housewarming party Jules gave, Marianne made a pass at Dylan. He rejected her…and the shit nearly hit the fan."

I read a little farther.

"He took Anna Belle and left. *I will never set foot on the Mercier property again, and my friendship with*

Jules is now in jeopardy as well."

"Whoa." Letty's mouth fell open. She took a deep breath. "I didn't see that coming."

"Wait until you hear the next entry." I didn't look up.

" *'October 3, 1925: This evening Jules and I met at the tavern. He'd called me earlier, the first time we'd spoken since that awful night. I arrived first, greeting others, and ordering our usual drinks. As he came in, looked around, and made straight for the table where I sat, I noticed he kept his head down, his hat pulled low. Was he ashamed of his wife's actions?*

'It was good of you to come, Dylan,' he said. Removing his hat and tossing it into an empty chair, he raised his head.

I was startled to see a large bruise on his cheek and several scratches, almost gouges, on his neck just above his collar. 'Jules, what happened? You look as if you've lost a fight with a bobcat.'

'Ran into a door,' he muttered, and to my utter shock, he began to cry, not loudly as a woman might, but with large, silent tears trickling down his cheeks.

Thank God no one noticed.

'That's what I tell everyone, though they all think I was in a brawl somewhere. But I can't lie to you, Dylan. Not after what happened.' Gently, he touched the scratches and winced. They were very red and inflamed. 'Marianne did this.'

Before I could reply to that, indeed even get my mind to acknowledge the fact, he went on, 'It seems it's accepted that a husband may beat his wife but no man wants to admit his wife beats him. She does, however, when she's crossed.' He looked up at me, eyes clear behind his tears. *'Have I now lost esteem in your eyes as well as our friendship?'*

'You'll never lose my friendship, Jules, you know that.' I assured him.

'You say that now, but when you learn...' His gaze seemed to unfocus, as if he were seeing someone else. *'I'd thought by leaving Brunswick, we'd finally put it all behind us, but now...''* He took a deep breath. *'I have to tell you.'*

'Brunswick? I thought you were from Savannah.'

The waitress brought our drinks and he paused until she was out of earshot. He took a large swallow of his beer, and a deep breath, and the story poured out.

'When I met Marianne, I was bowled over, I asked her to marry me after a few weeks' acquaintance. My family urged caution, not to rush into such a serious state as marriage with a near-stranger, while her family seemed strangely relieved. I didn't wish to wait, my mind was made up, so we married.''

He paused to glance at me.

'What do they say, Marry in haste, repent in leisure? *Believe me, I've had no leisure. We had a lovely home with a garden and I thought to hire someone to care for it because I didn't want my wife working in the dirt.'*

Here he laughed ruefully.

'Ironic, eh? Since her husband now does exactly that? I found a bright, smart youngster, a handsome boy...too handsome. A week later, he quit without notice. I hired another. It wasn't long before I found Marianne in the garden whenever he was there. Shortly afterward she informed me she and the boy were in love and she was leaving me.'

'You mean, they were having an af—'

'I mean nothing of the sort,' he snapped. 'She did to both my gardeners the same thing she did to you. One was afraid I'd believe her so he simply quit. The other told his father, who came to me, Marianne railed at him, nearly attacking the old man, and he threatened to call in the police. It was only by offering the boy two months wages and his father another sum that I kept it quiet. My brother suggested I take Marianne away, to a place where no one knew us, so we moved...'

As it turned out, there had been another scandal there, this time with violence from his wife. Again, they moved, and again and again.

'It came to me,' he said, 'perhaps this was why my wife's family was so happy at my proposal...because someone else would take on responsibility for her.'

The longest they stayed in one place was Brunswick, where his two children were born. but after three years, it happened once more.

'...so we moved here, as far away from friends and family without going into another state. Things seemed to be going so well.' He caught my arm. 'I swear, Dylan, I had no idea...until you came though the kitchen door. I waited until after the party and our guests were gone and then confronted her. She answered with this.' He pointed to his neck. 'My friend, I'm so sorry. Whatever she's convinced herself into feeling for you, it's worse than any of the others. Dylan, you've become an obsession. Her every thought is of you."

He averted his gaze, head dropping. "We haven't shared a bed since we moved here.'

I think that admission shamed him more than the fact that she'd struck him.

'I sleep in the guest room.'

'Is that why you asked to have it made so much larger?'

He nodded. 'In our cottage, I shared my son's room. I didn't want another house, but she did and I've always given in to her wishes.' Here he gripped my arm tightly, staring into my eyes, his own wide. 'I've done everything I can to make her happy, but nothing works. Now...we'll have to move again.'

'Jules,' I said. 'You don't need to move. I'm not going to tell anyone. Not even Annie knows. What you need to do is get your wife help. She needs a doctor, perhaps...' I hesitated to suggest it. '...she may even require commitment because of her delusions as well as these spells of violence.'

'Don't think I haven't tried asking for medical help,' he said. 'By the time I can get a doctor to the house, she's over her rages, and then I look the fool because she seems so lucid and calm. I'm trapped, Dylan. I don't know what to do.'

'You've witnesses to her behavior,' I pointed out. '...the gardeners, and the others.'

'I don't want more of a scandal, for my children's sake.'

I understood that.' A thought occurred to me. 'Does she keep a journal?'

'Journal?...a diary, you mean?'

I nodded.

'Yes.' He frowned as if wondering what I was getting at.

'Do you have access to it?'

'I know where she keeps it, but I've never looked in it. To me that seems a betrayal of trust.' He shook his head. "No, that's wrong. I won't lie. I did read it once.

The things she put in there were unspeakable…things she and her imagined lovers did…demented. And her feelings for me… It makes me despair to think how wretchedly dark her mind has become.'

'Don't despair,' I told him. 'You have me as a friend, and if no one else will, I'll bear witness for you.' I thought of something else. 'Does she ever offer harm to the children?'

'So far, it's all directed at me. For thwarting her plans with her nonexistent lovers.'

That was good.

'Here's what you should do.' I told him what I'd been thinking as he talked. 'The next time she has such a temper fit—and you and I both know there'll eventually be another—take her and the diary to the nearest physician. Immediately. Before she can recover. If he reads it and sees what a state she's in, he won't delay doing something.'

He was silent a long time, then finished his drink and looked at me.

'I'll do it. It'll be like waiting for a bomb to explode, but I'll do it. Thank you, Dylan. You're truly a friend.'

I acknowledged that with a hand to his shoulder. 'Needless to say, for the time being, however, I think it'll be best if I stay away. My presence could make things worse. I'm sorry, Jules.'

'I understand.' He looked sad.

He left soon after. My God, that poor man. I feel guilty for being so lucky as to have a wife who is not only beautiful but also mentally stable. I hope this turns out well for him.' "

It was the longest passage Dylan had written.

I paused for breath. "Does Anna Belle have anything

to say around this time?"

Letty studied the diary. "Just that they went to the party. Dylan went with Marianne to look at the garden to advise her on furniture, then came back inside, spoke a little heatedly to Jules, and told her they were leaving. He refused to say what happened so she 'accepts his judgment and won't press him about it.' That woman was really trusting." She turned a page. "A few days later, she notes that Dylan met Jules at the tavern and returned very serious and thoughtful, and hasn't seen his friend since."

She glanced at the clock.

"It's nearly noon. Want to take a break?"

I shook my head. "There's only one more entry. Let's see what it has to say, and then we can stop."

That entry was so shocking I could barely read it.

" *'June 28, 1926: A storm is coming. Annie and I were preparing to take shelter in the root cellar when the phone rang. It was Jules.*

'Dylan, I need help. She's raving and I can't control her. I think the storm triggered something. She got one of my rifles. Said she was going to kill me.'

I didn't say anything. I was too shocked. What an inopportune time for Marianne to decide to have her temper fit.

'I've locked her in the bedroom for now, but I'm afraid she may break down the door.'

In the background, I heard the sound of loud thumps and a woman screaming, as well as a child's cries.

'Before I took the rifle from her, she struck me with the butt. I bled all over the nursery floor. I think this time she means to kill me.' His voice trembled.

'You can't handle her?' I didn't mean to be

judgmental though it sounded that way.

'You know I'm no weakling,' for a moment, he rallied as if I'd insulted him, 'but no…I can't handle her alone. She's as strong as a man when she's like this.'

'Do you have the diary?' I asked.

'I've wrapped it in oilcloth so if the storm breaks it won't get wet.'

I made my decision.

'I'll be there as soon as I can,' I promised. 'We'll take her and the diary to Dr. Walton.'

'Thank you, Dylan.'

I hated the desperate gratitude in that proud man's voice.

'You're a good friend.'

I disconnected the call and turned to see Annie standing behind me holding the baby.

'That was Jules, He needs me to help him put away some of his farm equipment,' I lied. 'Take Teddy and Ila and get to the root cellar.'

'Do you have to go?'

The look on her face made me want to stay, to ignore Jules and his mad wife and huddle with my family in the cellar and wait out the storm. I couldn't do that. I'd given my word.

'He needs my help.' That part was true, at least. I threw on my rain slicker and kissed her. 'I'll be back as soon as I can.'

I'm writing this as I sit in my truck before I leave. The storm is getting worse, but I fear Jules and I are about to face a storm of another kind.' "

I looked up. "That's the last entry. Apparently, he left, went to Jules' house, and…" I shrugged.

"The storm hit and they were killed?" Letty finished.

"Possibly. What does Anna Belle say about that night?"

" '*I sit in the root cellar with a tornado raging outside. The baby's asleep and Teddy is playing with a set of trains his father carved for him. The lantern doesn't give much light but he's quiet so I don't complain. Dylan went to Jules Mercier's to help him put away his farm machinery. Why did he go? It's dangerous to be out tonight, but Jules is his friend and he needed his help, he said. I wish he'd come back.*' "

"But he didn't," I finished.

She ignored that. "The next entry is the next day, about her calling the sheriff and the search party." She read a little farther. "She's defensive abut Marianne Mercier's story that Dylan and Jules ran away together. 'A horrid lie,' she called it. There's a short note a few days later. '*Dylan's truck was found at the Amesville depot. His journal was on the front seat and Ezra returned it to me. I won't read it for that would betray my trust in my dear husband.*' That poor woman. If only she had. Too bad Ezra didn't." She looked at me. "There's no entry for Bobby B's story, though there's a copy of the clipping."

She held it up.

I didn't take the clipping and she returned it to the diary.

"Anything else?"

"Only a notation, dated February 2, 1936, where Anna Belle met your…what would you call him?—your step-great-grandfather? And he wants her to have Dylan declared dead. That's it."

We stared at each other.

"Now we know what happened," I said.

"Not all of it. We still don't know where Dylan and Jules went. We only know up to that moment."

I remembered my dream. "I think I know."

"Well?" She waited for me to go on.

"Marianne killed them."

"Come on, Dylan." Letty looked scornful. "How? These were two grown men. Jules was as big as Dylan, and if Dylan was anything like you in size, he was a brute. How could she overpower both of them?"

I bristled slightly. *She thinks I'm a brute?*

"The rifle. She shot them," I said, "then drove Dylan's truck to the depot and walked back to Estonko to the sheriff's office."

I had to admire her fortitude, at least. That's a long way to go on foot.

"You sound mighty certain of that."

I decided it was time I came clean about my other dream. "The night I stayed at the house, I had a dream. I never told you…"

"…about Marianne's attempted seduction? Yes, you did."

"This was a different dream. I was running through the garden with someone. We were being shot at. I was hit twice." I placed a hand on my cast. "The first shot broke my arm, the second killed me. Marianne killed Jules and Dylan."

I made it a flat statement.

Letty looked as if she didn't want to believe it, but she said, "Okay, for argument's sake, say it happened that way. What did she do with the bodies?"

"You certainly like to play devil's advocate, don't you?" I muttered. "Maybe she threw them into the river. I don't know."

"Not the river," she argued. "We've still got the weight factor, remember?"

"Okay…she dropped them into the well."

"Same argument." She shook her head. "Anyway, the water tests ruled out any contaminants. Two dead bodies would've definitely been contaminating…and there would've been…remains." She looked a little sick as she said that.

"The garden, then. That's it…that's why all these accidents have occurred…to shut down the site, because when the house is finished, we'll start on the garden, and when we dig it up, we'll find the evidence that everything she said was a lie."

"What does it matter now? If victims and killer are both dead and have been for nearly a hundred years?"

"I don't know," I snapped. "Maybe the truth always matters to a ghost." Something she'd said much earlier suddenly intruded. "What's today?"

"The same as it was earlier. June 28."

"June 28." I dropped Dylan's journal on the couch and stood. "Letty, we've got to go to the house."

She didn't move. "Nope. Not with that storm heading this way."

"That's the reason we have to go. Today's the anniversary. There was a storm then and there's one now. All that's missing is Dylan Roth's presence. *He* can't be there, so *I* have to be."

I pulled her to her feet and she put her arms around me.

"I don't want you to go. Please, Dyl."

"I have to." I hoped she wasn't about to start crying. If she did, I'd cave and I knew it. "I think…tonight it's all going to come to a head, one way or another, and I have to be there."

Still talking, I turned and ran for the back door, not waiting to see if she followed.

"If you don't want to go, I understand. I think I can drive…"

"No, you can't, and you know it." She pulled her purse off the doorknob and pushed open the door.

Chapter 26

Neither of us spoke. The truck was filled with sullen, heavy silence. It would've been better if we were railing at each other instead of that ominous quiet.

Though it wasn't yet noon, the sky was heavily overcast and dark. In contrast, puffy white clouds were gathering above the band of gray, looking brilliant against the lowering sky. They piled on top of each other like luminescent whipped cream on a bank of lead-colored, mile-high thunderheads, a definite indication bad weather was on its way.

Beauty always preceded terrible weather.

The wind was also rising. Pine trees bordering the fields swayed, their branches trembling, needles swishing back and forth. A loose piece of newspaper skittered across the road in front of the truck, followed by an empty plastic grocery bag. The wind swooped them up and slapped both against the windshield with a smack of dirt, then swept them into the air again.

"You know what's going to happen, don't you?" Letty didn't take her gaze from the road. "That storm'll become a tornado and we'll be caught on the road, and…"

"…picked up and deposited who knows where," I snapped. "Of course, it's going to become a tornado. It has to. You didn't have to come," I reminded her. "I told you I'd go by myself."

She didn't answer. Instead, she tapped a button on the console, turning on the radio. A country western song blared out. As if to underscore what she'd said, the music abruptly cut off.

"We interrupt regularly scheduled programming for a weather announcement. Tropical Storm Iris, hovering off the coast, has now been officially updated to tornado EF-2 status. Winds are currently estimated at one hundred and twenty-five miles per hour, with an expected funnel diameter of one and a half miles across. Tornados of this size are expected to stay on the ground longer than lesser ones. Iris has already come inland, and there has been a sighted touchdown outside Savannah. It is now traveling in a slightly southwesterly central direction, and everyone in that general vicinity is urged to take cover immediately. Go to a basement or cellar or some inner room with no windows…"

I slapped at the button and the sound died. "I wonder if there's a record of the vitals on the one that night? It's be interesting to compare—"

"Will you please shut up?" Letty blurted.

Tears formed in her eyes and her mouth worked silently. She bit her lip. When she spoke again, it was with an effort.

"We're driving directly into the path of a tornado, and you want to compare it to one a hundred years ago? Dylan, have you gone absolutely crazy? We should be looking for shelter."

"I don't see you turning this truck around," I shot back.

What the hell am I saying? She was frightened out of her wits but she'd still come with me. Is that true love or what? I should be telling her how brave she is.

"That's because we've arrived."

She turned the wheel and the truck bounced across the culvert.

The wind was stronger now. Gusts struck the passenger side, making the door rattle and the chassis tremble. As a sudden blast slammed against us, I put out a hand, bracing against the dashboard. We were halfway down the track when Letty slowed the truck and let it coast to a stop.

"Why did you…"

I glanced at her. She was looking up.

Has the tornado already reached us? I followed her gaze.

There was a flicker of light through the trees. The waving branches made it twinkle. Above, the sky glowed, touching the underside of the clouds with gold.

"My God! Is the house on fire?" I stared at the illuminated billows as the wind swirled them about, tearing the cottony mass into wisps, then reforming them.

Letty didn't answer. She tapped the gas pedal, sending the truck jumping down the track. We rounded the curve and swerved to avoid rear-ending a car parked directly in front of the steps. She slammed on the brakes, sending both of us pitching forward, then bouncing back against the seats, in spite of our shoulder harnesses.

The house was ablaze with lights.

"That can't be." Letty looked at the house. "The wiring isn't finished. The power's not on." She gestured at the vehicle. "Whose is that?"

I slid out of the truck, staring at the car. It was a black Model-T sedan, looking fairly new.

Had Jules owned such a car?

Parked down the lane were a couple of antique trucks as well as some buckboards, mules or horses within the shafts. Nearby, several saddled horses were tied to tree branches.

The wind started up again, blowing Letty's hair into her face as she pushed open the driver's door. She struggled, trying to get out. I caught the door and held it, but her feet had no sooner touched the ground than a swooping blast ripped the handle from my hand, slamming it shut.

From inside the house, came the sound of voices, barely audible above the whistle of the wind, and...

I thought about the stories we kids heard repeated, of lights and sounds at night, and...gunshots...

A man shouted something.

"Come on." I caught her arm, dragging her up the front steps.

The door wasn't locked and I didn't hesitate but pushed it open and went into the foyer. The light fixture glowed with incandescence, highlighting a table and reflecting in the mirror above it, shadowing the passageway past the stairs. The ballroom was dark and also the parlor, but I could see the outline of a settee and several chairs and end tables, in a vaguely Victorian style, gathered around the hearth. Lamps on the tables had bowl-shaped fringed shades.

"Dylan," Letty whispered, "where did all this furniture come from?"

From upstairs came the sound of voices. There was a soft, solid thump and a cry of pain, followed by a heavy thud. A child began to cry.

Releasing Letty, I started up the stairs. She didn't hesitate, but followed. I put a hand on the banister, feeling the indentations and smooth curves beneath my fingers, Dylan's carvings, under my hand.

As we reached the top step, they came out of the nursery. Two figures, a man and a woman struggling against each other, their bodies becoming more solid with each step they took.

I felt a sudden wave of dizziness, a nauseating spin of vertigo. I managed to keep my balance, glancing at Letty, seeing she was affected, also. The very air seem to swirl as if we were caught in a small but invisible tornado.

Letty caught my hand. I put my arm around her, pulling her tightly against me, for as they became corporeal, I could feel our own physical reality slipping away. I could see my hand where it grasped her body. A moment later, I found myself looking through her at the wall as we faded into nothingness, our corporeal bond dissolving.

In the space of a moment, we became the ghosts and they the living entities...

****

Marianne fought him wildly. Jules simply tried to fend her off. In all her other 'spells,' he'd never seen her this frantic. Though she struck him with a frightening strength, fists landing solid, painful blows on face and chest, he still didn't fight back. She was his wife, the mother of his children. He'd never struck her yet, so how could he hit her now, even after what she'd done?

There was a swollen splotch on his cheek where the rifle butt had struck, already blackened and raised, broken flesh spread over the crooked ridge of his nose. His face was numb, blood streaming from his nostrils, spotting his shirtfront. He managed to catch her wrist with one hand, squeezing it so tightly she cried out while the other hand still swung frantically, reaching for something, fingers clawing.

The rifle. He held the weapon that had damaged his face out of reach of those grasping fingers as she continued trying to wrench it from him.

"Give it to me," she screeched. "I hate you. I'm going to kill you, and then Dylan and I are going away together. I hate you hate youhateyouhate…"

Her voice went up in an unintelligible wail. She screamed in sheer frustration.

Somehow, he managed to lean the rifle against the wall just outside the bedroom, leaving his hand free to grasp her other wrist. Twisting them behind her back, he grimaced as if in apology, then dragged her to the open door and flung her inside. She fell through and he slammed the door shut, taking a key from his pocket and locking it.

Immediately, she began pounding on the other side. "Let me out. If you don't, I'll kill you! I'm going to him and you can't stop me…you can't…"

"Oh, God…" Jules leaned against the wall, resting his forehead. That sent more blood running down his chin and dripping onto his shirt.

The sputter of an engine made him raise his head. A door slammed and someone ran up the steps. The front door opened.

"Jules?"

"Up here, Dyl." He straightened, looking toward the stairs. *He's here. Thank God.*

There were hurried footsteps on the stairs.

****

Floating in our hazy ectoplasmic fugue, I looked

down the stairs, saw someone coming up them, a dark shape enveloped in a poncho-like garment glistening from the raindrops coating it. He removed his hat, tossing it aside and slinging water. I started to step back, to make room for him to pass but he didn't stop, and…

…walked through us.

Letty shuddered. I felt encased in ice. I stared at the man who'd been my great-grandfather, and I also trembled, because I was looking at myself.

****

Dylan stepped onto the landing.

"What the hell happened?"

"I don't know. She's been so normal I was beginning to hope… She was putting Edward to bed. I was in the nursery…the next thing I knew, she was coming at me with the rifle, telling me she was going to kill me, that she was meeting you and…"

"You're bleeding something bad, Jules." As usual, when Dylan got emotional, his voice took on a foreign intonation.

"Yeah." He gave a breathless little huff. "Rifle butts are pretty hard. Think she broke my nose." Jules pulled a handkerchief from a back pocket and began to wipe the blood from his chin and upper lip.

"Dylan, Dylan, is that you?" The pounding on the door started up again. Marianne had heard his voice. "Darling, help me. He's locked me in." Her plea became strident with hate. "Kill him, sweetheart, and get me out of here!"

"Good Lord." Dylan looked at the locked door in horror.

From across the hall came a watery whimper.

"The kids…they all right?"

314

"Eddie's in his room. I told him to stay there."

"Have you got the diary?"

Jules patted his hip pocket. "Safe and sound. How's the storm holding?"

"It's only raining so far. Damn, what a night she picked to…" Dylan shook his head.

"What are we going to do about the kids?"

"We'll have to leave them for now." Jules started across the landing.

He disappeared into Eddie's bedroom, returning a few moments later with his son in his arms. The little boy was wearing a nightshirt and had been crying. He burrowed a tearstained face against Jules' shoulder. Jules carried him into the nursery and set him on the floor. In the crib, eighteen-month-old Ila lay on her back, waving her arms, completely oblivious to the drama going on around her.

"Damn, Jules, that looks like a lot of blood." Dylan stepped over the puddle on the floor.

Jules didn't answer. Dropping to one knee, he put his hands on Eddie's shoulders. "Son, I have to leave for a bit."

"Where you going, Papa?" Eddie snuffled.

"I have to take Mama to the doctor."

"Will he make her well so she'll stop yelling?"

Marianne chose that moment to shriek as loud as she could, and he flinched, face primping as if he were going to burst into tears again.

"I hope so. I want you to stay with Ila and make sure she doesn't cry. You can play with your horsey Uncle Dylan made you." He gestured toward the fireplace.

Next to it the wooden horse moved gently as the wind blowing down the chimney sent it rocking.

"I'll be back as soon as I can."

"I love you, Papa." Eddie flung his arms around his father's neck, giving him a stranglehold of a hug.

"I love you, too, son." Gently, Jules unclasped his arms. He caught the child's face in his hands and kissed his cheek. "Be good until Papa gets back."

"Yessir…" Lower lip quivering, Eddie wrapped fingers around one of the spindles on the crib.

Jules stood, looked at Dylan. "Let's get this over with," and stalked out.

Dylan followed, standing beside his friend as Jules locked the nursery. Marianne's struggles against the door had since ceased. Walking to it, Jules slid the key into the lock. He looked at Dylan.

"Ready?"

Dylan nodded. Jules turned the key and threw open the door, thrusting the key into his pocket.

Neither was prepared for Marianne's violent rush toward them. She came out fighting, waving something long and black, a fire poker from the set on the hearth. She swung at Dylan, catching him on the temple, sending him sprawling, then brought it down against Jules' shoulder and kept striking brutally, driving him backward as he tried to escape. Arms wrapped protectively around his head, he hit the banister, overbalanced, and toppled over it. There was a thud as his body hit the steps, rolled down two more, and stopped.

Marianne ran around the newel post.

Dylan recovered, reaching for Marianne to stop her from going down the stairs. She spun. Her first blow sent him reeling as the metal rod struck again and again while he dodged and, like Jules, tried to protect his head.

"Why didn't you help me?" she screamed as she raised the poker again, dealing Dylan a blow driving him to his knees. "He locked me in. I love you. Why weren't you here?"

"Marianne, for God's sake, you're going to kill him," came Jules' agonized cry from the stairs. He reached for the banister, struggling to pull himself to his feet.

"Kill him?" She glanced down the stairs, not pausing in her attack. "Yes, I'll kill him. He should've been here. You'd never have stopped me if he was. This is all his fault."

Dropping the poker, she looked around, saw the rifle, and dashed for it.

Raising his head, Dylan pulled himself to his feet and ran to the stairs, catching Jules by the arm as he passed.

"We can't handle her. We need help. Can you walk?" He put an arm across Jules' shoulder, helping him down the stairs. "Come on, we've got to get out of here."

They managed to reach the bottom step before Marianne was behind them, carrying the rifle. She leaped from the middle of the staircase, landing at the bottom unhurt, righted herself and raised the weapon, cocking it, as Dylan reached for the doorknob.

"Stop right there!"

Both men skidded to a halt. Dylan slid his arm from around Jules' shoulders. He stepped away from the door. It swung open as both men turned. A gust of hot, wet air blew into the foyer.

"You betrayed me," Marianne grated, eyes narrowing. "You told me you loved me, but you weren't here when I needed you."

"Marianne, you know that's not true..." Futilely, Dylan tried to reason with her.

"Shut up!" She waved the rifle.

Jules flinched.

"Get away from the door."

They obeyed. Marianne moved so she stood between them and escape. Behind her, the door swung back and forth, blown by the wind.

"Marianne, please..." Jules spoke.

A sudden blast of wind surged through the door, sending it slamming against Marianne's back, making her stagger.

As she struggled to regain her balance, Dylan grabbed Jules' arm. "Come on! We'll go through the woods."

They dashed to the kitchen, flinging open the back door and jumping down the steps into the garden.

Marianne recovered, running after them. "You're not going to get away!"

Outside, the storm was gathering. Clouds swirled and collided as they were ripped apart by the wind.

"We'll follow the creek to the road..." Dylan puffed. "...walk back to my place...use the phone..."

They ran across the garden.

Marianne raised the rifle.

She fired. Caught by the wind, the shot went wild, striking a tree. The two men didn't stop but continued running through the dark, skirting bushes, dodging in a zig-zag.

The storm grew in intensity, ready to break. Thunder cracked, and the sky lit up as bright as the incandescent lights in the foyer.

Marianne stopped near the well. She raised the rifle to her shoulder.

Jules glanced back. "Dylan, look out!"

She fired again.

Dylan went down, clasping his arm.

A second shot whizzed over his head, striking the water oak at the entrance to the baptismal pool. Marianne pressed the trigger again. There was a loud click but it didn't fire. She lowered the rifle, jerking back the bolt handle. The spent cartridge ejected, joining the other on the ground. Digging into her apron pocket, she pulled out two more and reloaded, feeding them into the chamber.

Lightning lit everything as clear as day. Jules bent over Dylan.

"Get up, Dyl. Come on." He pulled his friend to his feet.

Marianne fired a third time and Dylan's body jerked as a hole was punched in his forehead. His head slung backward and his body spun out of Jules' grasp, collapsing on the ground. A red mass struck the water oak, clung to the bark a moment, then dripped down it.

"You bitch!" Jules looked from the body of his friend to his wife. "You've killed him!"

"Good," Marianne snarled. "He got what he deserved. No man spurns me, Jules."

She shot her husband in the chest.

The echo of the rifle's crack swirled around and around, loud in the sudden silence as wind and rain abruptly died.

Instead of falling immediately, Jules took a single step. Then his knees buckled and he toppled head-first into the baptismal pool. The splash his body made was barely audible.

Marianne ran to the pool, staring at the body lying on the steps, facedown in the water. Raindrops from the water oak's leaves dripped around him, making tiny rings in the pool as his body gently floated back and forth.

Leaning the rifle against the tree, she caught his ankles, tugging him backward onto the ground and rolling him over.

She didn't hesitate but ran back to the house and around it, appearing a few moments later, lugging something in a burlap bag. It rattled and jangled, metal striking against metal as it bumped along the ground. She dropped the bag, then seized Jules' arms, and with many grunts and groans, tugged him around until he lay awkwardly atop it. Fingers fumbling at his belt buckle, she pulled the strip of leather from around his waist and pushed it under him.

Then she knelt beside Dylan's body.

His eyes were open. A trickle of blood running from the bullet hole in his forehead had dripped into one eye, making the iris a startling blue in the middle of a red puddle.

"Don't stare at me," she cried and began to sob, voice falling to a whisper. "Why weren't you here? You could've prevented this." Straightening, she went on, "Now I have to hide you and Jules and make certain no one finds out how you betrayed me."

It took some time for her to drag his body to where Jules' lay. After a struggle, she dropped Dylan on top of her husband's corpse.

It began to rain again, a prelude to the storm's arrival.

The burlap bag was closed with a drawstring in a

wide loop. Squatting in the wet dirt, she managed to thrust one of Jules' arms through the loop, tying it in a tight knot.

Opening Dylan's belt, she slid the end of Jules' belt through the buckle, locking the tongue in place. The rain made it slippery. It took her several minutes to draw it tight over Dylan's chest, Thrusting the other end into the buckle of Jules' belt, she bound bag and bodies together.

By now, it was raining steadily. Marianne was soaked, her hair coming loose from its pins, sticking to her forehead. Shoes, stockings, and the hem of her dress were thick with mud. With a sudden heave, she shoved both bodies toward the steps, falling forward onto her hands in the waterlogged soil. They rolled down the steps, tumbling into the water, the metal in the bag clanging as it struck the bricks.

For a moment, they floated, Dylan's dead-blind eyes staring at the sky. Then their buoyancy shifted and Jules momentarily rolled to the surface, submerging Dylan. His corpse bounced gently as the wind stirred the water. Finally, their clothing filled with water, and that and the metal's weight pulled the bodies under.

Through it all, Marianne watched silently. When only a trail of bubbles and a single ripple remained, she sighed and it was a satisfied sound. Picking up the rifle, she swiped at her dripping face with one muddy hand. Then, she started around the pool, looked up, and stopped.

"Dylan?"

****

She looked directly at me.

Letty and I, the ephemeral spectators, had followed them…down the stairs, through the house, and out into the garden, watching futilely, unable to do anything…but what could we do?

Letty had screamed when Dylan was shot, then wept as Jules died. She tried to run to him. I held her back, afraid we'd suddenly become visible.

Now, with the crime completed, we had.

I didn't move, didn't make a sound.

"It can't be." She glanced back at the rain-spattered surface of the pool, then started toward me. "I killed you. I…" She saw Letty. "Is *she* why you betrayed me? For your puling little wife? Wait a minute." She peered at her. "This isn't Anna Belle. You were two-timing me? You bastard!"

Before either of us could move, she caught Letty by the wrist. Spinning, she swung her off her feet, sending her flying over the wall and into the water.

Letty sank without a sound.

"You bitch!" I caught her shoulder, swinging her around, and without the least hesitation, backhanded that vicious, pretty face with my uninjured hand.

She staggered, shocked that I'd dared fight back. With a scream of rage, she flung herself at me, fingernails stabbing at my eyes. I jerked my head back just in time.

The wind grew more furious, the rain beat down…

…and the storm broke.

Lightning crashed, and the wind howled as it whirled around us in a blackened, roiling mass. As if out of nowhere, a dark funnel hovered directly above. I was caught in its suction, could feel it pulling, lifting me off my feet, making me stagger. Surely, in a moment, I'd be airborne.

I had to do something. Escape, yeah, but this was

also my one chance to make it right. Somehow.

"You aren't going to get away this time, bitch." With my one good hand, I caught Marianne's wrist.

Like a discus-thrower, I put myself into a frantic turn, all my weight behind it, and spun, swinging her into the air.

The black sucking cloud swept her upward.

She knew she was done for. She stopped her attack and clawed at my hand in an attempt to grip it. If that happened, I'd be pulled into the storm with her. Her eyes got wide, burning with black intensity, then went blank. I could see through them, the wind whirling around as if inside her head.

With a vicious jerk, I wrenched my hand away. Her fingers slid from mine and I clamped my hand into a fist.

No way was she touching me again.

With a scream of fury, she was swept away, the sound spinning around and around until it was swallowed by the storm's roar.

Her eyes got wider and wider until their blankness melded into the funnel's dark mass. Her skull crumbled, one bit at a time, wafting away like dust blending with the tumbling clouds.

Marianne's body twisted, losing its human shape. It stretched to spider-web thinness, translucent as the deluge in which it floated, spinning around and around, then separated, torn into wisps of whirling cloud until its very molecules vanished into raindrops and dispersed into vapor…

…with the echo of a spiraling wail…

The funnel disappeared. The rain stopped. Rain dripped from branches, striking the pool's surface with loud sharp *plops*…leaves rustled and settled in the aftermath of the dying breeze.

"Letty!"

I ran to the pool, splashing down the steps, arms outstretched to keep my balance on their moss-slippery surface.

A bubble broke the surface, Letty surged upward as if thrown, struggling and gasping. It had probably been only a few seconds since she hit the water, but it seemed hours.

I waded to her, reaching out. Coughing and sputtering, she splashed toward me in little fits and starts, rising and falling as if carried by an underwater current…

…and something came with her, clinging to her waist, pushing her along with clutching, boney fingers…shreds of what might have been the remains of a rain slicker floating around its neck.

As my hand touched hers, it released its grip and slowly sank beneath the water again.

I backed away, pulling Letty to the steps. We staggered out. Standing at the edge of the pool, I hugged her body to mine while the sodden world dripped Iris' aftermath around us.

Chapter 27

My cell phone was waterlogged. I had to go back to
the truck and get Letty's from her purse.

Sheriff Benson himself answered my call. He was
immediately attentive when I said I wanted to report a
double murder, but didn't appreciate it when I told him
it happened ninety-six years ago. It took me some time
to convince him I was serious. After that, it wasn't long
before his car came barreling down the track, lights
flashing, siren howling, even if there was no real hurry.

Dylan and Jules weren't going anywhere.

As for Marianne...I hoped her torn-apart body had
been swept directly to Hell.

The sheriff asked me to repeat again what I'd told
him over the phone, recording it into his own cell. With
the aid of a flashlight, he examined the pool.

"You sure they're down there?" He looked up at me
as he squatted near the steps. "Because, boy, if you're
lying..."

"I swear I'm not." I assured him, partly ticked off at
being called 'boy' since we were the same age. "My
great-grandfather and Letty's are at the bottom of the
pool, weighed down with a burlap bag full of metal."

All it took to verify our story was draining the pool.
At the bottom, half-covered by a century of muck,
leaves, and submerged twigs, lay two skeletons, weighed
down with an almost decomposed bag of rusted

carpenter tools.

There was also a very water-damaged rifle lying near the bodies.

"Too bad my great-uncle was so intent on covering up Marianne Mercier's lies," the sheriff said. "Otherwise, he might've noticed a few things...like cartridge casings, or brain matter clinging to a tree, and solved this case then and there." He shook his head. "To think they've been right here the whole time."

There was a coroner's inquest, though it was more of an information-gathering and a verdict-rendering.

All the old evidence from the original missing persons case was reviewed. That can of worms Letty once mentioned was now open and wriggling free, jogging the memories of an older generation and giving gossip fodder to a newer one.

What with the current waves of family scandals, murders, and whatever filling the media, however, the world in general ignored our small-town drama. It didn't even rate a headline on Yahoo.

Letty and I testified, without mentioning the ghosts, of course, coached by Sheriff Benson to be circumspect about that, as if we had to be told. My reputation as a former investigative reporter held us in good stead. *Professional curiosity* was a plausible enough excuse for what we'd done.

DNA samples taken from Letty and me were enough of a match to establish identification. The body they determined was Dylan's had a broken left arm, which could've been caused by a bullet striking the bone, the coroner said. Cause of death was very obvious: the hole in his forehead, as well as the fact that the back of his skull was partly missing. He'd been wearing a chain around his neck, with a little gold cross suspended from it, a man's cross. On the back was the inscription *To DMR from ABR.*

Jules' body showed evidence of a blow to the face as well as a shattered rib near the sternum. The bullet killing him was lodged in his spine.

Because the rifle had been in the water so long, they were unable to do any ballistics tests, but the bullets found in the bodies were the proper caliber for the rifle. It was noted that some used rifle cartridges had been found when the well was being excavated, though they had been thrown away.

Miraculously, a good portion of the clothing each body had been wearing was still intact, and in Jules' back pocket was Marianne's journal, wrapped so tightly in oilcloth it was barely touched by the water it had lain in for ninety-six years.

The journal and the other two diaries were given to Dr. Allan Moore, one of the county's expert psychiatric witnesses, who rendered the opinion: "Comparing the entries in the three diaries, I believe it is safe to say Marianne Mercier suffered from erotomanic compulsive-obsessive-dissociative-disorder. That is, she had sexual fixations centering around someone who didn't return her attentions. Apparently, she'd indulged in this behavior many times, causing her husband to pay off the object of her obsession and move to another town afterward."

"Would such a person actually carry out the threats she mentions?" asked the judge. "Killing her husband, attempting to kill Dylan Roth's wife?"

"In my opinion, Your Honor, an erotomaniac is very dangerous and could easily commit murder without batting an eye. In recent years, we've had several examples of this in real life…a man convincing himself an actress would love him if he killed our president…a late-night television star stalked by an erotamaniac fan…" Dr. Moore took a deep breath. "From the written accounts of the people involved, I think when Dylan Roth got to the Mercier home, and Marianne Mercier learned he wasn't there to go away with her but to help have her committed, she again got possession of her husband's rifle and killed both him and Jules Mercier, weighting their bodies with the bag of tools taken from his truck and then throwing them into the pond."

"That would also explain why she stopped allowing the church to use it as a baptismal pool," the judge said.

"Exactly. It would also clarify her increased anxiety on the anniversary of their deaths, as evidenced by the news story written by Robert Bascom, and the fact that she was committed to the state mental hospital the following year on that date. Since she'd done away with the victim of her current delusion, as well as her husband, the guilt she didn't dare admit caused her to kill herself the next year while an inmate."

The single entry he read from Marianne's journal clinched it.

There was no problem reaching a verdict: Dylan Roth and Jules Mercier were shot and killed by Marianne Mercier during a period of insanity.

Case closed. Stop the presses. Film at eleven.

As we left the inquest and walked to Letty's car, I had one last thought about the scene in the farmhouse, wondering how many times it had been played out over the years, waiting for me to arrive and end it once and for all, wondering what might have happened if we hadn't come, if we'd sat out the storm, letting the house be finished and sold. Would the new owners have become the objects of Marianne's wrath?

We'd never know. Thank God.

****

From the diary of Marianne Mercier, June 28, 1926:

There's a storm coming. Of course Eddie's frightened. I'm trying to calm him. Thank goodness the baby's asleep. I don't think I could take it if she were crying also. The noise would drive me mad.

Jules is putting away the farm equipment. He intends to turn out the horses. They are giving him trouble. I wish the storm would hit and lightning strike him. Then I could go to Dylan. This storm would be a good cover for us to leave. I think... Yes, I'll do it. I'll settle Eddie, then get one of Jules' rifles. He keeps them in the corner of the bedroom where they're handy. I'll shoot him, then I'll drive to Dylan's and kill his wife and his brats and we'll be free to leave here and love each other as we really want to. I can't wait to be in his arms, to feel his naked body against mine.

Oh, Dylan, I'm so glad I thought of it. In a few hours we can really be together.

Chapter 28

We buried Dylan in the Roth family plot, next to Anna Belle and her second husband.

Jules was buried there, too. Letty's father felt that was more appropriate than taking him back to Savannah and placing him beside Marianne. He'd probably have floated out of his grave and gone back to Estonko in protest. There was a small memorial ceremony held at the graveside.

Afterward, Letty and I stood on the church steps, looking out at a rainswept but peaceful town going about its business as usual. For a place that had been hit by ferocious weather only a short time before, as well as experiencing the discovery of such a calamitous crime right under their noses, it was an exceedingly calm scene.

"Well," I said. "We've solved a mystery, cleared our great-grandfathers' names, and closed a downright frozen cold case. What should we do for an encore?"

"Why don't we get married?" Letty suggested. "And live happily ever after?"

"Great idea."

So we did.

PS—I wrote the book, fiction, of course, and Bobby B got his copy. Autographed.

Epilogue

From the diary of Anna Belle Rowen Roth, February 2, 1936:

I have met someone for whom I have formed an affection. He wishes me to have Dylan declared dead so we can marry. Alec Troup is a fine, church-going man and I think he'll be a loving husband and a good father to my children.

June 30, 1936: Court date today to have my husband declared legally dead. Oh, my darling, where are you? Please appear in the nick of time, like in one of those movies. Come back to me before it's too late.

June 30, 1936 (later): I am now officially Dylan Roth's widow. I will put an obituary in the newspaper, late as it is.

August 1, 1936: Today I will become Mrs. James Alexander Troup, but in my secret heart I will always be Dylan Roth's wife. I love you, Dyl.

A word about the author...

Toni V. Sweeney has lived 30 years in the South, a score in the Middle West, and a decade on the Pacific Coast and now she's trying for her second 30 on the Great Plains.

Since the publication of her first novel in 1989, Toni has written 94 novels, with 89 of them having been published. This includes several series.

Visit Toni at:

https://www.facebook.com/profile.php?id=100048587829251

Thank you for purchasing
this publication of The Wild Rose Press, Inc.

For questions or more information
contact us at
info@thewildrosepress.com.

The Wild Rose Press, Inc.